HEARTS
of CLAY

Dosun Adeleye

HEARTS *of* CLAY

© Dosun Adeleye, 2018

Cover design and formatting by John Amy
www.ebookdesigner.co.uk

To those in pursuit of love and happiness,

may you remain fearless in your quest

for what sets your soul on fire.

Contents

CHAPTER ONE

Lagos, City of Lessons

IT was my twenty-second birthday and nothing was going to dampen my spirits, not even the stationary traffic I was stuck in, on Lagos' Oshodi–Apapa Express Way. Try as I might, I never got myself accustomed to Lagos' daily road traffic – it's heart-wrenching!

My heart always skipped a beat when I watched impatient motorcycle riders and even bus drivers wriggle their way through tiny gaps between car lanes, something I never thought could happen in the 21st century. But it was happening in 2004 on Lagos' roads.

To be fair, road rage is rampant everywhere, even in England where I had lived for twelve years, a little over half of my life. You often hear/see people curse or pull horrible faces at you for very petty reasons; respectable individuals turning into frustrated clowns the moment they got behind the wheel. It made me wonder when human beings would stop taking out anger on people they didn't know.

My friend Chelsea once laughed so loudly when I came up with the term 'crazometer'. "It will be the greatest invention of all time," I said, as I wiggled my finger in the air.

"To measure the level of craziness on busy roads?" Chelsea asked, before adding, "there is no need for that, London measurements will be high for sure, but Lagos measurements will skyrocket so much so that your stupid invention will shatter into pieces and cause even more havoc on the roads." We had giggled at the thought.

I wasn't giggling now though, as I assessed the situation on the ground. I realised I was going to be stuck on the road for a while, without anything to keep me entertained as my car stereo was faulty. 'How am I supposed to survive without my favourite gospel music, or Lagos 96.5 FM?' I wondered, as I let my eyes wander across the road to where women, men, teenagers, and even children as young as eight-years-old, hawked various goods between the lanes of traffic. I was always inspired by their spirit of hustling, but it didn't take away the pity I felt for them as I watched them risk their lives, running from one vehicle to another to advertise their wares.

One little boy in particular pulled at my heartstrings as he proactively advertised his goods. He looked about eight-years-old and also completely out of place, as his skinny body was dressed in a hooded jumper with GAP inscribed on the front, fashionable jeans, and a pair of decent trainers. I wondered how he managed to look so comfortable in such warm clothing on a hot afternoon of about 36 degrees. I was curious, I needed to find out more about the little boy. I felt drawn to him and wanted to know his story.

You may not know it looking at me now, and whilst I have enjoyed some privileges in my life, I have also experienced hardship; and my heart especially goes out to children from rough backgrounds. I cannot help myself but want to do everything in my power to help them. I decided to attract his attention.

"Oni bread!" I called, and all the other bread sellers, both old and young, ran towards my car like an army of ants will crowd around a heap of sugar.

Even though I only had eyes for the youngest of the mob, I didn't want the others to know. So I wound down my window, which immediately allowed a gust of hot hair into my air- conditioned BMW 5 Series car.

The bread sellers started shoving their loaves of bread in my face whilst shouting out reasons their own bread was better than their counterparts'. To make it fair, I bought a loaf each from the younger hawkers, leaving my favourite child and the grown-ups.

"Aunty," the little boy called as his eyes pleaded with me, "I only have three loaves left, please buy them so I can go home to study for my Common Entrance Exam. I haven't been to school today Aunty, please Aunty."

I quickly did my calculations and realised that I had underestimated the little boy's age, he was probably about ten-years-old if he was going to secondary school next September. He was older than he looked, his little body most likely stunted in growth through malnourishment. As I was about to ask more questions, one of the adult bread sellers barged in. "Smallie, shut up, commot from here! You don' sell almost all your bread, na only you?" he said in broken English, "Madam, my bread sweet, I also get Milo chocolate powder too o."

I ignored the jealous bread seller and turned my attention to the boy. I told him, "I will make you a deal. If I buy the three remaining loaves of bread, will you let me drop you off at home?" I motioned to the road, "Look, the traffic is already moving."

"Yes Aunty, God bless you!" he said, as he quickly opened the back door to place his tray on the seat, then jumped in after it and made himself comfortable, even before I asked him to hop in.

"Sola!" called one of the female hawkers, "Are you crazy, you want her to sacrifice you for money rituals?" She wagged her finger at him. "If you go with that lady I am going to tell your aunty," she warned, but Sola didn't listen. He was more concerned with adjusting the air vent such that cold air from the AC blew directly onto his little face.

As I watched him from the corner of my eye, I wondered how a boy so young could have so much confidence in him. He seemed to have a wisdom older than his years, streetwise and sassy, but smart too. I thought, 'With some support and guidance in his life, he could have real potential…'

"Aunty, I like your car o. It is fine!" he said, interrupting my thoughts.

"Thank you dear, have you had lunch today? It's my birthday and I was going to treat myself to some hot amala and okra soup at Sweet Munches," I said, keeping my eyes on the moving traffic.

"Aunty, don't waste your money, I know a great canteen near my house. If you buy a plate of amala, vegetable stew, ponmo kika and ogunfe – I mean proper goat meat, you will find yourself licking both front and back of your plate. Mama Sewa's food is so sweet and very plenty for the price!" he said.

The way Sola dramatised the quantity and taste of Mama Sewa's food made my mouth water. I knew exactly what he meant, street food on Lagos' streets was always cheaper and tastier than the overhyped and usually overpriced food in most of the fancy restaurants, so I asked him to lead the way.

As soon we stepped out of the car and walked towards the canteen, people started hailing Sola for bringing back an empty tray as usual; and it seemed they couldn't praise him enough for his unbeatable enterprising skills. It was the same when we got to the canteen, everyone seemed to love the little boy and he enjoyed all the compliments and attention. When we found a table, the canteen owner personally came to take our orders, despite having waitresses around.

"Sola, who is this fine Aunty?" she asked as she smiled knowingly. "I already know 'Ronaldo's' usual, what you will eat ma?" she asked, in broken English.

I smiled. "Ronaldo? Why are people calling you Ronaldo, are you a football player?" I asked the boy.

"Yes, I am a wonderful football player and Ronaldo is my favourite," he said, looking very pleased with himself.

"That's great!" I grinned. "If you want to be a football star, you must put in all the effort. How often do you train and who takes you there?" I asked.

"Nobody takes me!" he said, as he looked in the direction of the kitchen. "After I was born, my mum left my daddy because he was poor, and she left me with him. We heard she has remarried and lives somewhere in Abuja with her new husband and children. For a long time, it was just me, my daddy, and his younger sister, Aunty Tinu, until my daddy got a student visa to study Law in London. He promised to come for me as soon as he settled, but he hasn't been back for the past three years, because life in London is very difficult. But he plans to come for me when things are a bit better. In the meantime, Aunty Tinu will continue looking after me until my daddy returns."

Now I had heard a little of his story, I was even more curious. "If your dad is in the UK, why have you been hawking bread on the streets of Lagos? You are too young for this kind of thing – you only need to concern yourself with your studies at this age, and you should be looked after by an adult. Doesn't your dad send you and your aunty money for your upkeep?" I asked, in an attempt to know more about this little boy who I was growing to love as much as everyone in his neighbourhood seemed to.

"My daddy sends money to Aunty Tinu every month, that's what she uses to pay my school fees and support her bread business," he replied, before calling out for Mama Sewa. "Mama, where is our food now? I am hungry!"

"Just a few more minutes Ronaldo," she replied.

"Aunty Tinu asks me to help out over the weekends, and some Fridays when she has to visit her boyfriend in Ibadan for the weekend," Sola said.

I couldn't believe what I was hearing; I wanted to find his so-called 'Aunty' Tinu, slap her across the face, then ask her why. No one in their right senses will leave a child unattended for three good days, let alone asking him to market her bread. I thought reading about child labour annoyed me enough, but seeing it first-hand fired me up beyond my imagination.

"When your aunty isn't around, who looks after you?" I asked, as I watched his captivating eyes light up as he saw the waitresses bringing our food over.

"I look after myself," he said proudly, "I get to study, play football and sleep all I want... Aunty, don't look so worried, I actually like it when Aunty Tinu is away, in fact, I always look forward to it."

After we had finished our lunch, it was time to part ways with Sola. I gave him 5,000 naira, the equivalent of £20, but I couldn't let him go without knowing where he lived, so I asked him to show me his house. I thought seeing his house, in some way, might help me feel that he would be ok. At first, I just wanted him to indicate which of the old bungalows was his, but then my curiosity got the better of me, so I let him talk me into coming to visit. We had already walked about 0.8 miles and Sola kept pointing to the distance saying, "That's it over there; it's the white building just around the corner."

"Sola, are you sure we aren't lost, do you know where your house is?" I asked, when we had been walking for about 15 minutes. If I had known his house was more than a mile away, I would have driven him home, instead of us walking under the scorching hot sun.

"Aunty, this is the place," he said, as we entered a tall building.

Two hefty men were sitting on the veranda of the house, playing some sort of board game. There was something about them which made me feel uncomfortable, and I wondered if I had done the right thing in following Sola home. When the men noticed they had company, they called out what sounded like two native Nigerian names, and two equally sturdy men emerged from the house and walked towards us. They took their places either side of me, like guards.

"Sola, are you sure this is your house?" I asked nervously, beginning to worry for my safety, but Sola just ignored me and walked up to the guys on the veranda. He started speaking Yoruba to them and my heart sank as I realised my gut instinct was right, and I was in some kind of trouble. If it wasn't for the burly guards, ready to grab me if I dared move an inch, I would have run for my life.

"I didn't even try you know," Sola boasted, "She just stepped into my trap so easily…. big bros, we are blessed! When I realised that she is not from around here, I knew I had to take the opportunity – no dulling at all! I think she is from London, because she sounds just like the Uncle you asked me to trail last month."

As soon as the men heard 'London', the guards immediately grabbed my arms and started leading me into the house.

I was terrified, but I tried to keep my cool and reason with them, appeal to them. "Gentlemen, I am a woman," I said, "Please handle me with care." But they all just burst out laughing and snatched my handbag off me, containing just my car keys and phone, and tossed it to one side.

"English, keep blowing your grammar around!" one of the men snorted, a wicked smile on his face. "Gentlemen!? Ha!"

As they dragged me down a corridor to a room ahead, I tried again to speak sense to them. "But, what do you want from me?" I pleaded, "Why me?" But they just ignored me and threw me forward into the room, so that I tripped over my own feet and landed in a heap on the floor. "Your room m'lady!" laughed one of the men, in a mock English accent.

I gave up on the men and tried with the boy, who had only a short time ago been my new friend. Now this. "Sola, why are you doing this?"

I cried, "You should have considered how nice I have been to you this afternoon, I even had plans to take you to your father…why are you not thinking of your future? Just talk to me Sola!" But he did not, he didn't even look at me. They just closed and locked the door, and left me there.

At first I hammered on the door tirelessly, continuing to call out for Sola, but there was no response. All I heard were the muffled sounds of Sola and the older men laughing and bantering. They were laughing about how easy their victory was, how foolish I was. Suddenly, I was overcome with a mixture of shame and shock, as the severity of my situation started to sink in. The way I felt could only be compared to when I had discovered my own mother had betrayed my own father and I. You see, there were similarities between Sola's story and my own, which is one of the reasons I felt so drawn to wanting to help him. Well I had helped him alright, and now I felt so stupid and betrayed, by a small child who I saw as a charity case – a child I was planning to save and lift out of abject poverty. In some way. I had never thought for one second it would be this way, with me as the new victim of the tale.

My head hurt as I replayed the afternoon's events in my mind, round and around, like a movie stuck on a loop. I just couldn't get my head around how a little boy so easily wrapped me around his little finger! Before I knew it, I had worked myself up into such a state of agitation, I thought my heart would beat its way right through my chest. As the adrenaline coursed through my veins, I started to shake and I was scared I would have a heart attack right there and then. I needed something to stop my body from shaking, maybe some food, even though it had not been long since I had eaten. Then, thinking of food, I realised with horror that I had left my insulin in my car.

'Stay calm Grace,' I told myself, 'If you stay calm you will find a way through this, you always do.' I took some deep breaths and tried to quieten my racing mind. I tried to concentrate on just one thought: if I was to die, it should not be as a result of my kindness.

I think what scared me the most, was the fact that for the first time as an adult, I had no control over my situation. For starters, I couldn't predict how dangerous the men on the other side of the door were. They had not hurt me, yet, but they were hardly charming hosts. For all I knew, they could be kidnappers, ritualists (if the Nigerian movies I had watched had any atom of truth in it), local rogues, or even worse, rapists.

As I took in my environment and looked around helplessly for a possible escape route, the door opened and in came one of the hefty men. He just stood there and stared at me, licking his lips as his eyes traced the shape of my body. I squirmed and shuffled back against the far wall, shaking my head and wondering if there was any way I could run past him and out of the open door. He seemed to read my mind. "Oh no you don't!" he barked. "Don't worry, we are not going to hurt you, we won't even touch you if you do what we say. If you are lucky, someone will love you enough to come for you. And we will be rich."

With his words, it became horribly clear that I had casually strolled into a kidnapper's den; and I had no one to blame but myself. He saw the look of realisation and resignation on my face and he nodded. "Now be good!" he said, as he left the room, slamming and locking the door behind him.

A few minutes passed and I noticed the house was a little quieter, so I guessed the men had gone to ransack my car, keep what they considered valuable, and sell the car to the highest bidder. None of that worried me, most things can be replaced, but my concern was for the suitcase I kept in the boot. This suitcase contained my insulin kit, my British and Nigerian passports, and my wallet containing all my bank, credit and ID cards, aka my life – all you need to do is go through my wallet and you'll know everything there is to know about me. I was sure it wouldn't be long before they called my mum for a ransom, my poor mum who was incapable of handling stress as it was. It was bad enough that I insisted on traveling to Nigeria without her, she had tried to stop me and, in failing to do so, had turned to relentlessly nagging me about it, she was so worried some harm would come to me. Now she was going to hear that I had been kidnapped.

Thinking about it broke my heart and, at the same time, I blamed her for the predicament I found myself in. After all, my mission to Lagos in the first place had come about directly because of her, because of what SHE did. No wonder she was so worried about it, maybe not just for my safety either, but for what I might find here – secrets and lies. My MOTHER, the one I trusted with my life, had also played poker with my life and I wasn't sure I would ever forgive her for it. Now, in a strange way, it felt as though my being kidnapped was not through my own fault, but was my mother's punishment, many years after she did what she did to change the course of my life.

CHAPTER TWO

Lost in Thought

I was born in Lagos on the beautiful Sunday morning of 16 September 1982. This is why I was named Grace Abosede Olokose as, in the South-Western part of Nigeria, my middle name Abosede (Bose for short), means female child born on a Sunday. I interchange between my first and middle name, depending on who is asking.

Shortly after I was born, my dad relocated to the UK leaving my mum and I behind. Apart from pictures and telephone calls, I didn't really know my dad. My mum, however, was my world until I turned five-years-old and my dad came to take her away from me. She dropped me off at my maternal grandparents' house in Ibadan and relocated to the UK with my dad. Mama, as I used to call my grandma, was so happy to have me, in fact it was her dream come true but a nightmare for me. Despite loving Mama to bits, I found it difficult to adjust to my new life and all of Mama's efforts to fill in the void proved abortive, as I was either moody, crying, or asking after my mummy. As days turned into weeks and months into years, Mama gradually became the centre of my world, with only occasional reminisce of Mummy's love. Dad, however, was my greatest scorn, I couldn't forgive him for taking my mother away from me, knowing too well how difficult it was for us to be torn apart.

Mama was a petty trade businesswoman and the stronger and more independent partner in her marriage, she sold firewood and kitchen utensils and, wherever she went, I followed. We travelled from one town to another to supply goods to her ever-increasing customers and the icing on the cake, for me on those long trips was stopping over at roadside canteens to eat pounded yam and bushmeat stew (my favourite). Even when I started primary school, my grandma would pick me up from school and off we went on her business trips. One day, my class teacher called Mama into her office and told her she was putting my life at risk by taking me on those business trips.

"Mama, as you know, Grace is a bright kid, but I reckon additional studying at home will do her some good, especially now that her Common Entrance to secondary school is forthcoming," she said and, to my surprise, Mama heeded Mrs Kolawole's advice.

She recruited the best teacher in Ibadan for me, Mr Taye, who was also a teacher in my school. He was indeed a clever man, but that wasn't the only reason parents and pupils liked him, it was his playful and jovial nature too – he knew how to make learning fun for pupils and, in return, he produced dedicated and outstanding scholars. My grades were hitting the roof within weeks of extra lessons with Mr Taye and I started to worship him in a way, as he became the strong, nurturing, male figure in my life. I loved my grandpa, but he could never fill the shoes of my dad. Whereas Mr Taye had stepped in where my father stepped out. At least, that is how I felt back then, so young and innocent.

One evening, Mr Taye had just finished marking my Common Entrance mock exam papers and it was time for him to go home, but he couldn't leave because there wasn't an adult at home to watch me. Grandma hadn't returned from her business trip and Grandpa hadn't returned from his evening walks. So Mr T, as I loved to call him, volunteered to stay with me until they returned. To while away the time we started playing silly games, such as doing impressions of people where the other person had to guess who it was. After a couple of rounds of this, we were both in fits of giggles.

"Grace, oh Grace…" he laughed, "You are so good at this and so funny too. Do you know your chubby cheeks wobble when you laugh!"

"My cheeks aren't chubby and they do not!" I snapped, playfully.

"Yes they are, and your tummy too!" he teased.

When I said my tummy wasn't chubby either, he asked me to prove it by lifting up my dress. When I hesitated he just laughed more and told me, "Ah yes, you have a chubby tummy for sure! You must have, to be so shy of it – I bet it wobbles like your cheeks do!"

"It does not!" I said, now wound up, wanting to prove him wrong above all else and lifting my dress in defiance, "See!"

When I saw the strange look on Mr Taye's face, I suddenly felt awkward and the blood rushed to my cheeks in embarrassment. 'Why is he looking at me like that?' I thought. I wanted to smooth my dress down again, hide my shame, but then his face lightened and he grinned and looked like the Mr T I knew and loved again.

"Don't feel ashamed Grace," he encouraged me, as though reading my mind, "I was just admiring you. I like the colour of your pants. Who bought them for you? Come closer, let me feel the texture."

As though on auto-pilot, I moved closer to him, but then he started to fiddle with my groin area. I pulled away, confused about his sudden change in composure, but he reached out his arm to me in a friendly fashion. His voice was thick when he spoke, "Come on Grace, come sit here with me. You don't want to disobey your teacher now, do you?" His extended arm closed around my waist and pulled me towards him again. His attention was no longer on me as his pupil, all he was interested in was my body.

"Stop it Mr T, I don't like what you are doing. Mama told me never to show my nakedness to any man unless I was old enough to be married," I protested, as I observed his shifty countenance.

He shrugged. "But you are not naked. You are just showing me your pants and I am just feeling the texture, because I love how it feels." He said it so nonchalantly, as though it was such an everyday occurrence and quite normal. Then he smiled. "Do you want to feel mine? Then it will be fair. But you must never tell anyone, it will be our little secret."

In my little head, I thought it was only fair to get even with him as he had already seen mine. I was also an inquisitive child and was curious to see what his underwear looked like. He had just taken off his trousers when we heard a key in the front door; it was my grandpa.

We were right by the dining table, in full view of the hall, so anyone who came through the front door would see us. Mr T started behaving erratically and I could see panic in his eyes as he turned his head this way and that, trying to decide if it was best to put on his trousers, or just make for the nearest exit. In the end, he jumped over the dining table, trousers and shoes in his hands and ran past my grandpa, who was too shocked to react.

Grandpa knelt in front of me and asked, "Abosede, did that man touch you?"

I was too confused and ashamed to tell him what I had done because, as young as I was, I knew I shouldn't have shown Mr T my pants. I had just wanted to please him and I didn't think he would hurt me. In my eyes, Mr T knew best. So when Grandpa repeated his question, I remained mute.

"Where did Mr T touch you?" he asked and this time, I pointed to where.

"Mo ku o, e gba mi!" Grandpa exclaimed. Meaning, "I'm dead, save me!"

Then it dawned on me that I was in trouble, so I left him there, still kneeling on the floor, collected my books from the dining table and headed to my bedroom. The moment I was dreading eventually came about an hour later – Mama was back. Grandpa must have told her what happened because all I could hear was Mama cursing on the top of her voice, whilst Grandpa spoke soothing words to try and calm her down.

"You are a weakling, someone raped your granddaughter and you let him walk? What kind of man are you? Move out of the way!" she yelled, "Baba Adunni, I said move out of my way and hand me the keys!"

"It's too late Mama Adunni, we will go after him tomorrow when we have reported this to the police," Grandpa cajoled.

Grandpa must have hidden the front and back door keys, because the next thing I heard was the sound of her footsteps, followed by Grandpa's.

"Abosede, I thought I told you never to show your nakedness to any man until you get married," Grandma cried, "What did he do to you?"

"Nothing, he only asked me to show him my knickers and he felt the texture – that's all. Mama, I'm sorry," I said as tears started rolling down my cheeks.

"Sweetheart, there is nothing to be sorry about. You are a child but he should have known better. So, he didn't ask you to take your pants off?" Grandma asked.

"No, he didn't, but he took his trousers off to show me his own knickers," I said as I watched her and Grandpa exchange looks.

"Did he take his knickers off?" she asked, as she stared at me intently.

"No, he didn't," I replied, followed by a simultaneous sigh of relief from my grandparents.

The following day, through my classroom window, I saw Grandma, Grandpa, and a bunch of policemen matching towards our headmistress's office. Fortunately, I was kept out of it at the school, but the drama didn't stop there. When I got home I heard Mama narrating the incident to my mum over the phone.

"I don't know how you and your husband are going to do it, but you have to come back for your daughter as soon as possible. As you've heard for yourself, she is no longer safe here," Mama said, before continuing.

"You promised to come for her as soon as you'd settled, it's been five years and you haven't looked back since…What kind of mother are you?" she lamented and still didn't stop there.

"I don't understand how you can live comfortably without your daughter, especially now that she has a young brother. I keep telling you, siblings should grow up together, how else are they meant to bond and love each other? Sibling rivalry is deadly you know?" Mama said, matter-of-factly.

"Adunni! Adunni!! Adunni!!! How many times have I called you?" Mama asked and I imagined mum saying, "three times!" because there was a pause before Grandma continued.

"This town has nothing to offer Grace, she is too clever to waste away here, come and take your daughter to the UK where she belongs. If your father didn't come in when he did, who knows what would have happened to the poor girl?"

As I sat on the dining table I wasn't only wondering when Mama would get off the phone so I could speak to my mum, I also pitied my mother because I don't think Mama allowed her to say anything in response – whenever Mama was angry, she never let anyone get a word in.

All I can say is Mama's yelling has had a positive effect on my life, because within two weeks of the incident with Mr T, my mother landed in Nigeria and, within a month, I was living with my parents and little brother in the UK.

As if to compensate for lost times, or maybe it was just the guilt of neglecting me for years, Mum spoilt me rotten. At first, I thought the pampering and overindulgence would subside after the initial weeks of homecoming celebration, but it didn't stop – all I had to do was ask and the boundaries were pushed even further. I had more than I needed for love, attention, latest toys, food and, as one would imagine, I milked every bit of it. After all, my little brother, Femi, was equally a spoilt brat.

In year 9 of high school, only four years after I left Nigeria, I was diagnosed with Type 1 diabetes at the age of fourteen. It came as a surprise to everyone, including the doctors who thought I should have shown some sort of symptoms before. Our journey home after the hospital appointment changed my world around, such that it became even more confused than it already was. Mum and Dad had started their usual argument about me, but this time it wasn't just about Dad scolding Mum for spoiling me rotten.

"I have always told you that overindulging this girl will do no one any good! You see where you have led her to?" Dad said, and before he could complete the rest of his sentence, Mum barged in.

"Did you not hear what the doctor said? It's not only about being overweight or eating unhealthy food, it is caused by hereditary factors," she argued.

"Well, if it runs in the family then you need to check you and her father's lineage for answers, there is no diabetes in my family. Go and ask her real father!" Dad snapped back.

At first it didn't make any sense what my dad was saying, I had to replay his last sentence in my head several times before the penny finally dropped... "Go and ask her real father... her real father... real father... " In that moment, all I could hear was the sound of cars zooming past and that of my own heartbeat, along with the feeling of something tightening inside my chest. I couldn't decide if the tightening was due to my newly diagnosed disease, or the hurt of being lied to for many years by the people I trusted the most.

Suddenly, it became clear why Dad and I never really got along, and why I always thought he only loved Mum and my baby brother (his biological son). I was obviously his least favourite and he didn't make any effort to hide it, this would explain it all.

'No wonder I always felt like an intruder in my own home whenever he was around,' I thought.

When we got home, I confronted Mum about the issue. To this day, I believe she would have kept it a secret forever if she had the chance, but her skeleton was out of the closet. She refused to go into detail, but confessed that she was dating two men at the same time, fell pregnant to the one she loved the most, but pretended the father was the man who loved her the most. It didn't make any sense to me, so I called Mama and asked her to shed more light on the matter. I knew Mama would tell me the full truth.

According to Mama, my mum and my real dad had been lovebirds who were planning their wedding. In fact, both bride and groom's families had been formally introduced, but everything went downhill when Mum met a new man, a rich man. She dumped my biological father, robbed him of his unborn child, and eloped with her rich lover to Lagos.

To say I was heartbroken and disappointed in my mum was an understatement. I felt as though the only thing that could return happiness and comfort to my life, would be meeting my real father. I promised myself to find him as soon as I could, as soon as I was old enough and had earned enough money to travel to Nigeria on my own. Until that time, I decided I must look after myself and make myself fit and well for my most important journey ahead.

As the doctor suggested I started making some changes to my diet, became more active, learnt how to inject myself with insulin, and took it up a notch by recycling the kind of friends I kept. They were all selfish and irresponsible brats, just like I was, and that had to change too. I wanted to be a better person, not just for myself, but for my real father; I wanted to make him proud by being the best daughter I could be for him and wipe away any poverty in his life to compensate for what my mother had done to him by rejecting him for a richer man. I wanted to show him that money was not everything, but also to help provide for him.

By the age of seventeen, my baby fat had disappeared and boys who had called me "Chubby Grace" at school were all in awe of my transformation. I had grown into a tall, slim and, as many people told me, beautiful girl. In fact, they would tell me I was a classic African beauty, with my smooth honey-coloured skin, long hair, and curvy hips. When I looked in the mirror I still saw part of the old me deep inside, but I also appreciated the woman I was becoming.

To top it all, I gained admission to the University of Oxford to study Mechanical Engineering and, before I knew it, I was selected for the Best Graduating Student award and landed myself a job as a junior Mechanical Engineer at BMW Oxford. After six months' worth of salary, I started writing about my mission to find my biological father in open letters to Nigerian newspapers and blogs. It wasn't long before my media started gaining interest; one of BBC Lagos' top journalists, Chelsea Bala, was touched by my open letter to Hello Lagos and decided to invite me for an interview in Nigeria.

Mum tried her best to talk me out of it and I was surprised to discover my adopted father tried to dissuade me too, when part of me thought he would be glad to see the back of me, but I had my mind made up. I wanted to meet my Real Dad and no one was going to change that.

CHAPTER THREE

The Hostages

I must have fallen asleep despite my determination not to, as I found myself lying flat on the mattress I had perched on the previous day, the only piece of furniture or comfort in the room of my capture. If not for what I call the Natural Nigerian Alarm Clock – that is, the sound of roosters crowing as early as 5am, local Imams and/or pastors using their megaphones to sing and pray in their respective places of worship, and mosquitoes singing in your ear even in the morning – I wouldn't have woken up.

I had been dreaming about my childhood, my innocence lost, and the family I had left behind. And for what? I hadn't come very far before finding myself in this predicament. I hated myself for sleeping a wink, not only because my dreams had made me feel nostalgic and wishing I could turn back the clock, undo a couple of decisions and free myself, but also because I knew too well that my family, especially my grandma, would have been worried sick about my whereabouts.

I knew nature had to take its course but it didn't stop me from feeling guilty, as I hadn't really taken the time to talk to my mum the previous day when she called to wish me a happy birthday. I had promised to call her back, explaining that I was helping grandma as she was upset about losing her 18 Karat gold necklace. In fact she hadn't lost it at all, just done her usual trick of forgetting where she had put it.

Mum and I briefly joked about the number of times Mama had been convinced that someone had stolen her stuff, when in fact she had just misplaced it. This time the jewellery was found in Mama's glass cup cabinet of all places. I had meant to return my mum's call, but got sidetracked. Now it was me who was lost and I wondered how long it would take for anyone to find me.

As I was about to take a peek through the keyhole of the locked door, I heard footsteps approaching. I quickly ran back to the mattress and wore the most miserable face I could pull. The door opened and in came a tall young man who looked about the same age as me. I had not seen him the day before and he did not seem to have the same menacing air as the others; he seemed more gentle in his nature. I wondered who he was.

"Good morning, hope you had a good night's sleep?" he asked, as he placed a tray in front of me. "This is your breakfast, make sure you finish it so that you'll have enough strength to speak to your parents this afternoon...that should be morning in the US," he said, looking intrigued by the time difference between America and Nigeria.

"How do you know I'm from America?" I asked, as I eyed the tray of bread and what seemed like an omelette island surrounded by a pool of vegetable oil. Despite the unattractive appearance of the food, my stomach rumbled with hunger.

"I just know, they don't tell me anything here, I'm just a cook. Eat up!" he advised.

I nodded like a good, obedient captive, but my mind was racing. He was obviously in the dark because, if my kidnappers had spoken to him, he would have known I was from the UK, not the US. That meant he wasn't one of 'them' and, whilst this didn't make him any better in my eyes as he still worked for the kidnappers, I realised this naïve young man could perhaps become my ally and even my escape ticket. As he was about to leave, I decided to try my luck.

"So, what's your name? I'm Grace!" I said, in the sexiest voice possible, looking up at him from my seat on the mattress and batting my eyelids in a subtle yet seductive manner. The way he stopped mid-step in a twinkle of an eye assured me that my plan was already working. I saw his body relax and he smiled down at me.

"My name is Sunday, I am from the eastern part of Nigeria," he said, showing his big white teeth in a friendly grin.

"Oh, wow, you are my namesake then, I was also born on a Sunday! In the Yoruba culture, girls born on Sunday are called Bose or Abosede in full, that's my middle name," I explained, as I carefully analysed his body language. "I believe nothing is a coincidence, God must have brought us together for a reason. What do you think?" I asked and, when he didn't say a word, I continued.

"Namesake, I got myself into this mess because I was trying to be nice to a little boy called Sola. I thought if I helped him reunite with his father in the US, I would have done one child a favour, little did I know that he had other plans. If you get me out of here, I promise to take you to America instead," I promised, searching his face for a positive reaction and wondering if I had jumped too quickly to asking him for his help.

"Ha! Ha!! No o!!!" he said, as he eyed the doorway suspiciously, "Den go kill me, I am sorry, I can't help you. I don't want to die yet, no one will look after my parents – I'm all they've got."

But I wasn't giving up so easily and changed my tone to a firm and encouraging voice, one which I hoped might sway him. "Sunday, this is why you have to help me, so that I can help you. They can't kill you if you get to them first. Don't you know you are the most powerful person in this house? The cook has the ability to wipe out a whole nation, just be attentive and listen to me, everything will be alright."

He did not speak, but he did not leave either, so I continued. "When you leave here today, go straight to a chemist far away from here, make sure nobody recognises you, and ask for the strongest sleeping tablet they've got. I don't know what they'd prescribe here in Nigeria, in the UK something like Zopiclone is the best. What time do you normally make dinner?"

He shifted from foot to foot and I could tell he was thinking about it. "I start cooking around 7pm, food is usually ready by 8 o'clock," he said, "But I don't...."

I interrupted quickly, while I could still see him wavering, considering it. "Make sure you buy enough tablets to make them sleep for eight hours straight – but not enough to kill them. Blend the tablets, add the mixture to their food or drink, and when they're all asleep, come and get me and off we run to safety. Can you do this for me?" I asked.

Sunday was silent for a moment, then he took a deep breath and stood up very straight, as though to attention, and I realised with great excitement that I had won him over. His voice was firm when he said, "Yes. Yes I can, but on two conditions. One, you will take me to America; and two, we will have to free the other hostage, he is a nice guy too."

"Of course," I responded immediately. I had a vague memory of Sola mentioning a male hostage the previous day, but I didn't know he was still in the house. Sunday and I gave each other a nod of knowing agreement and he left the room, locking the door behind him. As soon as he was gone, I started munching my breakfast like it was my last. It was also a lot tastier than it looked, perhaps thanks to my new-found hope of escape.

In the afternoon, I expected someone to bring me lunch, or at least check up on me, but my door remained closed. I found this frustrating because I had been looking forward to speaking to my family, as Sunday had told me I would, and now I wasn't able to assure them that I was ok. Still, if all went to plan, I would be out of my prison and reunited with them before too long.

It was evening by the time the door finally opened and, with my heart in my mouth, I thanked all the action thriller movies I had ever watched, as it looked as though my plan had worked. Sunday tiptoed into my room, followed by a tall, dark-skinned and terribly ungroomed man. I had never seen a man with so much beard in my life, you could hardly see what he looked like underneath it! I wondered how long he had been held captive to become such a state and grow so much facial hair. But the mammoth beard, as horribly fascinating as it was, and all my questions surrounding it, would have to wait. It was now time for us to make good our escape.

The three of us crept down the corridor like thieves in the night, and around the kidnappers who were already lying, snoring, on different sofas in the living room, with alcohol bottles and unfinished food on the centre table. I think I must have held my breath the whole time, scared of making any sound which might rouse them from their slumber. Sunday put his hand on my shoulder and whispered in my ear, "It's ok Grace, I used plenty of pills, just like you said, they will sleep until morning for sure." Still, just so I could be sure, I continued to hold my breath until we were through the room, across the veranda, and I could once again feel the air of freedom on my face. Then, we ran. We ran as though chased by lions, with Sunday leading the race.

We had to follow him because it was already getting dark and he knew where we were going. So we sprinted after him through the dusk, huffing and puffing, as fast as we could, until we were far enough away from the kidnappers' lair. We stopped to catch our breath when we felt it was safe to do so and I saw we had made it to the ever-busy Lagos' Oshodi/Apapa Express Way. Even if they had woken up and come after us, which was doubtful, they wouldn't be able to recapture us here so openly, without drawing attention.

I breathed in the dusty air and even the traffic fumes smelled and tasted sweet to me. I flung back my head, raised my face to the sky and extended my arms, as though to hug the world. Then I started to laugh, quietly at first, before it took over my body, shaking my shoulders and bringing tears of joy to my eyes. For some reason, I remembered Mr T teasing me about my "chubby tummy" and asking me if it wobbled when I laughed. But that just made me giggle even more, as it didn't matter anymore, none of it mattered – I was free.

When I stopped laughing, my mind turned to more practical matters. "Sunday, could you lend me your phone please?" I asked, but he just carried on walking down the Express Way as if he didn't hear me. "Sunday, do you have a phone I can use to call my grandma please?" I repeated, "I need to put my grandma's mind to rest, she hasn't heard from me since yesterday morning and will be worried sick."

"Let us get a taxi first, we should not be lurking around carelessly. You can call her later," he snapped, "Keep moving, both of you."

Then for the first time, my fellow hostage spoke. "Sunday, did you remember to grab my British and Nigerian passports?" he asked, his voice coming from deep within his beard.

Only then did it occur to me that I had been short-sighted all along; thinking only about leaving the house and not how to return to the UK, or about my health. "That's true, Sunday... where are our passports... and did you find my insulin kit?"

Sunday's face twisted into a smile which wasn't quite as friendly as before. "Your passports are at my house, you have no choice than to follow me home. You guys must think I am dumb? You've got to remember I am a Lagos boy, always a step ahead of you," he bragged. "I drugged your kidnappers in the afternoon, retrieved your passports, went to keep them in my house, and only then did I come back to get you two. Why didn't you correct me when I said you were Americans? Let me guess, your plan didn't include me, you just wanted to use me as your pass to freedom then flee without looking back? Guys, if you want your passports, you have to follow me to my house, and do whatever you have to do to take me to the UK with you. Now, stay there while I get us a taxi!" He wandered off into the traffic to negotiate with one of the drivers.

My movie-plot inspired escape plan had worked, but I had underestimated Sunday and now found myself in a new predicament.

"From the frying pan to the fire!" my fellow hostage and I cried, simultaneously. I think I was becoming a little hysterical from all the excitement by this point, as our comment in unison made me start laughing again. I wondered if any further harm or peril could come from trying to make a new ally, one in the same situation this time. 'Nothing ventured, nothing gained,' I thought to myself.

"What's your name?" I asked, turning to the bearded man.

"Felix Ajao," he replied. I found it odd that he felt the need to include his surname. "So sorry, I should have introduced myself before, but I am so disorientated right now. I was kidnapped about four weeks ago and these bastards have been bleeding my mum and uncle dry of their life savings after making them believe I'll be released imminently. And now this, when I thought I was finally free?" he sighed. As if he suddenly remembered something he added, "What's your name and did I hear you say insulin? Are you diabetic?"

"Grace... Abosede, you can call me either," I responded, as we watched Sunday make his way back to us, having negotiated a fare with a taxi driver.

"I prefer Grace," replied Felix, and the way his eyes twitched indicated he may have been smiling beneath the beard. Once again, I wondered what he looked like underneath it.

"Me, I prefer Abosede," Sunday interjected with an arrogant smirk, as he led the way back to the taxi.

"Sunday, where are we going?" Felix asked.

"To my house of course, I already told you."

"I know, but where in Lagos is home?" Felix persisted, but all we heard was silence as Sunday took the front seat of the taxi whilst Felix and I made ourselves comfortable in the back. I could tell Felix was getting really frustrated and impatient and, if I didn't do something to stop him, he was probably going to grab Sunday by the neck and shake an answer out of him. I was frustrated too and it may have been satisfying to watch Felix overpower the trickster and teach him a lesson, but we needed to keep good relations if we were going to get our passports and my insulin back. We couldn't trust the taxi driver either, for all we knew he may have been in cahoots with Sunday.

I tried a different style of persuasion. "Sunday, we have been civil with you all through, but it seems you are trying to hold us ransom just like your bosses did; I see no difference between you and them," I said, hoping to get a reaction. Sunday just stared straight ahead, as though he hadn't heard me. Never one to give up, I continued.

"When we get to your house, please give us our documents and let us go. We are not employees of the British Embassy so we are not able to issue you a UK visa to allow you to travel with us. The most we can do is invite you to the UK when we get back. May I also remind you that we can call the police on you right now, as you can see they are positioned at every junction, but we won't. Just give me your phone so I can call my grandmother and let her know I am alright."

"You people are dumber than you look," Sunday sneered, not even bothering to turn his head back to face us, "You just mentioned police and phone in the same breath, and you expect me to hand you my phone like a fool. If you want to call the roadside policemen, I'm not stopping you, call them and let's see who will lose out." He paused before adding,

"If it will put your minds at rest, my house is at Ikoko and that's where we are going."

Even though I didn't know Lagos well, I knew we were miles away. Ikoko was a small town on the outskirt of Lagos and it would take us a while to get there. We had better settle ourselves down for the journey. Sunday handed us each a bottle of water, I gulped mine down like a horse after a race, and so did Felix. I was so thirsty and so tired too. When the blackness descended upon me, it was almost welcome.

The next time my eyes opened, Felix and I were lying in a secluded room, legs and hands tied with only a local mat for furniture. My heart sunk as my eyes met with Felix's.

"What have we gotten ourselves into now..." I asked, but before I could finish my sentence, Felix butted in.

"More like what have you gotten us into?" he said. "You kept running your mouth in the car like you knew what you were doing. If you were smart enough, you would have known that dashing Sunday's hope of going to the UK was a bad idea, right now he has no reason to free us. He is probably thinking of how to sell our identities to the highest bidder, or use them himself. If you hadn't mentioned the police, he probably wouldn't have drugged us, now we don't even know where we are. This is all your fault, I was better off with the other kidnappers who had promised to release me after the final payout of five million naira... which I'm sure my family would have coughed up somehow."

When he finished his whinging, I didn't know whether to slap him across the face or bring his head to my bosom, give him a pat on the back and tell him everything will be alright. So, I just kept quiet and let him sulk for a little longer.

As I suspected, his tone soon changed again. "Grace, I am sorry for blaming everything on you, you've done what I should have done weeks ago. Whether right or wrong, at least you tried to get us out of that den,

I just sat there like a helpless he-goat and now I am sitting here pointing unnecessary fingers at you when all you've done is your best to get us out of trouble. Please forgive me," he said, as he half-crawled, half-writhed like a caterpillar, across to my side of the room.

"It's ok Felix, I feel your pain. You've been apprehended for weeks with minimal hope of getting out or seeing your family. Apart from your mum and uncle, is anyone else missing you?" I asked.

Immediately after the last sentence left my mouth, I regretted it because it was obvious I was asking if he had a girlfriend or a wife. I didn't want him thinking I was interested in his love life, especially when it wasn't my intention, not in our circumstances anyway. Or with the beard in the way, like a huge, hairy mask. Still, beard and all, I was starting to feel strangely attracted to him. 'It's just the situation you find yourself in Grace,' I told myself, 'All this drama is making your heart beat too fast.'

"Oh, are you hitting on me?" he asked with the widest grin I had ever seen a man wear. I wished the floor would open up and swallow me, so I looked away quickly.

"I am not 'hitting' on you, I just wanted to find out why you are in Nigeria and who might be looking for you in the UK," I said, defensively, as warm heat seared through my cheeks.

"I am just teasing you, I know what you mean – I only have my mum, sister and uncle looking for me," he replied and we both went mute for a while before he broke the silence.

"I read somewhere that most women fantasise about being held captive, you know – the whole shebang of being tied and gagged. Are you waiting patiently for Sunday, your master to come and untie you?" he asked, looking satisfied with his analysis.

From flushed cheeks, now I felt my blood boiling, with rage this time. I definitely wanted to slap him now. I glowered at him and imagined what it would be like to shake him by the ears, but Grace by name and Grace by nature, I chose decorum instead. "You read wrong mate, any women who fantasise about that clearly haven't been raped or fiddled with," I said indignantly. "When you think of cracking silly jokes, please think again."

Felix hung his head and, to be fair, looked thoroughly ashamed. "I am so sorry for making such an insensitive comment. I sometimes say silly things when I'm nervous – apologies!" he said, looking genuinely sorry.

I felt my anger subside a little. We were both under immense pressure, I doubt I was shining at my most brilliant best either. "That's ok!" I reassured him, but I still couldn't look him in the eye.

"I'm sorry," he said again, "I clearly crossed a line I did not intend to. Would it make you feel any better to talk about it? I will share my own sad story in return if you want?"

"My story is truly a sad one, you don't want to hear it," I said, not sure I was feeling in the mood to tell it either.

"It can't be as sad as mine, trust me!" Felix said as he shuffle-crawled backwards, so that his back was against the wall.

I shuffle-crawled backwards too, and we relaxed together as best as we could, considering the circumstances, against the wall. I rested my head on his shoulder. "So tell me and prove it," I said, and he did.

CHAPTER FOUR

Felix's Story

"**M**Y parents broke up immediately after my eighth birthday, my dad moved to the North of Nigeria and I haven't set eyes on him ever since. My mum was a primary school teacher in the private school I attended and, as you can imagine, it became increasingly difficult for her to pay for the life we were accustomed to, so we had to downscale by moving to a low maintenance house and an affordable primary school. In the year I turned thirteen, one of Mum's second cousins paid us a visit, he had just arrived from the UK and needed a teenager to help out in his London grocery store. He said his wife specifically asked for a boy which was why he was at our house.

"Richard, you are a callous man, you want my son to become your cheap houseboy in the UK. It's not your fault, if my useless husband had let me complete my university degree before getting me pregnant, I would have been a respectable bank manager by now and you wouldn't have been able to open your slimy dirty mouth to propose such absurdity," my mum said, as tears rolled down her cheeks.

When Uncle Richard left, I tried convincing my mum to allow me to go, but she wasn't having it, even when I pointed out the financial benefit to our family.

"I will not let you become anyone's slave – not my first-born child," she said.

Friends and family who heard about my mum's adamant decision advised her to seize the opportunity before it was too late. Mum's best friend said, "Mama Felix, make up your mind quickly o, I have a son who would jump at the prospect of relocating to the land of milk and honey. If you are sure London is not the place for Felix, please let me know, I'm happy for my David to go."

It wasn't long before my mum started reasoning along with everyone and agreed to the life-changing proposal which started the process of my relocation to the UK. Everything happened so fast and, within six weeks, I was in England.

Uncle Richard kept to his promise as he quickly enrolled me in the high school closest to home and, after school and during the weekends, I joined him at the grocery store to resume my shop assistant duties. This made me an easy target for bullies, not only for my Nigerian accent, but also because I was a shop attendant for a petty African store. When I walked to the shops they sometimes called out 'Slave of a slave' or 'Black Monkey', but I just carried on walking as my uncle had suggested.

"You are the one who has lots to lose, so don't ever retaliate unless you want to be deported," he would say, when my classmates came to buy jelly beans and chocolate bars only to shout racist words to me on their way out. I was very sure my mum would have encouraged me to stand up for myself, in fact the old me would have put them in their place for good, but like my uncle said, I wasn't in my own country, so I had to swallow my pride and let my emotions die inside of me.

Completing secondary school was a miracle, it still baffles me how I achieved straight A*s in my GCSE subjects. Unfortunately, all my hard work was for nothing as I wasn't able to get into University. I was an illegal immigrant because my uncle hadn't processed my papers to remain in the UK. His excuse was, the amount of money he sends home to my mum every month was exorbitant, which meant he was unable to afford lawyers.

Friends advised me to report my uncle to the authorities for child labour and human trafficking, but I couldn't because I wasn't prepared to starve my mum and sister to death. I continued working at the shop for free, hoping that one day, my dreams would come true.

A few years later my hard work at the shop was finally paying off, my uncle made me the store manager of one of his branches, and this time I wasn't working for free. Things were really looking up, not just for me, but also for my family at home. Mum confirmed that she had finally completed building her own house; Tomi, my little sister was finishing University soon; and Mum's mini-supermarket business was booming. All of these things gladdened my heart – all I suffered in the UK meant something after all.

Being a shop manager came with its perks. For example, all the ladies who behaved like I was an obnoxious pest, were finally flocking around me, even the ones who bullied me whilst in high school were finally coming around. "I love your hair", "You have such amazing eyes", "You are so tall", they'd say, whilst eyeing me lustfully. I was sometimes flattered by their advances, but I only had eyes for one girl in particular, Funmi, who I thought was the most beautiful girl on earth. When I slept, she was the one I dreamed of; in my subconscious, she was the one I thought of; on the streets, she was the one I looked for; but she didn't know I existed, she didn't even know my name.

One evening, on my way back from work, I decided to stop at the supermarket to get some groceries. At the canned food aisle, I bumped into Funmi who was putting some baked beans into her trolley.

"Hi Funmi, how are you doing?" I asked, but she didn't respond.

"Funmi, why do you always ignore me? I am just saying hello, the least you can do is respond," I said.

She looked me up and down. "Felix, I have no reason to speak to you, I can't stand cowards. Every time I see you, it reminds me of how you let people bully you when we were in high school. Why did you never stand up for yourself?" she asked.

I was shocked by her confrontation, because she never acted as if she knew me, or how my peers treated me.

"I don't remember you standing up for me either," I said defensively, "I never retaliated because my uncle advised me not to."

"Bullshit!" she said, "No matter what, you are a man who should always stand up for himself. If you don't, how are you supposed to protect your woman? Would you believe it if I told you that you were my crush in school? I just couldn't bring myself to talking to you because of your sheepish attitude."

"Funmi, I think you and I aren't that different, you saw how your friends treated me in school but you never stopped them, sometimes you even joined in. Being a coward and a hypocrite is a very nasty combination you know?" I said, as I watched her eyes soften.

"I am so sorry Felix, we've wasted too much unnecessary time apart, there's nothing stopping us from making up for lost time now," she said, as she took my shopping basket off me, placed it on the shop floor and put her arms around me.

It was the first time I held a girl so passionately and before I knew it, her lips gently brushed mine, waiting for me to reciprocate. At first, I didn't know what to do, so I returned the gesture by pecking her lips – they were soft and succulent. My instincts told me to go a step further, but I didn't know how to. As I had read in books, her pupils were dilated, her lips engorged with passion, so I let my instincts lead the way as I embraced and locked lips with her. The rest, as they say, is history.

Funmi and I became inseparable, she was either at mine or I was at her halls of residence in Uni. We were even talking about getting married as soon as she finished Uni, not only because we were so much in love, but also to legalise my stay in the UK.

One day, Funmi and I were on bus 279 to Seven Sisters African food grocery store when a dozen Immigration Officers got on the bus.

"Present your bus pass and a form of ID – it could be your driving licence or passport. Get them ready before we get to you!" one of the officers shouted, as they reviewed passengers' IDs.

They were halfway down the bus and I still hadn't thought of what to say. Funmi looked worried but didn't say a word as she got out her driving licence; I only had my library card and some cash on me, I didn't even own a provisional driving licence.

"Library card is not acceptable," an officer said, then another asked, "What is your name, how old are you and where do you live?"

I answered all their questions, but they didn't seem satisfied, so they probed further and, after a few more questions, they found out I was illegally living in the UK. Right there and then, they put me in handcuffs and I knew they were going to deport me.

"I am not a criminal!" I screamed, "I went to school in the UK; I practically grew up in this country; it is my country and I have never caused any troubles; my fiancée is British so you can't remove me just like that."

"Your fiancée's parents don't want you in this country, they think you are a waste of space," one of the officers said, as they dragged me out of the bus.

I looked back to reassure Funmi that everything was going to be ok, but was surprised to see her sitting on the bus like a cold chicken, with a blank face that made it difficult for me to determine whether she was happy or sad about my situation. Watching her emotionless face confused the hell out of me, it made me wonder who on earth I had been spending my life with for the last year – her actions still haunt me up until today.

"Which school did you attend and how long have you been in the UK?" another officer asked, and when I told him, he advised me to leave the UK voluntarily and then get myself a lawyer to help me return. I took his advice because it was better than facing a ten-year re-entry ban into the UK.

Going back to Nigeria was a blessing in disguise because I was able to spend ample time with my mother and sister. The condition in which I met my family was better than I imagined. All the money my uncle and I had been sending to mum for years was put in good use and she already had five supermarket branches across Lagos, and a bakery.

When I had been in Lagos for about three months, Mum asked me what I wanted to do with my life. She gave me the option of furthering my education in one of the Nigerian universities, or in the UK. I was already accustomed to the UK way of life, most of my friends lived there, and of course I wanted to look Funmi in the eye and ask her WHY. Why she never called to check up on me, especially when she had several opportunities to do so. As you would have guessed, with the help of my lawyer, I returned to the UK.

Uncle Richard said he bumped into Funmi on several occasions but she did everything in her power to avoid talking to him. What Uncle Richard didn't tell me, until I returned to the UK, was that she was heavily pregnant. 'Who by?' was the question running through my mind, as I sat on the train from Birmingham to London, on my way to go and confront her. When I got to her rented apartment I didn't need to knock on the door as I already had a spare key. I just opened the door and there she was, my first love, almost unrecognisable.

The shock on her face gave me such a sense of satisfaction, I wish I had taken a picture, framed it, and kept it on my fridge so I could see it every day, just for my own amusement.

"What are you doing here? You shouldn't be here!" she screamed.

"Calm down, you shouldn't be shouting in your condition," I said, her unwelcoming reaction spurring me on to speak the truth. I continued, "The horror on your face is out of this world, I wish I had brought a camera with me, the picture of your face is worth framing and hanging on my bedroom wall at the University of Birmingham's halls of residence." My words had an instant effect and her face looked even more confused than it already was.

"Funmi, I only have two questions for you," I said. "One, did you ever love me? Two, is the baby you are carrying mine?"

In answer to my questions, all she kept saying was, "I'm so sorry!" as she shed few crocodile tears, (well, that's what it looked like to me).

I had no sympathy for her and I wasn't going to leave until she explained herself, she owed me and 'Sorry' wasn't going to cut it. When she realised I wasn't going anywhere until I got what I wanted, she started talking.

"My first love and childhood friend, Dotun, cheated on me with a girl from his University in Wales. When I found out, I felt betrayed and wanted to hurt him back. Even though he apologised, I was determined to make him pay because I knew I wasn't capable of breaking up with him. Then I met you at the supermarket, I knew you liked me since our high school days, so I thought I should give you a chance, but I didn't intend for us to get that deep.

"After a few months of us seeing each other, Dotun found out about us and reported me to my parents because he knew how much they loved him. In their eyes, he was already my husband and they were prepared to remove any obstacle in their way. I tried to play it cool with both of you, because I kind of loved you both and I couldn't make up my mind who I wanted to be with. I was still trying to figure it out when the immigration officers came to take you away – for the record, my parents did that, not me or Dotun.

I am sure the baby is Dotun's because I was always careful with you; we used protection most times. I am getting married to him after the baby is born. I am so sorry to have hurt you like this, I hope someday you'll find it in your heart to forgive me," Funmi explained.

As the saying goes, the truth is bitter and sometimes better left unsaid. When Funmi finished her sob story, I felt sick in my stomach, as I realised the long and short of Funmi's story was that I was her second best, aka her pain reliever. The knife in my heart pierced even deeper – I regretted making the journey to find out the truth and I cursed the day I met her."

CHAPTER FIVE

The Masquerade Festival

BY the time Felix finished telling his story, I must have cried a gallon of tears. I thought my life was the worst until I heard about his. I just wanted to give him a big hug and kiss away all his pain, but instead, he was the one who comforted me.

"I am so sorry Felix," I wept, "I had no idea."

"It no longer hurts Grace," he said, "In fact, I never told anyone the full story, not even the girlfriends after Funmi. I am glad you asked, and you are such a great listener." He paused, before adding, "And in answer to your question, I am as single as number ONE, I'm not romantically involved with anyone." As he spoke those last few words, he moved even closer to me. By this time, our faces were only a couple of inches apart.

"I don't remember asking if you are single or involved," I mumbled, wondering if the hot sensation I was suddenly feeling came from his body heat, or from somewhere deep inside my own body.

"Yes, you did!" he whispered in my ear, his breath making the hairs stand up on the back of my neck.

Using his tied hands, he gently lifted my chin such that our faces met again. We held our gaze for a while, then I looked away again because I was feeling the familiar butterfly sensation at the bottom of my belly, and I didn't think it was the place or time for such frolicking. 'Oh Grace,' I told myself, 'Compose yourself! It's just the drama of the situation heating you both up, nothing more.' As if he read my mind he quickly dropped my chin, although he made sure our eyes met again in the process. He said nothing.

This time, I found myself unable to look away. We just stared at each other and communicated with our eyes. I found it easy to read his thoughts and I believe he was able to read mine too. His eyes seemed genuine and pure, just what I needed at the time. The purity in his eyes, stripped even more bare by the situation we both found ourselves in, was in stark contrast to the many hidden agendas and lies of too many people who had mucked me about in my lifetime. Then, as if to break the loud silence between us, Felix spoke in the sexiest voice I had ever heard.

"I will get us out of here my lady," he said, his eyes blazing with the determination in his words and the passion in his body. As respectful as he was being, I could tell his mind was in conflict with the animal nature of his body. His eyes burned into mine and he leaned forward, suddenly pecking my lips lightly with his own as if he was asking for my approval, before pulling away again.

'Ooops!' said my own inner dialogue, 'What were we just saying about composure, Grace?', but my body told another story. My rationale and reasoning chided me like a strict aunt, but my sexuality welcomed his advances.

When I didn't move or show any sign of disapproval, his lips met mine again and I found myself responding. I was surprised to find my thirst for his kiss was so great that I didn't even mind his beard. In a way, the rough nature of it just added an erotic frisson to our caress. At first it was gentle, as we explored each other's mouths for the first time, then it gradually escalated into something a little more aggressive, as if the kiss was the required antidote to cure us of the circumstance we found ourselves in.

Even though our legs and hands were tied, it didn't stop our tongues from taking over our bodies. We writhed lustfully against each other and, in a matter of moments, I was lying on my back and Felix's groin was getting harder as it rubbed against my thigh, making me want every inch of his body inside of me. It surprised me that my body so desperately yearned for a man I barely knew; not only did my body want him, I wanted him too…

Unfortunately, before we could get further carried away, the fact we were handicapped by our shackles brought our bodies crashing back to reality, followed by our minds, as our joint fantasy of escapism through sex flew out of the window and we reluctantly parted, breathless and frustrated. "How I wish!" said Felix, panting with desire.

"We'll just have to make do with what we have," he added, before bringing his lips to mine again, but this time I did pull away because we heard footsteps approaching, further shocking us back into reality. Felix quickly crawled back to his side of the room and I sat up against the wall on my side, acting like a helpless miserable moose, painfully aware of how hard and fast my heart was beating. I wondered if it had been so loud, that it alerted our kidnapper to come and pay us a visit.

The door opened and in came Sunday, this time with a remarkably pretty young lady who looked slightly younger than him. She certainly did not look like a kidnapper, but she was clearly not a captive either. I wondered who she was.

"These are the people I was talking about," said Sunday, nodding to the mystery woman and gesturing at me and Felix.

The young woman cast a glance at us and rolled her eyes. "Sunday, you are as blind as a bat," she said, "I see no resemblance between the lady and I, none whatsoever, except…maybe our complexion, physique…I mean, that's it. And the man looks nothing like you, period." She laughed, "Sunday, you are blind and a fool! This will never work!"

In that moment, I realised that Felix's prediction was spot on.

Sunday and his girlfriend, or whoever she was and her identity was bugging me as she did look vaguely familiar, were trying to steal our identities. After all, Sunday still had our passports and, if there was a resemblance between us, it wouldn't be too difficult to pull off.

The thought scared the life out of me, because Sunday was actually right about the mystery young lady and myself – she could at least pass as my younger sister. We had the same skin tone and height, same curve of the jaw and cheekbone, and she even had wide hips, just like mine – even her hair had the same glossy thickness as mine. There was just something about her and I couldn't shake the feeling we were more than just similar in looks, but related by blood. My curiosity took over and I had to know more.

I sat up straight and looked her in the eye. "What's your name?" I asked, smiling in my most persuasive fashion.

She shifted from one foot to the other, eyeing me suspiciously, as though mirroring my own curiosity and questions. She was silent at first, then sniffed and nodded. "Morolake, but my friends call me Mo," she replied.

I took my opportunity to communicate further. "Oh, what a pretty name, I have always loved that name. If I were you, I will never let anyone shorten my name, it robs it of the richness. Correct me if I'm wrong, Morolake means 'I have someone wealthy to care for', right?" I asked.

"Yes, it means just that – I have riches to look after in the form of this child," she agreed, "But I prefer Mo, it sounds foreign and cool." She cocked her eyebrow, a small smile starting to form on her face.

"What's your surname?" I asked optimistically, in an attempt to find out more about her, but she suddenly went on the defensive.

"Why are you interrogating me? You have no right to ask me questions, if anyone should be asking questions it should be me," she snapped.

My inner voice berated me, 'Grace, you just pushed it too far, too fast, again. Slow it down.' I took a deep breath and gave it another go. "Calm down Mo, I was just trying to have a conversation with my lookalike," I said gently to her, before turning my attention to Sunday.

"Hang on a minute, Sunday," I challenged him, "Do you really think you can steal our identities?" I paused for effect before continuing, "She's right you know, you and Felix look nothing like each other, and even if you do, it's not just a matter of landing at Heathrow airport with our passports and walking through the borders without being caught. If I may ask, how do you intend to step into our lives and fit in? The system will find you out in a matter of minutes because your fingerprints won't match ours and you definitely won't be able to do our jobs as you aren't qualified."

Pleased with my little speech of reasoning, I settled back and observed its impact. I noticed Mo, more than Sunday, was seeing things from my point of view, so I carried on pointing out the facts – both true and false, I didn't care anymore, I just wanted to get the hell out of their smelly room.

"Your best bet is to allow us go back to the UK and I promise to invite you and Mo over if you feel that's the best thing for you. I understand you are doing this because you want a better life for yourselves, but it doesn't have to be this way. Once we return to the UK, Felix and I can send you guys a substantial amount of money to start up a business of your own. The UK is not as rosy as you think, Felix, tell them!" I said, but Sunday didn't give Felix the chance to respond before he interjected.

"You these abroad people must think we are daft in Nigeria! If the UK or US is as bad as you say, why did you and your family leave your fatherland for a white man's country with no intention of returning?" he asked. "Look at your fresh skin and clothes, expensive enough to feed a whole family for a week and you sit there telling me that I'm better off staying in this shit hole country? You are talking about starting up a business, do you know how much money has gone down the drain by some patriotic optimist who believed in this system? At first the business may seem profitable until a competitor opens up their shop next to yours, and that's if lack of electricity hasn't ruined the business before then." Sunday finished his speech by throwing his hands up into the air.

Felix stepped in to support my argument. "Sunday, I see your point, but Grace is right. Living in the UK is not as easy as you think; every penny you earn in the western world is never by accident. You work your socks off only to pay most of it back to the government in tax. At least in Nigeria you stand a chance of starting something the proper way, and making it big because it's your country. Don't believe what you see when people like us come back home to show off, trust me, there are poor people in western countries too."

Sunday snorted and waved his hand at Felix, "But no matter how poor they are, food won't be a problem. Before I got that job as a cook, I could hardly feed myself one square meal a day. So, no matter how bad you say the UK is, I think it is better for people like us."

"Ok," said Felix, slowly and intentionally, "If you insist on leaving Nigeria, Grace and I can help you with the processes. But first, you have to give us our travel documents, follow us to the UK embassy where we can help you complete your visa application and, in the next few weeks, you will be able to relocate to the UK." He winked at me on the sly.

Also on the sly, I could tell Mo had been continuing to watch me out of the corner of her eye. I could almost hear her brain ticking out loud. For all the unfortunate incidents which had led me to this point, I started to wonder if they were all part of fate's plan and, indeed, my path to find my blood father.

Mo's voice was firm when she spoke. "Sunday, their suggestion is fair, we can't just barge into a foreign country with someone else's ID," she said, before turning her attention to me. "Abosede, we will let you go on one condition," she continued, "This may seem strange, but the condition is that you follow me to my father's house and meet him. I mean you no harm and this sounds crazy, but I have a feeling we are related…" She trailed off, but I nodded at her to continue.

"My father," said Mo, "A few years ago he found out he had a daughter, a daughter he has never met. Apparently, the mother gave the child to another man and they both eloped to the UK. Ever since he found out, he has been on the lookout." Mo trailed off again, chewing her lip and twisting her fingers together nervously, before continuing, "I just think it's more than a coincidence that we look alike and you are here in Lagos, from the UK, on whatever mission you are on. Who knows, you might actually be my long-lost big sister. I don't know, but I have a feeling that you might be. My father, he will know the appropriate questions to ask to find out for sure, like your mother's name."

Hearing her speak left no doubt in my mind that my own suspicions were founded, as her words poured into the part of my soul which was wanting to find my biological home. Even if we were not blood sisters, we were sisters in this need for belonging. If I had just found my blood sister, then I had also found my father. The similarities were striking and my grandmother had told me my father was originally from a small town on the outskirts of Lagos, but she wasn't sure of the exact location. After they came for the formal introduction ceremony at my grandparents' house in Ibadan, the plan was to return the visit, but Mum had called off the wedding before they had the chance to.

"I will come with you," I said, "Please tell me, what is your father's name?"

"Mathew Fadiro," Mo replied, confirming what I already knew in my heart – I had finally found my father and a half-sister I didn't know existed. Everything was starting to make sense – the heavy traffic I was stuck in for four hours, the bread seller, Sola, and the kidnap were obstacles I had to overcome on my journey to meet father. My head was swimming as all the pieces fell into place.

"Am I allowed to come with her?" Felix asked, snapping me out of my thoughts. I was so excited by these new revelations, I had almost forgotten he was part of my story. Sunday, mollified by Mo's argument, nodded his agreement and Mo shrugged. I could tell she didn't care either, she was as intrigued and thrilled as I was. Emboldened by our positive responses, Felix asked another question, "Can we stop over at the nearest chemist to get Grace some insulin?"

My heart warmed. 'How sweet of him' I thought, 'He remembers and he cares.' It was clear Sunday had only rescued what he deemed to be the most important items from my car, our passports and ID, and not my insulin. Felix had noticed this and acted on it.

Although I'd only just met Felix, I couldn't help but compare him to my previous boyfriends who left the moment they heard I was diabetic. To them, I was a walking corpse and my illness was contagious. One of my ex-boyfriends, Michael, who I adored so much, had vowed to give me all the support I needed, but his actions showed the exact opposite.

"It scares me when I see you stabbing yourself like this. Doesn't it hurt? I just hope you won't have to do this forever," he once said, and when he saw the expression on my face, he quickly added, "I am only asking because I feel sorry for you, especially if you'll need to inject yourself with insulin on your wedding day or in front of your children. What if they inherit your disease, that will be a disaster for a child."

I wasn't sure if Michael was genuinely sorry for me, but it was blatantly clear that he was removing himself from the equation – he obviously didn't see a future with me. Before he came up with a reason to dump me, like the others did, I broke up with him as soon as I could and the relief on his face was evident. It was also the last time I heard from him.

Back to the present and, as suggested by Felix, we stopped at the chemist on our way to my father and Mo's house. Sunday paid for one bottle of insulin which should last me for the rest of my stay in Nigeria. Even though we still had a long way to go on our journey to freedom, I felt myself relax, knowing I now had my medicine should I need it. All I needed now was somewhere private to inject myself, because I didn't want to do in front of Felix. Whilst I was sure he wouldn't mind; the reactions of Michael and others had made me self-conscious.

"How far away is your house Mo?" I asked, hoping it wasn't too far so I could inject myself there upon arrival. When she said it was close by, I handed her the insulin bottle to keep safe in her handbag as we made our way to the bus stop. We had been waiting for about twenty minutes, without a taxi, motorcycle, or anyone else in sight. The road, which seemed like one that was supposed to be busy, was deserted. I wondered what was going on.

"Oh, my God! I forgot, the Ikoko Masquerade festival starts today," Mo announced, "I forgot because I spent the night at yours."

"No, it doesn't start until tomorrow," Sunday replied.

"Sunday, there was a curfew two days ago warning all women, children and non-natives to stay indoors because the festival had been pushed forward," Mo confirmed, "Just look at the road, there is no traffic and this is why."

"What do we do now?" I asked, hoping someone had a good idea, as I was increasingly keen to reach our destination for a number of reasons.

"The festival won't start fully until the afternoon," reasoned Sunday, "So if we walk really fast, we can be at Mo's house in forty-five minutes."

"That's too far," said Mo, tossing her head in disagreement, "Why don't we walk to the neighbouring street, it is meant to be busier. I am sure there will be random taxi or bus drivers waiting to earn quick money before the festival starts," she suggested and we all agreed.

As we walked across the streets, we heard the sounds of the festival approaching, loud sounds of drums, tambourines, and men chanting strange songs.

"Disobedient and inquisitive women will have themselves to blame, peep through the keyhole and lose your sight; look through the window and lose your head. This is a festival only for men, only for princes, only for kings. Women, women be warned!" they sang aggressively. This festival did not sound too friendly!

"We must run back home right now!" Sunday and Mo cried, but it was already too late, the masquerades and their boys had already spotted us and were running towards us with their whips.

They continued singing and drumming loudly; some of them danced dramatically, whilst the others ran towards us in excitement. We all stared at each other in panic. We knew our lives may be at stake, as implied by their songs, so we started running in the opposite direction as quickly as we could. Felix, Sunday and Mo were able to run faster than me, probably because my blood sugar was running high due to lack of insulin in two days. In fact, I was surprised to have lasted that long without it. I kept running as fast as I could, but my body wasn't cooperating with me and it gradually slowed down, until I fell when my foot hit a stone. I tried to pull myself up and once again run for my life, but my body felt weak and my head felt dizzy and I was struggling to orientate myself. The sound of the men's feet, stamping ever so loudly, was closing on me ever so quickly, and I concluded there was no point in even trying to run. I couldn't even stand up without a superhuman effort which felt beyond my capabilities right then. All I could do was slump there, spent of energy, and wait for what was coming next. The noise grew closer and, when I looked up, all I could see were several barefoot men, with angry faces, gathering around me.

"Get up, idiot!" one of the men shouted, but I was too weak to move. All I could do was look in the other direction to check if Felix, Mo and Sunday were out of harm's way. Through the legs of drummers, masquerades, their handlers, and the dancers who were still beating their instruments furiously, I saw Felix. He was being pulled away by Sunday, seemingly against his wishes. My eyes blurred with tears as I saw him try to break free and run to me, to rescue me. He almost wriggled his way out of Sunday's grasp, but Mo ran back to help Sunday and the two of them eventually overpowered him. It was the last scene I saw before I closed my eyes.

CHAPTER SIX

Ikoko Town

THE next time I opened my eyes, I found myself in a white mosquito net tent with fluffy pillows strategically placed around me. 'Is this what heaven's like?' I wondered, confused and still groggy. I didn't know I was thinking out loud until a middle-aged woman came to my bedside. She moved slowly, with an easy air and a ready smile.

"You are not in heaven, my dear, you've been given a second chance," she said, gently placing her hand on my forehead and stroking my hair back from my face, "It's up to you, use it well. We almost lost you, thank your lucky stars and the gentlemen who brought you to the palace yesterday."

"The palace?" I mumbled, now even more bewildered than before, "What palace? Where am I? What happened to me?"

"Sshhh dear," she replied in a kind voice, "Don't agitate yourself, you are safe now. All in good time my dear."

I sat up and perched amongst the cushions. "Tell me, please tell me," I demanded.

The woman sighed, "Alright dear, I will tell you all I know. Rumour has it that the masquerade handlers apprehended you, raped you till you passed out and, when they thought you were unconscious, they left you in the middle of the road to die. The King's right-hand, Otunba, found you and made sure you were brought to the palace with the hope that our chief priest would be able to resurrect you. After hours of appeasing the gods, you came back to life. Like I said, you are a very lucky girl!"

I was dumbfounded and couldn't believe what I was hearing.

"Can one be raped without knowing?" I asked, as I used my fingers to check my crotch area for any visible evidence, "Can one almost die without knowing? How long have I been here, and what time is it?"

"So many questions my dear!" she chided, "I cannot answer them all. They brought you to me yesterday, the king and chief priest asked me to watch over you and cater to your needs. It is now morning and you slept all through the night. You were dreaming, you were talking in your sleep, asking for someone named Felix, but I do not know who that is, you were alone when you came here." She fussed around me, plumping my pillows and making soothing sounds, like a mother with a child. "What's your name, anyway?" she asked.

I debated on which name to give her, since I was in a traditional environment, I thought it was best to go by my traditional name.

"Abosede," I replied.

"Abosede, the chief priest predicted you will be very hungry when you wake up. What would you like for breakfast?" she asked, "The cook can make anything you like."

The chief priest knew what he was talking about because I was starving, but the mention of a cook brought back a flood of memories... about how Sunday had abused his position as a cook to rescue me and Felix, just to con us again, and how they had all abandoned me to the attackers. I had a flashback to Sunday and Mo holding Felix back as he called my name, and I felt sick. Before I ate anything, I wanted to know more about my current situation and how 'safe' I actually was this time.

"Ma'am, you are right, I am very hungry, but before you find me something to eat, it's important to tell me when the chief brought me here," I said, "If all you say is true, the palace has gone to some trouble to save me – why? Why me? Or does the chief go around scooping up any lost woman he finds lying on the street?" As the words left my mouth I realised this last comment made me sound a little churlish, so I added, "I am sorry, I am immensely grateful, I am just confused and trying to make sense of it all."

"I am sorry too my dear," she replied, "I do not have all the answers you seek. After breakfast you will feel stronger and then you can speak with the chief and the king, they will know better." She paused and looked at me with added interest, "You don't sound like you are from around here, you have a foreign accent, similar to that of my British lecturer at Teacher Training College. Where are you from?"

"I am from the UK," I replied, remembering that Sunday still had my passport, so I had no way of proving my identity.

"Oh, poor child!" declared my kind nurse, "What brought you here? Did you not know yesterday was a stay at home day? The streets are dangerous during the festival!" She tutted in a disapproving fashion, before adding, "Where are your parents, they must be looking for you by now?"

"Yes," I agreed, "They must be worried sick by now, especially my grandma, I need to call them to let them know I am alright." I had started to relax a little. "Please may I use a telephone and, yes, please may I have some breakfast?" I pondered on what to ask for; I needed something fast so I said, "Fried eggs and a couple of slices of bread would be nice. And can you send someone to a nearby chemist to get me Lantus – my insulin injection, I am diabetic and I need my medicine."

"Insulin? What does that mean?" she asked, as she retraced her steps back to my bedside, "I know what diabetes means, we call it 'Itosugar' but you are too young for that. It's an old person's illness and people who've been diagnosed with it are warned to stay away from anything sweet or starchy. Instead of pounded yam, they are asked to eat wheat or amala made out of plantains. For breakfast, they usually eat oat... I know how to make oat, I make it for the king's mother every morning. Would you prefer that to bread?"

I felt relieved that I didn't have to explain my illness further to her, she knew more than my grandma, who refused to believe anything was wrong with me.

"There are two types of diabetes," I explained, "The king's mother probably has the adult-onset of diabetes called Type 2, which means it is not insulin dependent. I was diagnosed with Type 1 when I was fourteen, it's the child-onset of the disease and is insulin dependent."

Despite my hunger and need for insulin, I was definitely starting to feel more like myself again and wasn't in any pain in my body. I considered the rumours of the severity of my attack may have been exaggerated. "You know, I really don't think I was raped yesterday... I remember collapsing and blacking out, but surely no one in their right senses would rape a semi-conscious person," I said, before adding, "Please can you tell me your name ma'am?"

"You can call me Mama Soji...my only son, Soji, is in University studying Medicine, you will get to meet him when next he visits the..." she said, as she smiled with the distinctive look all mothers wore when they wanted to show off their child. I knew if I didn't stop her, we could be there for ages while she told her proud stories, so I butted in.

"Mama Soji, you can tell me all about Soji later, please get me something to eat first, my body is shaking," I said, feeling bad for cutting her off mid-sentence, but she didn't seem offended.

"Don't worry Princess, I will be back with a delicious bowl of oatmeal, just give me five minutes." She handed me a glass of orange juice, "Here, drink this, your breakfast will be ready soon," she advised, before leaving for the kitchen.

True to her word, she was back within minutes, carrying a tray of food. As she approached my bedside, I noticed there was the promised bowl of porridge, but it was accompanied by something which looked like my favourite food of all time.

"Moi wrapped in banana leaves?" I cried in delight.

"Yes, my dear, it is, I wasn't sure if you'd like spicy steamed bean cake," she said, as she placed the tray on my lap and the delicious aroma immediately filled my nostrils.

"I love Moi Moi, especially when it's made in leaves; it gives it an authentic local taste. My mum and grandma have the best recipe in the world," I said, as I started unfolding the wrap and completely ignoring the piping hot bowl of porridge.

"I can bet my last dollar you will take your words back when you taste this Moi Moi; the secret recipe was passed down to me from my great, great-grandmother. Just so you know, this one was cooked in an Ikoko Amo on firewood, you will never get the authentic smoky taste if you cooked it with an electric or gas cooker," she explained, and I could testify it to be true – just one bite convinced me that Mama Soji's Moi Moi was the fluffiest, richest and tastiest I ever had.

"I know about cooking with firewood, but what is Ikoko Amo?" I asked, as I continued eating my delicious breakfast.

"Ikoko means pot and Amo means clay," she replied.

"Alright! So how come this town is named after a pot?" I asked.

"Good question, I will tell you the story my grandmother told me about the genesis of our town!" She readjusted herself in her seat, with a twinkle in her eye.

"Our town is named after the first King of Ikoko. The king of neighbouring town, Salolo, was going to give his daughter, Sade, away in marriage to any young man who was capable of making the best Ikoko Amo in town. So, he called for a competition. Princess Sade was very beautiful, every young man's dream wife. The king also mentioned that the newlyweds would inherit acres of land on the other side of town, to call their very own. The pressure was on for the youngsters, so they all went away to sharpen their pottery skills.

"On the day of the competition, one of the potters, Kola, intended to create a huge masterpiece, but the pot he was shaping was curving dangerously outwards. He was perplexed. To make matters worse, when he looked around him, he noticed his rivals were already creating perfect-looking pots, maybe not as huge as what he had in mind, but they were good enough to win the competition, if he didn't do something fast.

"Just before he went back to readjust his pottery, he saw an incomplete clay pot in the distance with no one minding it, so he quickly went to pick it up, added it to his craft and reshaped it into an astoundingly beautiful model that won him the competition. He married Princess Sade, became a very powerful king, together they had seven boys and a daughter, and they lived happily ever after!" Mama Soji finished her story with a big, satisfied smile.

"Hmmm," I said, "Are you saying he won the competition by stealing someone else's unfinished work?"

"Well, I wouldn't call that stealing, it was unattended. His clay pot was going pear-shaped, he had to do something to bring it back to life, so he did what he had to do," Mama Soji replied. When she noticed I wasn't totally convinced, she added, "You've mapped your life out perfectly, along the line, something threatens to ruin it, wouldn't you do something to put your life back on track?"

"I will, as long as I don't hurt someone else in the process," I replied.

Just before Mama Soji could reply, we heard a knock on the door. It was a guard with my insulin medication. "Thank you!" I said as I collected the kit from him and made for the en-suite, away from the prying eyes of Mama Soji.

Now I had my breakfast and my medication, I felt like a new woman and as though I could conquer the world. In my head, I had a list of activities to accomplish – first and foremost, I wanted to thank Mama Soji for looking after me, then thank the king's chief, Otunba, and the king for saving my life, and ask if one of them could spare me a few bucks for transport fare to get me out of town.

It was high time I went back to Grandma's and, eventually, back home to my family in the UK. A part of me still wanted to find my biological father, but it was clearly costing me too much – kidnapped on my birthday, freed the following day, only to be drugged and kidnapped again, then almost losing my life whilst running from some traditional masquerade revellers. I didn't feel like it was worth the effort of staying another day in Nigeria, I just wanted my easy life back. As the saying goes, 'You never know what you have until you lose it'.

I knew I would return to Nigeria in future, but I'd be better equipped next time, with security agents to drive me around. If I was still keen on finding my father, I would recruit a detective to locate him, and that shouldn't be difficult because I already knew where to look.

"We need to get you ready for Kabeyesi," said Mama Soji, interrupting my thoughts, "He will like to see you before he starts his day and it's my duty to make you presentable."

"I can't wait to meet the king, but I don't need to dress up for him, just get me something clean to change into…a pair of jeans and clean T-shirt will do," I said, but Mama Soji was already navigating her way through the wardrobe, which was filled with expensive-looking traditional ball gowns and matching shoes.

"Mama Soji, are you even listening to me?" I asked.

"I can hear you loud and clear my dear, but you are not listening to me. You are going to be our next queen – our Olori. Before Otunba brought you here, the oracle informed us of your homecoming," she said.

"You are proof that our forefathers haven't completely deserted us, they are still very much potent. The oracle said you will be sent from above and, when you arrive, we should treat you like the queen that you are."

Now I was confused again. "What are you talking about ma'am?" I asked, "I am not a queen. I am not even a princess."

"Ah my dear, hush now," soothed Mama Soji, "But you are. We didn't understand it then, but now we know, you are indeed from above because your aeroplane flew in the sky from abroad. We had decorated and equipped this room last month in preparation for your arrival, we also have a befitting lounge on the other side of that door which adjoins your room and that of Kabeyesi's. The other wives have separate apartments on the other side of the palace. You are really a lucky girl, and a godsend to this town and palace. Olori Abosede, there is no point in looking at me like I am speaking gibberish, you are going to be the king's third wife!"

I didn't think I could take any more shock in my life, but there I was looking dumbfounded as Mama Soji placed a stunning ball gown at the foot of the bed.

"Now hurry up, go and have a bath," she added, shooing me in the direction of the bathroom, "Get ready for your king!"

However, I stood my ground. For all the craziness I had experienced in the last few days, now things had become quite simply ridiculous. "Mama Soji, listen to me and listen good, I don't know which gods or chief priests have brainwashed you, but the moment I step out of this bed, and out of this room, it will be to go home. Make sure you stay out of my way, or else you will regret ever setting eyes on me," I snapped, indignantly, before continuing, "I haven't come to Nigeria to find a husband! I have a purposeful life ahead of me and it does not include being some loser's third wife. Not even a first and only wife, but a third wife, one of many! In case you don't know, I am somebody's daughter...don't you or your Kabeyesi realise that. And even if he really wants to marry me, doesn't he think he must ask me first? Then ask my parents for their approval? What world do you guys live in? I'm not just a stray dog you can keep without finding its owner. Please don't annoy me any further, in case you can't tell, I have been through a lot and I am starting to lose both my patience and my temper."

Letting out a bit of steam felt good, even though I knew snapping at Mama Soji was shooting the messenger and also unfair, as it was not her fault and she was just following her instructions. Still, it was the kind of outlet I needed to pour out my frustration and mask my fears, because deep down in my heart, I knew I was in big trouble. I was smart enough to know that Mama Soji's calmness was based on the fact that guards were waiting outside my room, listening and ready to restrain me the moment she gave the order.

However, I still had a big fight in me, and I wasn't ready to sit back and watch my life, my freedom and my personal choices go to waste because of some ridiculous prophecy. In an instant and before Mama Soji could stop me, I leapt out of the bed and made for the door – shoeless, unkempt and determined. 'Queen Grace?' I thought, to my own private amusement, 'I'll give you Queen Grace! Here she is, behold!' As I flung open the door I realised my intuition was right, because there were two armed guards standing to attention outside.

"Good morning guys!" I sang, aware that I probably looked like a mad woman and caring not a jot. When neither of them responded, I greeted them in Yoruba. "Ekaro o!" I said, but they both remained mute. They didn't even look me in the eye; rather they kept their eyes downcast, and their hands on their weapons. I realised further attempts to communicate with them would prove fruitless at best, and potentially dangerous at worst.

I gave up on the guards and ignored Mama Soji, who was now fussing around behind me, trying to persuade me back into the room before I got myself into any more trouble. "Please my dear," she cajoled, "If you just come and get yourself ready for the king…"

"Ah yes!" I cried, "The king! Of course, I wish to meet the king – right now!" Realising I was unable to push past the guards, I resigned myself to standing in the doorway and screaming at the top of my voice, reckoning my cacophony would alert the king, if he really was in the room next door. "King of…Oba of Ikoko, or whatever you may call yourself, I am going to call you once and if you are not a coward, you better come out from your hiding place and let me go. I am being held captive against my will by your staff, come out and do the needful!"

I was half expecting the guards to grab me and throw me back into the room, but they did not move. "Please keep quiet, do not disturb Kabeyesi" said one of them, cautiously.

I realised they were just for show and were not allowed to hurt a single strand of hair on my body. In fact, they probably weren't even allowed to touch me. Their frustration was almost palpable. Taking advantage of this revelation, I stalked past them, into the corridor, and headed for the door to the king's room. To my amazement, nobody even tried to stop me, so I hammered on the king's door with my fists.

"Come in!" called a deep, calm, and amused-sounding voice on the other side of the door. Hearing his voice loud and clear, with just the touch of laughter in it, made me exceptionally furious because it meant he had heard me all along and, worse, found comedy in my plight. I flung open the door, ready to spit fire, but there was no one in sight.

The bedroom was huge and heavily adorned with glitter, animal skin decorations, lanterns, traditional mats, expensive-looking furniture and hardcover books. A part of me wanted to wander around and explore the room further, especially the bookshelves, but there was no time for that right now, I was a woman on a mission… where was he? I looked around the room again, now noticing a soft breeze and, following it, I saw the silhouette of a man on the balcony, leaning on the railings and looking out onto a view of mountains, valleys and tall trees, as relaxed as you like, as though he wasn't expecting anyone to come in and disturb his space.

The fact he seemed so relaxed infuriated me even more. He didn't even bother to turn around and I found this incredibly rude. I dislike talking to someone's back, king or not, but I finally had my audience, or at least the back of his head. "Sorry to disturb you 'your royal highness'" I began, my own voice sounding sarcastic in my ears, "I am here to thank you for your hospitality and to ask for your help." What I really wanted to say was, "Can you turn the fuck around and tell me why you are holding me captive in your palace for no reason? Tell your guards to set me free this minute!" But I knew it was easier to at least try to follow protocol and behave like a dumb sheep, in order to get the results I desired.

"Now that's better," he said, in a voice which sounded like dark rich honey, without turning around, "I was starting to think you needed lecturing on how to address royals. Come and enjoy this scenery with me. Waking up to this view is always the highlight of my day."

I bristled, but I knew I had to play him at his own game if I ever wanted to leave the godforsaken palace, so I took exactly twenty agonising steps from the middle of the room to the balcony. Only then did he turn around to face me.

I don't know why I imagined the king to be a middle-aged and potbellied man. On the contrary, I was surprised to discover he was young, about five years older than me, tall, lithe and handsome, with skin which matched the dark, rich, mahogany colour of the door frame. I was aware I was staring at him, most likely with a gormless expression on my face, and I suddenly felt self-conscious of my downtrodden appearance. His eyes, so dark and full of confidence and power, hypnotised me. When I managed to tear my own eyes away from his, they betrayed me by travelling straight to his lips. His mouth was firm, yet looked as though it would be delicious to taste, and his beard looked so full and well-shaped that I wanted to run my fingers through it. He must have been enjoying the look on my face, because he just stood there staring back at me, grinning like a tomcat who had just caught the juiciest of mice. The grin was all I needed to jolt me back to reality and dig for the anger which seemed to have diffused like a teaspoon of sugar in a cup of tea.

"What's your name and where did you get that accent from?" he asked, as he bent his head to get back through the doorway and into the room.

I took a deep breath and, when I began to speak, the words flowed out of me like a river. "My name is Abosede. I was born in Nigeria; relocated to the UK to join my mum and my dad; returned to Nigeria to find my biological father; got kidnapped on my birthday; escaped the following day only to be kidnapped by another thug who, with the help of my newly-found sister, agreed to take me to my father, but I passed out in the hands of your masquerade revellers and their handlers; was rescued by one of your chief councils, and now kidnapped by you. That's the story of my life in a minute, now can you get me out of here or shoot me right now?" I asked, gasping for air, not sure if my breathlessness was due to speaking too fast, or caused by the astonishing beauty who stood before me.

I couldn't help but wonder why the hell I was behaving like such a bitch on heat, it was the same thing I did the previous day – and that resulted in kissing a total stranger. Now, in the unnerving company of the young king, the memory of kissing Felix faded away like mist across the ocean. After all, he had abandoned me to the masquerade attackers, so he was hardly the hero I had hoped. Rather, it was this man who had rescued me, even though his mercy was a two-edged sword as I found myself trapped again. 'Don't look at his lips Grace,' I told myself, 'Don't look into his eyes. In fact, just don't look at him at all!' For want of something better to do, I started at the floor and at my own grubby naked feet.

"Abosede…" said the king, slowly, as though savouring my name on his tongue, "I like you!"

"You like me?" I asked, incredulous, "That's all you've got to say after I tell you about my bad experiences in my own country of birth? In your country! Do you realise that I have people looking for me right now? People who love me and are worried about me, my family who are desperate to speak to me, as I am desperate to speak to them. You hold me here against my wishes and all you have to say is I like you?" I flapped my hands at my sides, then brought them up to my downturned face as I felt myself start to cry. "I…" I began, "I just….", but my sorrow took over and the tears started rolling down my cheeks.

He touched me on the shoulder, gently. "I am so sorry, I didn't mean to upset you, please don't cry my angel. A drop of your tears mustn't touch the floor, please stop," he said, as he put his arms around me and led me back into the bedroom.

A sudden wave of helplessness engulfed me, once again it felt like I no longer had control over my own life. It also made me realise that I hadn't cried in a very long time, in fact the last time I cried was when I found out that Dad wasn't my real father. Ever since that day, people had always disappointed me and I kind of expected nothing less from them. If my own mum could betray my trust the way she did, why on earth would I anticipate something more from an outsider? The tears kept streaming down, uncontrollably; it was as if my body was taking over and doing all it could to get rid of all my pain.

"Listen, I feel your pain, and you know why? Because you and I are cut from the same cloth," he said, as he placed the palm of his hand on the small of my back and pulled me closer to him. With his other hand he cupped my chin and lifted my face, so that our eyes met. I was thankful for how my tears blurred my vision, as though I was watching everything through a pane of glass. I felt utterly wretched and just wanted to curl up into a little ball and wish myself home.

"What can I do to wash away your tears?" he asked, in a voice as rich and smooth as molasses, and I felt his beard brush against my cheek as he brought his face closer to mine. Then, ever so gently, he started to kiss away the salty water of my sorrow.

His mouth traced the path of my tears down my face, until his lips reached my own. 'Oh no Grace,' I thought to myself, 'Not again, not like this…' but I was so desperate for comfort, in both my body and my heart, that I felt myself start to yield to him.

His kiss was tentative at first, then it advanced into something more passionate as he pulled me closer to him and parted my lips with the powerful thrust of his tongue. I felt my body melting into his masculine torso, dancing to a tune of its own, one which I could not fight. There was no need for words, as we communicated with our tongues and lips. It was almost like we were taking our time to tell each other everything about ourselves, all within that kiss, holding nothing back.

Whenever I shared a kiss with a man, no matter how lost in the moment I was, I always found myself pulling away first. Sometimes to clear my head and compose myself, other times simply to get some air, or stop or initiate the next move. But this time, I didn't even think it, let alone pull away, and if there hadn't been a sudden knock on the door, I don't think either of us would have left the magical world we were being transported to.

"Kabeyesi!" called one of the guards, peeking through the door, "Otunba is in the Palace, he will like to see you urgently." I noticed it was the same guard who asked me not to disturb the king with my noise. I wondered how long he had been watching us.

"Adewale, but Otunba and I have a meeting in an hour's time, why can't he wait until then?" asked Kabeyesi, his tone sharp at having been disturbed.

"No, your highness, it sounds really urgent, I've never seen him so rattled," the guard added.

"Ok, tell him I will be downstairs in five minutes," Kabeyesi said, waving the guard away.

As soon as the door closed behind Adewale, Kabeyesi pulled me back into his body and slid his tongue up along my neck until he reached my ear. He whispered, "This isn't over, let me go and see what Otunba wants, I will be back." He pulled away, smoothed down his robes and grabbed his horse tail tassel from his bedside table.

"You should come actually, you haven't thanked him for saving your life," he added as an afterthought.

I nodded in agreement. "Yes, I want to thank him, but I need to freshen up and change into something decent before coming downstairs. I will join you in a few minutes," I said, thinking the prospect of a bath and a ball gown now seemed rather appealing.

"Ok, I will tell him you are coming to see him, don't take too long though!" retorted the king, stalking out of the bedroom.

When I re-entered my room, I found Mama Soji making alterations to the dress she had chosen for me. The fabric was the colour of golden sunshine.

"You are still here; can I have a clean towel please?" I asked, making sure that our eyes didn't meet. I was sure that she knew, that everyone would be able to tell just by looking at me, that I had been cavorting with the king just moments previously.

"Fresh towels are in the bathroom, but before you have a bath, please come here and let me see if this dress fits, I don't like making alterations based on assumptions," she said. If she did know, she didn't let on and I doubted she would have been spying on us, as the guard had.

As I tried the dress on, the perfumed fabric rustled and settled against my body, like a second skin. The gown looked like it was specifically tailored for me and I loved the way it highlighted my dainty curves and enhanced my bosom. I almost didn't recognise the reflection that stared back at me in the mirror – I looked like a queen. A queen in need of a bath, it was true, but a queen all the same.

"You've done an amazing job in a very short space of time Ma'am," I said in admiration, and watched a smile of content form on Mama Soji's lips.

"Thank you my dear, I take it Kabeyesi has charmed you with his gorgeousness. You like him, don't you?" she asked.

I shuffled uncomfortably. "Did you say towels are in the bathroom?" I asked, in an attempt to avoid her question. Luckily, I was dealing with an understanding woman, so she let the question go and nodded in response to my question.

CHAPTER SEVEN

The Throne

I waited at the entrance of the throne room with guard Adewale, until Kabeyesi signalled us in. As I approached the throne, my heart started beating really fast for reasons I couldn't comprehend. I noticed that Kabeyesi wasn't in control of himself either, as he stuttered through his conversation with Otunba, who was also staring at me.

"You can blame Mama Soji for making me this beautiful dress, she is an amazing cook, seamstress; only God knows what else she is good at. Please thank her for me," I said.

"She is amazing like that, everyone loves Mama Soji," Kabeyesi said, eyes still on me.

I turned my attention to Otunba. "Good morning sir, thank you very much for saving my life yesterday. Without your intervention, I probably would be dead by now. May God repay you and bless you and your family immensely," I said, expecting Otunba to say something, but he didn't. He just sat there staring at me and, to my surprise, I realised he was crying.

"Otunba, get a grip, she is talking to you," Kabeyesi snapped, which seemed to jolt him back to reality.

"Did the boys touch you yesterday?" Otunba asked, a touch of badly-concealed concern in his voice. He was twitchy too and there was a strange atmosphere in the air.

"No, they didn't, I fainted because my blood sugar was high," I replied, wondering why everyone was acting in such an odd fashion.

"I got a call from your mother this morning," continued Otunba, "Stating that you had been missing for the past three days. Your sister also confirmed that the masquerade handlers attacked you yesterday on your way to my house…"

Even though Otunba carried on speaking, I didn't hear anything past that point. What did he mean by us being on our way to his house? What did he know of my mother and half-sister?

"Abosede… Abosede…" the sound of my name being spoken roused me from my thoughts. It was Kabeyesi. "Listen Abosede," he said, "You must listen."

"I am sorry," I replied, biting my lip and swallowing the hundred questions which were bubbling up in my mind, seeking answers. "Otunba, please continue."

Otunba smiled at me. "I couldn't believe it either," he said, "But it is the truth. I still can't believe I carried your almost-lifeless body in my own hands, without knowing you were my first child – my daughter." He got up and walked across to me, opening his arms to give me a hug. "You are such a beauty and the spitting image of me, no wonder your mother hid you away from me."

Time stopped for a moment while I observed the man in front of me – my father. I had dreamed of and longed for this moment for so long, and now it was here all I could do was stand there like a fool, lost for words. "Thank you," I muttered, as I wondered what he was chewing, "What are you eating?"

"This is Kola Nuts, you want some?" he asked, "Take it, it's good for you, it fights off all the English man diseases from the body."

Still in a state of shock, I took some of the nuts and tried one. "This can't be good for you," I snapped, as I spat out the nut as soon as I took a bite; it was so bitter that I felt it could only be poison. I threw the rest on onto the floor, "Yuck! Are you trying to poison me already?"

Both Otunba and Kabeyesi started laughing. "She is so lost," my father said and they carried on laughing. I bristled that they were laughing at my expense, but my annoyance did not last long.

My father continued, "I thank the gods for keeping me alive to see this day. If not for them, I would have lost you on the day we were supposed to meet. Your mother is such a wicked fellow, a very heartless woman indeed, I keep saying it, women are pure evil." Then he started to cry again, a grown man, the king's chief and right-hand man, my biological father, sobbing uncontrollably.

All I could do was accept his embrace and put my arms around him, as we cried together and Kabeyesi looked on.

When I daydreamt about meeting my father, I never envisaged it to play out as a sob story. It was meant to be a joyous event, after we might have connected automatically just by setting eyes on each other. Apart from the fact that I was trying to comfort the man whose arms I was in, I felt nothing for him. He looked older than I imagined and overly traditional for my liking, but hey, he was supposedly my father.

"How would you feel if I asked for a DNA test?" I asked, and Kabeyesi and Otunba looked at me as if I had just slapped my father across the face. "In this day and age people don't just assume, we need facts. I need a test to prove that you are truly my father," I added.

"You are just like your mother, too clever for your own good. You think I won't recognise my own daughter when I see her?" Otunba argued back.

"You didn't recognise me yesterday," I retorted, "You're most definitely my father, I just need to rule out any doubt in my mind."

"You don't need to sugar coat it my dear, I am not the father you imagined. I'm not a wealthy or educated man, what I am however is an honourable man, no evil blood runs through me. Everybody, and I mean every single person in this town, old and poor, respects me for the man that I am – my name means something around here," he said, before adding, "If you think I will follow you to one stupid hospital for a blood test to prove my paternity, you must be joking. I am your father and your mother robbed me of being a dad to you. Didn't you see the resemblance between you and Morolake, my other daughter? If you want proof then go and ask your greedy mother to come to Nigeria and tell us all why she gave my child to another man."

It was obvious to anyone listening that my supposed father was very bitter towards my mother and rightly so, but that didn't give him the right to be rude towards her or me. I wanted to shut him up for speaking evil about my mother in front of me, especially in the presence of Kabeyesi, but I didn't want to add more salt to his wound. So I changed tack.

"Kabeyesi, thanks for all your help, but its time I went back home. My grandmother and mother will be worried sick about me. Please may I use your phone to let them know I am alright?" I asked.

"Of course, here is my mobile. But you can't leave the palace until we have performed all our pre-marital rituals, the chief priest's message was as clear as a whistle," Kabeyesi replied.

"Pre-marital rituals? Chief priest? Please, what are you talking about? Why are you guys so backward thinking?" I asked, as I looked from Kabeyesi to Otunba. "Listen, I am not a fetish and I am not a resident of this town, so I don't need to take orders from a fellow human being. You are all insane and Kabeyesi, I wish I had never kissed you! I must have been insane too, your madness rubbed off on me! As soon as I finish speaking to my people, I am out of here, I have had enough of this country!" I snapped, snatching the phone and dialling my grandmother's number.

"Shut up, you spoilt child! You are originally from this town, this is where your ancestors are from and you will do as the gods say, you will do as I say. I won't let you bring a curse to my household and certainly not to this town. You will marry Oba Adetoro Ajagbe – and that's final!" Otunba shouted, using Kabeyesi's full regal name.

His orders were almost laughable, because I knew what I was capable of and what I would and would not put up with. From Kabeyesi's facial expression, he also caught the drift and he could tell that my obstinate nature would make their lives and that of their gods difficult. I wished my biological father had known that no one could talk me into doing something I wasn't prepared to do. Given the chance, my mum and adopted dad would have warned him not to sound so commanding, as being ordered to do something only made me rebel in the opposite direction. Luckily, I didn't need to respond immediately, because I could already hear my grandmother's beautiful voice on the other end of the mobile phone.

"Mama, it's me!" I cried in delight, "I am alive and safe!"

Initially, the phone line went dead, but it was immediately followed by a huge sigh of relief and a scream loud enough to rupture my eardrum, as I heard her call my grandpa and her neighbours.

"I am not a cursed woman; my granddaughter has been found!" she cried repeatedly, before bombarding me with a hundred questions per minute.

"Mama, I will call my mum as soon as I hang up…Yes, I will call her, but you'll have to hang up first. Yes, as soon as I've spoken to Mummy I will be on my way to yours," I said as reassuringly as I could.

Hearing my grandma's voice was such a breath of fresh air, reminding me of the great life and family I had been blessed with. I was on the verge of losing everything just because I craved the presence of a biological father who, in fact, wasn't proving to be the best of fathers after all. He only just met me and was prepared to marry me off to a stranger just to appease his gods, like I was a sacrificial lamb of some sort. Ignoring him and Kabeyesi's curious stares, I dialled my mum's UK number.

"Mummy, it's me!" And that was all I needed to say.

"My Sweetheart, Grace, Abosede, Tioluwani, Abeke, thank God you are ok. Thank you for calling, we have been worried sick about you. Where are you? Are you hurt?" she asked.

"It's a long story, I don't even know where to start, Mum," I said.

"You will start from the beginning when I see you tomorrow, I am flying to Nigeria tomorrow. In the meantime, summarise your ordeal. Why haven't we heard from you in three days? You promised to call back on your birthday and you didn't. Why are you still punishing me for something that was beyond my control?" my mum asked. So I explained the events that led me to the Ikoko palace and how my supposed father was now trying to betroth me to the king.

As if I had just added petrol to fire, my mum's voice became unrecognisable when I told her that Otunba was in the throne room with me.

"Give him the phone, give the phone to the ingrate!" she shouted, and I did what she asked. I have no idea what was being said on the other end of the phone, but whatever it was added more fuel to the inferno.

"She is my daughter too, I can do whatever I like with her. You had her for over twenty years, now it's my turn. If you like, bring a battalion of soldiers, she is going to marry the king, Oba Adetoro Ajagbe," Otunba retorted with maximum conviction.

I noticed that whenever my father mentioned the king's full name, he made it sound like an achievement, almost like the name was worth more than gold.

"Guards, take her to her room!" my father instructed, his eyes now blazing with fury.

Even though the mobile phone wasn't on speaker, I could hear my mum's voice as she interjected. Kabeyesi heard her too, as when the guards approached on the orders of Otunba, he stopped them. "No, leave her alone!" commanded Kabeyesi.

As if my father's wings had just been clipped, he quickly hung up the phone with mum, as if to hide his diminished power. He stood there like a chastised dog, fearing the wrath of the king.

"Otunba, you can go home now, leave Abosede and I to talk this through," Kabeyesi added, banishing him from the room.

I watched as my father left the throne room and I wondered what was going on in his mind. A part of me felt sorry for him, but my sympathy was totally with my mum. If there was one thing I knew, it was that my mum always had my best interests at heart. I know that parents are advised not to have favourites, but deep down in my heart, I knew I was my mum's favourite. And this was why I couldn't bear to think of how scared she must have been, listening to my father threating to marry me off to some local king.

"Kaybeyesi, could you lend me your phone one more time please?" I asked, explaining that I needed to call my mother back to reassure her.

"Mummy, please calm your nerves, there is nothing to worry about," I said as soon as she answered the phone. "I'm not going to marry a king who already has two wives, I am coming home with you. Just make sure you come for me tomorrow."

"You mean you are going to spend another night in that godforsaken palace, why don't you just go to your grandma's today?" Mum asked.

"Mummy, I want to wait here for you. Besides, you need to introduce me to my father properly," I said, but as soon as the words left my mouth, I knew I was just making up an excuse to stay the night with Oba Adetoro Ajagbe, as my father loved to call him.

"Olori Abosede, you've made the gravest mistake in staying the night, now I am going to make you stay forever," Kabeyesi joked, when I had finished speaking to my mother, but I knew the probability was zero. After all, he already had two wives, he didn't really need a third, and I was sure he would forget all about me fast enough.

"Stop calling me your queen, I'm not your Olori," I sulked, but a part of me liked it. I was curious to experience a small part of what it might be like to be his queen, even if just for one night. At least I wanted to see around the palace.

It amazes me how emotions sometimes win the battle against self-determination. Despite my previous tantrums about hitting the road as soon as an opportunity arose, there I was hanging around and waiting for prince charming to show me around his kingdom. 'What on earth am I thinking now?' I wondered, but there was something about Kabeyesi which urged me to feed my heart and discover what could have been between us, making me lose all sense of reasoning.

"Are you ready for the tour of my kingdom Ma'am?" Kabeyesi asked, as he took my hand in his and led the way.

When we stepped out of the building, a blast of humid hot air pressed on my face immediately, reminding me of the continent I was in; I had almost forgotten how hot it was outside, as the palace was adequately air-conditioned. As we walked down the sidewalk, I contemplated going back to change my outfit because, not only was I overdressed, the fabric, especially the lining, was beginning to feel uncomfortable as it clung to the insides of my thighs. It made me wonder how people coped with wearing complete African attire, or even worse, four-piece English suits, in such high temperatures. In my opinion, when it comes to dressing, Africans should be the skimpiest of all the continents, but culture and religion won't allow it.

"Kabeyesi, I need to change my outfit, I don't think I'm able to endure this heat any longer. Please give me a couple of minutes to change into something more appropriate for this weather," I said, and when he looked at me like I wasn't making any sense, I added, "All I need is a pair of shorts and a tank top to go with it."

"I don't think you will find such clothing in this palace, we don't dress like the English here…" he gestured to the guards, who always seemed to be hanging around, "Olalekan, or Adewale, either of you, go and get me three strong hand fans from my living room. And while you are at it, ask Niyi to join us, we will need an extra hand to fan the queen," Kabeyesi commanded.

"Yes, my lord!" Olalekan said, as he hurried back to the palace.

"Kabeyesi, this is unnecessary, I don't need anyone to fan me," I said, but he just ignored my protest.

"You know you don't have to call me 'your Royal Highness' all the time, when we are alone, please feel free to call me Adetoro," he said.

To be honest, it was a much-welcomed suggestion, because calling him Kabeyesi all the time kind of put a mental wedge between us making it difficult for our conversation to flow nicely. Secondly, I found it a little difficult to pronounce the word, I knew the correct intonation in my mind, but when the word left my mouth it sounded completely different to how the locals said it – all thanks to my British accent.

It wasn't long before Olalekan returned with another guard and the three of them started fanning me vigorously. As we approached what looked like a garden, Adetoro asked the guards to leave us, explaining that the garden was airy and with enough shade and trees to keep us cool.

"Adetoro, I thought we were going to meet the queen mother, your wives and children, why don't we do that first?" I asked, "Won't they find me terribly rude to be a guest in their home, without having met me?" The truth was, I didn't really care to meet them and wanted Adetoro all to myself for the brief time I would be there, but would have hated to be seen as just some interloper who didn't know how to follow protocol correctly.

Adetoro just brushed away my concern with a smile. "Say my name again, I love the way it sounds with your accent," he said, but I couldn't bring myself to say it again as I felt too shy.

"Ok, we will see my family after I have shown you my secret garden, it is where I do most of my thinking, a place where I can shut out the world and just appreciate nature and be nurtured in return," he said, humouring me, as we walked through the garden. It really was a place to behold, an oasis of beauty and peace, and I understood why he loved it so much.

"It's beautiful," I said, as I admired the glorious blend of colours, a rainbow spectrum of all the hues of nature, with the scents of a hundred floral perfumes. I let the delights of the garden flood my senses, relaxing my soul and warming my heart.

"How well do you know your flowers? This is my favourite of all, do you know what it's called?" he asked, as he handed me the stalk of flower with a red bloom.

"I love flowers but I hardly memorise their names. The only ones I know are red roses, sunflowers, orchids and lilies. What is this called?" I asked, noticing the way he looked longingly at me, or maybe it was just pure admiration because, for all my western ways, I was still able to name a few flowers.

"It's called Crown of Thorns. It's my favourite because it sums up the life of a king," he said, as he rotated the stalk in my hand. "At a distance, the crown is glorious and desirable – until you are the one wearing it. Look at these beautiful red petals, they signify the crown from afar, but when you look closer, there are thousands of thorns that prick. It's ok when it's the odd prick here and there, but when it keeps happening you end up with a big wound and, if care is not taken, it will rot until it kills you."

"You sound sad, aren't you happy being a king?" I asked.

"I am not sad, but I could be happier," he sighed, "The life of a king is not all glory."

"No life is all glory," I encouraged him, aware that our time together was ticking by and desiring to learn as much about him as I could before my mother came to take me home. "Let's sit on this bench, it has perfect shade from the sun. Please tell me your story. I want to know how you became king, married two wives in the space of…how many years? Or did you marry two of them at the same time? You must have started young, because you don't look much older than me, unless you have great genes," I teased him, as we both sat down.

Adetoro began, "My father, Oba Ajagbe II of Ikoko Kingdom, ascended the throne when his cousin, King Adetunji, died in 1994. Exactly two years after his coronation, my father died of cancer. None of us, except Mum, knew that he had been battling the disease for years. It was a trying period in our lives, because Dad wasn't just your regular father, he was a martyr who went extra miles for everyone else apart from himself. In just two years of his reign, Ikoko Kingdom saw the benefits of crowning an educated king – his hard work put our town on the map.

"His first project was education, he used his influence with the Lagos state and Ikoko government to ensure that an outstanding primary and secondary school was built. He also singlehandedly built Folarin Specialist Hospital for terminal illness (now we know why). He was in the middle of negotiating a deal to build us a university when he died. Now that he is gone, I sometimes wonder if his kindness was a result of knowing his passing was imminent. Despite all of Dad's good attributes, including his kindness and generosity, like every human being he had his flaws. Unfortunately, these built a huge wedge between him and Mum for years.

"Mum, Olori Adetutu Ajagbe, was a beautiful woman with the most ambitious enterprising skills I had ever seen. She was also kind, loving and caring, but showed it in a different way. As usually is the case, there was always one strict parent in a family, and that was Mum. She was a no-nonsense mummy who specialised in pushing everyone around her to their limits and we all loved and respected her for it, including Dad. It was all well and good if Mum's pushy nature ended with her children, but it didn't. She extended it to friends and family, both young and old, and dad was the biggest sufferer of her bossiness. In my opinion, it is what drove him into arms of other women.

"Like I said, Dad had his flaws and his main one was a weakness for women, he would sleep with anything in a skirt. As one will imagine, it was a big issue in their marriage, especially when the majority of Mum's home helps, shop attendants, or apprentices were her rivals. The moment the girls started sharing Dad's bed, the signs become evident to Mum because they tended to flaunt it in her face by rebelling against her. Even the apprentices, who had paid Mum to learn how to sell African lace materials, forfeited their fees for their relationship with Dad. He would have made them feel as though they were the most special women on the planet and didn't need to spend hours learning how to fend for themselves, when he was happy to pay their bills.

"Oyekan, my brother, being the first child, was however slightly affected by Dad's bad behaviour. He was the spitting image of him, and by default, worshipped the ground Dad worked on. He didn't see anything wrong in Dad's irresistible quest for girls. When my sisters and I turned our nose up at Dad's ill-mannered behaviour and comforted mum during one fling or another, Oyekan cheered Dad on, and it wasn't long before he started having girlfriends himself - fourteen to be precise. My sisters, Adenike and Adewunmi, especially Adenike, would constantly scold Oyekan because she lost a handful of friends to his unquenchable thirst for anything in skirts. And when she had insulted him to her heart's content, the next person to face her wrath was Mum.

"She would say, "It's all your fault, you condone Dad's behaviour by forgiving him all the time, now look, your first child is a man whore. How could you let this happen? You are rich independently, why can't you just divorce Dad so that your sons can learn consequences? God forbid any man born of a woman treat me with such disrespect, I will either kill him or cut off his…erm, erm, I will cut off his stupid dangling thing." This would always end up in a good laugh between her and Mum, and their anger at Dad would be momentarily forgotten.

"But Adenike and Adewunmi weren't alone. I also often wondered why Mum allowed Dad's excesses; she was strong, independent and beautiful. I found it hard to believe her excuse of staying with him for the sake of us, their children. In my opinion, I think it's because she loved Dad too much, was ridiculously attached to him, and maybe pity had something to do with it because she knew he was fighting cancer.

"When Dad died, my brother took over the throne and, as I said, he loved everything that came with being a king; the power, influence, money, travelling and, of course, the women. Even though Oyekan had married his university sweetheart, Simi, right after their degree – which surprised everybody at the time – he was still a full-time player. And like Mum, Simi condoned his bad behaviours, so when he became king and decided to take a second wife, she was kind of prepared for it. I wouldn't say Simi liked having a rival in her home, but she stayed.

"My brother's second wife, Remi, was a very young lady, a second-year student at the University of Lagos. I have no idea how she met my brother, but I heard she wasn't as inexperienced as perceived, because she already had a child with a man out of wedlock. A man who had just graduated from university and was hunting for a job, so when she met rich and handsome King Oyekan, she left her lover and son to find a better life for herself.

"Remi and Simi were always at loggerheads, fighting over one thing or the other. In fact, Simi almost drowned Remi once and, in retaliation, Remi threatened to drown my nephew, Simi's youngest. The only way my brother thought he could solve his problem was to marry a third wife, which made me realise just how dumb he was, even though he graduated with a first-class degree in Pharmacy.

"If Oyekan was without gumption, what confused me, however, was Mum, because I couldn't understand why she never advised him. She was living in the palace with him, his wives and children, so she was seeing everything first hand, yet she did nothing. For some strange reason, her loyalty was always with Simi. If I had to be honest with myself, I also had a soft spot for Simi, because Oyekan never saw her as his queen. In fact, whenever he went out on his world trips, he went with Remi and none of us could understand why.

"When he married his third wife, everything changed. The fighting between Simi and Remi stopped and the king's attention turned to the newest addition to the family, Toke. Even though I thought the king was stupid to have taken another wife, I had to admit that it was all the family needed at the time. Toke's arrival brought ample love, peace and accord to the palace and, for the first time, I saw my brother deeply in love with a woman. He was no longer interested in other women, he didn't even look at them twice. Unfortunately, it was all short-lived because Toke died during childbirth – neither her nor her child made it.

"Rumour has it that Simi and Remi teamed up to get rid of her by putting poison in her food, but I think that's bollocks. She had a very tiny frame and the doctor confirmed that she was severely anaemic. Toke's death was a shock to Oyekan, he went into a very dark place that no one, not even our mum, could help him out. He mourned Toke for months until his grief advanced into depression. A couple of years after Toke's demise, my dear brother, Oba Oyekan Ajagbe III, did the unthinkable – he took his own life.

"My heart wasn't only broken when I heard of his death, I was devastated and angered. I know one shouldn't talk ill of the dead, but I must say, Oyekan was so damn selfish. He had always been. Even when we were younger, he would create a mess or get into trouble and expect me to take the rap for it, only this time I wasn't able to yell at him for it. I wasn't able to ask him why he did what he did, knowing fully well how his actions would impact me and our entire family. He was aware of my plans to travel out of the country, he was there when I received my admission letter to study Economics at Yale University, he knew I had been granted an American student visa, yet he took his life, thereby stopping me in my tracks. In a nutshell, he made a mess of his life, and left me to pick up the pieces just like old times, except this time it was final and with a lot of baggage.

"Ikoko's traditions state that if an Oba dies on the throne before his twenty-year term, his son would take his place and, if the son dies within the said twenty years, the next son would take the throne until their twenty years is used up. At the time of Oyekan's death, our family had only ruled for eight years, so I had to ascend the throne as Oba Adetoro Ajagbe IV of Ikoko Kingdom and be stuck with the crown for twelve years.

"Not only did I become the king, by tradition I also had to inherit my brother's wives and children, because they were too young and of childbearing age.

"Ever since I ascended the throne two years ago, I have been looking carefully for my own wife, because those women are not mine and never will be. Luckily, they don't want me either, so all I do for them is look after them and their children, financially. Can you imagine how backwards our culture is sometimes? My nieces and nephews who had been calling me uncle Adetoro would suddenly have to call me Daddy.

How awkward would that have been? As a result, I insisted they continue calling me 'uncle', or 'Kabeyesi."

Adetoro finished his story and lapsed into silence.

Chapter Eight

The Royal Lunch

AS I listened to Adetoro, I wondered how human beings often made their lives so complicated by subjecting themselves to such heart-wrenching situations, all in the name of beliefs and cultures. I couldn't understand why any tradition would demand such responsibility from a young boy who had his whole life ahead of him. I thought inheriting his big brother's wives and children, all in the name of culture, was just too much. 'What if he already had his own wife and children? Would cousins then become siblings? If Adetoro impregnated one of his late brother's wives, technically, some of her children would be his, whilst the others will be his late brother's. How sick is that?' I thought.

"Adetoro, your culture is crazy!" I said, turning my nose in disgust.

"Don't forget it's your culture too, technically!" he replied and we both burst out laughing.

"Is it me, or are you also hungry?" Adetoro asked. As if he had just signalled my tummy, it began to rumble as if I hadn't just had breakfast a couple of hours earlier.

"Let's go and meet my mother and the wives," he said, "Now you know the story it will be easier. Plus, if my memory serves me right, Mum is in charge of the cooking today, so you are in for a treat."

The walk to the family quarters was further away from the king's quarters than I imagined. As we approached, it felt as if we were entering a less civilised city compared to where we were coming from.

"Why are you so far away from your people and why is your part of the palace more civilised compared to theirs?" I asked, as the flurry of guards rushed around us again. I had enjoyed our time alone in the garden and resented their re-appearance.

"Guards, please give us some space!" Adetoro commanded, either reading my mind, or feeling the same in his heart.

"In answer to your question, because of you my angel!" he replied, "I didn't know who my wife was, but I knew I had to build an empire for her and my unborn children and, most importantly, shield them away from my brother's wives – and my mother, even though I love her to bits. If the truth be known, I also felt I deserved a beautiful separate quarter for myself, having given up the life I wanted for this." He touched his crown for emphasis, before continuing, "But now I have found you, and I can be happy."

As warm as his words were, they also filled my heart with sadness. "Adetoro, I don't want to raise your hopes, so let's be straight with each other," I explained, "I can't be your wife. I am only waiting for my mum to come for me tomorrow. I am so sorry to have led you on with the kiss earlier this morning, it was great, but not enough to make me stay. I am sorry!"

"Abosede, I won't force you to stay because I know you will. You are my wife, I knew it from the moment I set my eyes on your almost-lifeless body. Forget about the chief priest's prophesy, I myself was in communication with God as we prayed for you yesterday. I promised to make it my responsibility to look after you if he spared your life. And he did. You aren't going anywhere, sweetheart, can't you feel it?" he asked, as he pulled me into his arms, "Olori Abosede, tell me you don't feel what I feel."

I tried to resist his embrace, but it was like fighting against myself, in a battle I was unable to win. So I let my body melt into his and I looked into his eyes, only to find everything I was looking for. No man had ever looked at me the way he did. He was so sure of himself and certain that I was his, no matter what. I didn't feel the need to rush back into his embrace again, I took my time, and so did he. And when I was ready, my eyes must have spoken to him, because his lips met mine and the magic commenced again. This time, it lingered on as we nibbled and played with each other's lips, as if he wanted to drink me like a glass of wine. He pushed my hair back and held my jaw in both of his hands as our tongues intertwined. When my knees started to tremble, I pushed back for a split second and then leaned back into him, as he squeezed my bum and pulled me even closer. I didn't want the moment to end as I melted into his broad chest. Instinctively, he held me even tighter, which immediately made me feel safe and secure in his arms. Security was a new feeling for me, and I welcomed it with an open heart.

"Let's go and have something to eat, my love," he said, jolting me back to reality.

The queen mother was an astonishing beauty, despite her age. The first thing I noticed was her long and natural hair as it fell neatly on her shoulders. Her eyes were exactly like Adetoro's, so was her nose, smile, and complexion.

"Is this Kabeyesi's wife, my daughter-in-law-to-be and the Queen of Ikoko? May the gods bless this day. Come here my daughter, come and sit with me," she said with open arms as I approached her and knelt before her.

"Ah but you are welcome my dear," she smiled kindly, as she helped me up from the floor, "Get up and give me a big hug instead."

"It's good to finally meet you my dear, you are such a beauty. I hear you are Otunba's first daughter, you look just like him," she added.

"Mother, which of these guards gave you this information? And don't give me the 'I have ears everywhere' line," Adetoro said. "Even Otunba only just found out about his long-lost daughter today and told me about it this morning. There is no way anyone could have told you about this, apart from these guards."

"Calm down son! I keep telling you, your guards don't tell me anything. Otunba himself stopped by this morning to give me the good news," she said, before turning her attention back to me.

"What will you like to eat my dear? We have fried rice and chicken, I cooked that especially for you because I was told you are from the UK. You might not like our local food," she said, which made me chuckle nervously, because contrary to her assumption, fried rice wasn't a British delicacy, rather it was either African or Chinese.

"Fried rice is fine Ma'am, but honestly, I would eat anything. I am not fussy with food," I said.

"Ok, the choice is yours. We made your husband's favourite too, pounded yam and egusi soup," she said.

'Husband?' I mused to myself, 'Now she is at it too. When will they listen?' But there was something about the queen's stern, yet smiley, countenance that made me bite my tongue.

"I will have a bit of both Ma'am, I am very hungry," I said.

"Good! Now go and help your seniors with supervising the maids, they should be rounding up by now," she replied, shooing me on my way.

By seniors, she meant her daughters-in-law, the people Adetoro was trying to shield me from. So I looked at him for help, but his eyes were on his mum, like he was slicing and dicing everything she was saying and analysing her every move.

The dining room was the biggest I had ever seen in my life, even larger than the ones seen in posh Hollywood or Nollywood movies. In the middle was a delicate looking golden and silver table runner, with matching dishes placed strategically on top of it. On the sides of the table were about twenty dinner plates, evenly spaced. It made me wonder how many people were going to have lunch with us.

In the distance, I could hear children's voices and, when I followed the sound, I saw two women dressed in beautiful African gowns, similar to the one I was wearing. They were welcoming about eight children who were accompanied by a couple of teenagers and a couple of janitors who carried their school bags.

"Hurry up children, go and change into your home clothes, lunch is ready…it's rice and fried plantain," one of the women said.

"Rice and dodo!" cried the children, as they ran past the hallway and up the stairwell.

After the children had gone, the women spotted me. "Good evening ladies, my name is Abosede, I was told to come and help with lunch," I introduced myself. They exchanged glances before the older looking of the ladies spoke to me.

"You are our husband's new wife, right? Where are you from, you don't sound like you are from around here?" she asked.

If I was paid every time someone asked me that in Nigeria, I would have been a millionaire. "I am Nigerian, but I grew up in the UK," I answered.

"So, they don't have husbands in London, that's why you came here to share ours with us?" the younger wife asked, as she checked me out. "By the way, how old are you? You should still be in school, not snatching husbands." She scowled at me, but the older wife leapt to my defence.

"See who is talking, you were not much older than her when you came to snatch my husband from me without a care in the world. Let the young girl be, you have killed our husband, let the fresh and young blood enjoy her life. It's her time!" she chided, before adding, "You are welcome my dear, my name is Simi, that's Remi. What's yours again?" she asked and, when I replied, she quickly walked me to the kitchen so we could move away from the rants of the younger wife.

When we entered the kitchen, I was surprised to see how huge it was, just like everything in Ikoko palace. It looked like a commercial and homely kitchen all wrapped into one. The aroma coming out of the room would make anyone hungry, even if they had only just finished a feast.

"Ladies and gentlemen, meet your new queen, she is from London. You must respect her and do as she says," Simi instructed and the maids and porters nodded in agreement, whilst bowing their heads. "Good afternoon my queen, you are welcome," they greeted me in chorus.

If they weren't all looking so serious, I would have burst out laughing at their mannerisms; I couldn't believe that, in this day and age, people still expected their staff to offer formal rehearsed greetings to visitors. 'Or was it because I was their supposed queen?' I wondered.

"Let's go back to the dining room, my dear. I am famished, what about you?" Simi asked, before leading the way.

When we returned to the dining hall it was filling my up quickly; there was the queen mother, Oba Adetoro, Mama Soji, Remi, and two old men who wore huge red beaded necklaces around their necks – chiefs maybe. As soon as Simi and I sat, the children all entered the room, fighting to occupy their favourite chair. The maids kept coming and going with various bowls of food; we were spoilt for choice but I stuck with my original plan. I had a very small portion of fried rice, fried plantains and fried turkey. And a smaller portion of pounded yam and egusi soup. My tummy was so full that I wasn't even able to have any fruit for dessert. If that was lunch on a normal day, then I wondered what Christmas dinner would be like. As soon as the maids started clearing the table, Adetoro asked for the two of us to be excused.

"Olori Abosede and I would like to leave now. We enjoyed the food very much and would come back for more tomorrow afternoon," he announced, as he helped me out of my seat, "Please don't expect us at dinner today, we will have a light meal in our quarters."

The room became dead silent, not even the children made a sound. They weren't the only ones surprised by his announcement and actions, I was too. Throughout lunch, and it was the longest lunch I ever had in my life, he didn't look my way once – it felt like I was non-existent. Between mouthfuls he made time to talk to his mum, the two chiefs, the children and wives, but he didn't even ask if I was enjoying my food, or endeavour to check that I was comfortable. I decided to make a stand and speak up for myself.

"Thank you all for your hospitality, the food was so delicious," I said, before adding, "It's a shame this is hello and goodbye from me. I won't be here tomorrow as my mum is coming to take me home. It was lovely meeting you…God bless you, until we met again."

I needed to set the record straight. 'If Adetoro felt he could speak for me, then he had better think twice in future,' I thought to myself.

The walk back to the new quarters seemed longer, probably because we didn't break the journey by stopping at the garden this time, or maybe it was due to the fact that we weren't talking to each other – I had never heard silence so loud.

If I had to guess why Adetoro went mute on me, I would say he was sulking over my little utterance back at the old quarters. He probably thought it was disrespectful of me to have embarrassed him like that. But I didn't feel bad at all. I was telling the truth; my mum was coming to get me the following morning. Also, he had no right to be upset when he hardly acknowledged me while surrounded by his family. Just because he was royal didn't mean he could be rude to me. Furthermore, his sulky demeanour was starting to make me go off his ample charms. As handsome as he was, and as much as there was undeniable chemistry between us, it took more than a pretty face and a fluttering heart to win me over. No matter how beautiful a face, a selfish soul spoiled it all.

CHAPTER NINE

Decisions, Decisions

WHEN we entered the palace, we both went in opposite directions; I up the stairs to my bedroom and him to a room that looked like an office. As soon as I stepped in the room, I took my clothes off, had a warm shower, and changed into my own clothes which seemed to have been washed and ironed. As beautiful as my room was, it lacked something very important, a TV. I took a second look around the room to see if I could find something to keep me busy before sunset, but I couldn't find anything, not even a book or newspaper to read. I lay in bed for a while, hoping I would fall into a quick sleep, but it wasn't forthcoming. So I did the only sensible thing that came to mind.

I opened my door and peeked to check for the guards in the adjoining living room. They were nowhere to be found – some of them were probably minding Adetoro's office and the rest still at the old quarters having lunch. I tiptoed across the living room and into the King's bedroom, with the hope of grabbing one of the many books I found on his shelf earlier that morning.

As soon as I opened the door to the room, I realised I had not been sensible after all, but actually rather dumb. I had gone bursting into someone else's room without knocking first. I froze at the sight before me and wished the floor beneath me could open and swallow me whole.

"You should have knocked…shut the door!" Adetoro exclaimed, "Or do you want the whole town to see me naked?"

"Where are your guards?" I asked, trying to act as casual as possible as I closed the door behind me. "I'm sorry, I didn't think you'd be in your room because they weren't out here. I was bored, so I wanted to borrow one of your books... Can you put some clothes on please?"

He grinned at me, clearly enjoying showing off his athletic body in all its naked glory. "I was going to have a shower, want to join me?"

"No, thank you. I already had one," I replied, making sure my eyes were looking everywhere but at his face, or below his waist. In fact, safer to just not look at him at all! I gazed off in the direction of his bookshelf.

"Ok," he sighed, "If I let you borrow a book, do you mind scrubbing my back then please? I promise I won't make you get in the shower with me, if you just promise to keep your eyes off my assets!" he laughed, gyrating around and trying to catch my attention. I could just about see him out of the corner of my eye and, although very difficult, I kept staring at the books.

"Adetoro, please go and have your shower, I am sorry to have invaded your privacy, let me just grab a book and return to my room," I said, as I made my way to his bookshelf.

At first I didn't hear him coming, but then I smelt his aftershave and felt his warm breath on my neck. He was only a step behind me, watching over my shoulder as I looked through his library of books. I could feel his body heat and was so aware of his nakedness, I could feel my heart beating like a drum in my chest. I tried to act oblivious to the fact, but the truth was the exact opposite. My body thrilled at his proximity and I wanted the anticipation to linger on for a little longer. So I continued to peruse the books, reading the covers and flicking through their pages, without actually retaining any of the information.

"That's a good one," he muttered, "You will love it! It's a story about the Yoruba river goddess called Oshun, known for her sensuality, beauty and power – she reminds me of you, actually."

"Ah yes, Oshun," I replied, without turning around, "Known mostly for being a goddess of love and beloved of King Shango. And I suppose you think if I am Oshun, then you are Shango!"

I heard him laugh again. "Do you know it is rude to talk to someone with your back to them? If you turn and face me, I will answer you."

I felt his hand fall upon my shoulder and he spun me around to face him. He was still naked and, even though I concentrated on looking at his face, I couldn't help but notice he was hard as a rock.

He stared deep into my eyes and, this time, I could not look away. "Did you know Oshun is also protector of the poor and mother of all orphans?" he asked. "She reminds me of you in many ways. Reading about her will give you an insight into your culture; we had our traditions and gods before the British brought theirs to us, you know? I can let you borrow the book, but it can't leave the four corners of this palace, only way you can read it is to stay," he said, as he placed the book in my hand. "Please stay, even if it's just for a week. Give us a chance, you can't kill whatever this is just because you are too proud to admit we have a connection. I can't explain it, but after setting eyes on you yesterday, even though you seemed lifeless, I had a strange feeling of déjà vu. Abosede, if after a week you feel this isn't working, I promise to let go. What do you say?"

Even before Adetoro's persuasion, I knew in the depth of my heart that I would find it difficult to leave just like that. I secretly hoped and prayed that Mum's visit to Nigeria wouldn't be a short one; it would be a great opportunity for her to spend some time with Grandma and, for my own selfish reasons, it would allow me extend my stay at the palace.

"Let me think about it… your royal highness," I said, feeling the undeniable chemistry between us, almost magnetic, pulling us together.

"Think fast," he growled sexily, as he literally swept me off my feet and onto his royal bed.

"I thought you were going to have a shower?" I asked, sarcastically.

"I already did, are you going to keep pretending you can't smell the soap and aftershave on me? You can't see me naked and go scot-free, it's going down today, beautiful!" he said, as he hovered over me and ticked my tummy until my laughter reached its threshold.

Then, as if to keep me quiet, he placed his lips on mine. The familiar magic started again; all worries gone in the wind, all pain washed away and replaced by a contented heart and a body ready for what was to come. Slowly, he took off my clothes piece by piece, before tossing them across the room in a playful manner. Without taking his eyes off me, he lifted my bum slightly to remove my panties. "Damn, you are juicer than I ever imagined," he whispered.

One juicy step led to another, until my body was on fire and trembling from the skilful collaboration between his fingers and his tongue – I wanted more. "C'mon!" I sighed, as I felt the big 'O' coming. As if to reward himself for giving me such a huge gratification, he slid himself inside of me as we embarked on the most pleasurable ride of my life…and didn't stop until we both reached climax and were left panting for air.

Everything happened so fast, I couldn't pinpoint when I could have objected to what had just happened. Nor had I wanted to object, and that confused me. Technically, I had just slept with a man on the same day I met him, and without protection too – everything against my principles. I had kissed many boyfriends in the past, but I always knew when to stop, unless I wanted to go all the way. And there I was, lying on the king's bed, yearning for more of Oba of Ikoko's sugar.

"Are you ok my queen?" he asked.

"I'm mesmerised," I replied.

"There is plenty where that came from if you're up for another round, just saying!" he smiled back at me, with lust in his eyes. And let's just say the smitten smile wasn't long-lived, because it was replaced by another explosive gratification, followed by another, and another, until we were both worn out.

When I woke up the following morning, the king wasn't in his bed, or anywhere else to be seen in the bedroom for that matter. I was disappointed for a split second, until I realised it was already 10am. I couldn't believe I had slept all through the night without waking once. If my memory served me right, neither of us had dinner the previous night, so I wondered how I managed to escape hunger pangs in the middle of the night.

I stayed in bed for a little longer, reminiscing on our previous night's encounters and hoping that Adetoro would return. When there was no sign of him, I got out of bed, put on my clothes, and peeped through the keyhole to check for guards, or anyone else, on the other side of the bedroom door. There was no one in sight, so I quickly tiptoed across the adjoining living room and headed back to my own room. To my dismay, Mama Soji was in my bedroom, making alterations to another ball gown. Thankfully, it was a knee-length dress this time.

"My Olori, did you sleep well?" she asked, without taking her eyes off the dress she was making – probably to save me the embarrassment. "Kabeyesi had to go downstairs to welcome your mum, she arrived this morning with Otunba and you've been asked to join them when you are up. Let's get you ready quickly, we don't want your mum thinking we are incapable of looking after you," she added, whilst raising her brows.

My elation from my night with Adetoro was extinguished as fast as if someone had just thrown a bucket of freezing cold water over me. 'Mum is around? I'm doomed!' I thought.

Mum always had a way of knowing when I was seeing a new man. I don't know how she does it, but she sure knows when I have been in a man's bed. After the very first time I had sex, as if by instinct, my mum came into my bedroom with a packet of condoms and asked me to use them wisely because she wasn't prepared to get another packet anytime soon. Although I was eighteen years old, it wasn't the kind of reaction I expected from her, considering what my friends had told me about how their mums freaked out when they found out they were sexually active. I suppose it was my mum's way of teaching me responsibility without being judgemental or hypocritical, especially as she probably started having sex about the same age herself.

I still question my mum's parental techniques to date but, as the saying goes, 'there's no right or wrong when it comes to parenting techniques', but that's a story for another day. The main task at hand was to ensure my mother wouldn't see any signs that I had slept with the king, that is if I wanted to extend my stay at the palace.

"Mummy!" I screamed, as soon as I set eyes on the constant love of my life. I didn't realise how much I had missed her until she had me in her arms again. We both sobbed and showered each other with kisses, as Otunba, my real father, and the king, my lover, looked on.

"We have your passport, your half-sister got it from one of the kidnappers…what was his name again?" she asked, expecting my father to jolt her memory.

"Sunday," he replied.

"It's time to take my baby home," Mum said, but the look of relief and joy on her face faded when she saw the expression on mine. She turned all her attention back to me.

"You are not thinking of staying, are you? Don't tell me you are about to throw your life away for some stupid superstitions, or are you swayed by all this glitter?" Mum asked, as she studied my face. "There is more to life than all of these you know? This time, I won't leave you to figure it out yourself, I will drag you back to the UK if I have to. What nonsense! You said you wanted to meet your father, and now that you have, please tell me what you have benefited from your reunion? No woman in her right senses can live with this man, very lazy, archaic and lackadaisical attitude to life – four children by four different mothers. Have you met your half-sister yet and her other siblings? That was the life I rescued you from…"

Mum hadn't finished spitting fire when my father barged in.

"Who are you to call me lazy? You, irresponsible slut! There is nothing wrong with my children, they are cultured adults worth tenfold more than the spoilt, ill-mannered brat you call a daughter," my father snarled, before adding, "She was asking me for a DNA test to prove my paternity yesterday. I told her to ask her promiscuous, gold-digging mother who her real father is."

"You haven't changed one bit, as frustrated as ever. I thank the good lord I left you and took her with me," Mum retorted, sticking her nose in the air.

"Like mother like daughter! Whether you like it or not, she is going to marry the king, and it will be my turn to be a father, not just any father, but the Queen of Ikoko's. Tell your rich husband to give or buy you another daughter, this one is mine by blood," he demanded. Mum looked so angry I thought she was about to hit him, and drag me home by my hair.

"By the power vested in me, I command both of you to stop this madness at once!" Adetoro suddenly shouted, stopping them both in their tracks like a pair of naughty children.

Mum and I looked at each other and, if we hadn't been in the middle of such a serious discussion, we would have collapsed in a pool of laughter. 'By the power vested in me, who says that these days?' I wondered, but I couldn't agree more with the king. It was complete and utter madness, as well as shameful, how my parents behaved. They couldn't even put aside their differences for my sake, instead, they were claiming ownership of me like I was some sort of trophy. Logically, I should have put an end to it before Adetoro interjected, but I was intrigued by Mum's behaviour, I had never seen her so upset and feisty. She and my dad had their fair share of arguments but it was nothing compared to the hatred I was witnessing.

"Honestly, I don't think it matters what you two say or how long you argue for, the decision is for Abosede to make," Oba Adetoro continued. "If she decides to stay, I don't think either of you can stop her. Having said that, madam, you have done a great job bringing up this treasure. If not for her foreign accent, one will never have guessed she isn't from around here. She is strong, well mannered, beautiful and with brain, a rare combination, and all credit goes to you ma."

Oba Adetoro's compliment seemed to soften Mum's contorted face for a second, before she replied sternly, "Kabeyesi, I don't mean to disrespect you, but do you have any children?"

"No," he answered.

"Then you can't understand where I'm coming from. This is my only daughter, the apple of my eye, I can't afford to let any harm befall her and that's what will happen if I let her stay here. Your gods will have to find an alternative option because my daughter isn't destined to be a queen, not in this village anyway. There is absolutely nothing for her in Nigeria and there's nothing either of you can offer her," Mum said, before turning to me.

"Grace Abosede, you have always asked me why I left your father and deprived him of knowing you. Now that the three of us are in the room, I can discuss it openly. I left because he was, and still is by the looks of things, a lazy and irresponsible man. I almost lost you in the first trimester of pregnancy because I went to bed hungry five out of seven days. This man would rather spend the little money he had on alcohol or gambling, depending on the mood he was in. I never bad mouthed him because I wanted you to find out for yourself, but seeing him unchanged and egotistical as ever brings back all the sad memories of my wasted time with him. The greatest decision I ever made was escaping with you for a better life, I have no regrets and you will thank me later," Mum said.

"Have you finished?" Otunba asked, as he stamped his feet on the floor, "There is no justification for robbing me of my first fruit – that was callous. You could have at least told me, even if it was a couple of years after you fled with your rich lover. But no, you didn't. I only got to know I had a daughter when she was already a teenager. You said I was lazy, remind me what you brought to the table yourself. If my memory serves me right, you were always sleeping, hardly cooked or did anything for me. The only reason you dated me was because of the little money I made from my petty business, some of which I used to fund our introduction party, single-handedly. The moment you found a better option, you took off and never looked back, that's what I call heartlessness."

When they had both said their piece and called each other every name under the sun, I thought it was time to intercede. I purposely didn't interrupt them because it was the only way I could hear both sides of the story and learn the truth about my existence. It was probably the only time I would hear both of them talking about me in the same room. Unfortunately, Adetoro was there listening to every word.

"I think you can both stop the blame party now, I am really not interested in who is wrong or right," I said, "Instead, we should all be thankful that we are all here, hale and hearty to witness today. Being alive is a miracle, I went through hell looking for you, Father. Thank God, I managed to overcome all the obstacles that tried to prevent me from meeting you. Mummy, this could have been worse you know? If not for him, who knows what could have happened to me? If I was still at the kidnapper's hideout, or dead, this wouldn't be the kind of conversation you'll be having right now. So, let's all move on and dwell on the future rather than the past." I paused for breath.

"Speaking of the future Mum, how long are you staying in Nigeria for?" I asked.

"A week, why?" she answered, looking at me suspiciously.

"I was hoping you might want to spend some time with Grandma and, if that's the case, I was going to ask if I can stay here for a little longer," I mumbled, holding my breath in anticipation of where this conversation was going.

"Why would you want to stay behind?" she asked, looking at my face and Adetoro's for clues. She then settled her glare at me as she confirmed her suspicion.

"Basically, you want to stay because of him, not because of your father?" she asked. However, instead of becoming angry again, I watched a cheeky smile form on her face. "That's ok, but what am I supposed to tell your daddy, brother and mama?"

"Did Daddy and Femi come with you?" I asked.

"Yes, they did. Your daddy was going to come with me but I insisted he stayed back with Femi at your grandma's."

"In which case, Mummy, I will come and join you, just allow me one more night with Adetoro…"

"Shut up, how dare you call our king by his name? You must call him Kabeyesi or Oba Adetoro!" my father snapped, without letting me complete my sentence.

"Mummy, please?" I asked, ignoring my father's rant. I was beginning to dislike him, as the picture he was painting of himself with his behaviour was as bad as the names my mother called him, but a part of me still wanted to give him the benefit of the doubt.

"Ok, but your dad and I are coming for you tomorrow morning, and that's final!" Mum agreed, as she purposely laid emphasis on the word 'dad'.

"Join us at breakfast ma, Mama Soji has set the table for four," Adetoro said, also ignoring my father's unnecessary outburst.

When I noticed my mum wasn't completely convinced, I quickly added, "Mummy, even if you don't have time for a full-on breakfast, you must try Mama Soji's Moi Moi, it's to die for. I never thought anyone could beat you and Mama's recipe, but this one does." I knew all too well that Mummy wouldn't say no to Moi Moi.

"Ok, if you put it like that, I might have few minutes to spare after all. But hey Grace, before breakfast, may I steal a couple of minutes to chat with you in private?" Mum asked.

I nodded and took her hand, excusing us for a few moments. "Of course," Adetoro consented, shooing my father from the room as he also left to give us some space to talk. "We will see you at breakfast, don't take too long."

As soon as we were alone, Mum began her impassioned speech. "Grace darling, please don't throw your life away for a man that doesn't deserve you, no man is worth it. You know I have never objected to any of your boyfriends, have you ever asked yourself why?"

"I don't' know!" I replied, "I have wondered that myself at times."

"It's because I believe you're smart enough to find them out in the end, but on this occasion, I can't just stand here with open eyes and watch you fall into a pit – a pit of snakes for that matter! I must voice out my opinion. I can see why you can be swayed by all this glitter and gold, and he is a handsome man too, but you mustn't forget your life ambition and your big dreams. How long do you think it will take for all of this to seem worthless to you? If you don't succeed in making your own dream a reality, trust me, you will end up resenting yourself and whoever got in the way of it."

She continued, "You must also consider your cultural differences with the king, remember he is a traditional man who may not fully understand your westernised ways. You were raised to question things, unlike their women here, who do as they are told. At first it wouldn't seem to matter, but along the line it will put a strain on your relationship. Finally, my dear, you won't just be married to him, you'll also be in partnership with this town, his wives, his children, his mother, his…"

"Mummy," I interjected, knowing she would go on for hours if I let her and aware we needed to join the king at breakfast. I was aware of the irony in my wanting to go trotting off after Adetoro, like a good little wife to be, but I did not want to waste the rest of the time we had together through arguing with my mother about it. "Mummy, I hear you loud and clear. I am not marrying him, yet. I'm only spending today with him, that's all. Besides, those women aren't really his wives, neither are the children. He inherited them from his late brother. Mama Grace, there's no reason to be concerned, I know what I am doing."

However, as the words left my mouth, they didn't even sound that convincing to my own ears. I realised my bid to reassure my mother had not worked and, if anything, she was probably even more worried about me now.

She put her arm around me and sighed, "Oh Grace, my love, I so hope you do know what you are doing, but I fear not." She looked as though she was going to cry, but she composed herself immediately. She kissed and patted me on the head as though I was still a little girl. "Come on, my baby, let's go to breakfast."

Farewell

MUM left after breakfast and Adetoro and I retired to his room to enjoy the rest of our time together in peace and privacy. We spent the entire day in his bedroom, lying in each other's arms in bed and watching Nigerian TV soap operas, ranging from, 'Super Story' to 'Fuji House of Commotion', and ending the day with English football.

Just before lights out, Adetoro pulled me into his arms and looked deeply into my eyes as he pleaded, "Abosede, please don't leave tomorrow!"

"The thought of losing you pierces my heart, let alone seeing you actually leave – it will kill me, my angel! Let's call your mum tonight… we can promise her that we will fly to the UK together in a few weeks' time," he said, as he kissed my forehead. "In a matter of two weeks, I'm sure I'd be able to get a visa to visit the UK."

"I don't know, Adetoro," I replied, as I ran my finger through his beard. "The UK is not, well…here…"

My mum's warnings about our cultural differences rang in my ears and I suddenly realised I had not read the book about Oshun. I wondered if he would let me take it with me.

"Think about it," he pleaded, "In a few weeks, you'll be the one showing me around your neck of the woods. Talking about showing each other around, I haven't taken you to the exquisite places in Ikoko, and we have a few. If you let me, I can show you the beauty of Lagos, Ibadan and Abuja. We can paint Nigeria red before continuing our sightseeing adventures in the UK. What do you say my angel?"

"I don't know," I sighed, "Please give me a moment to think."

Adetoro's argument for me to stay longer was more appealing than his suggestion to follow me back to the UK. His promises to take me sightseeing made my thoughts travel back to when I arrived in Lagos the previous week...

When I had first arrived in Nigeria, Chelsea, the journalist who invited me to Lagos, came to pick me up at the airport because I landed at night and I didn't want to worry my grandma with the task of collecting me. I was pleasantly surprised to discover that Chelsea was about the same age as me; she was young, bold and full of life.

That very night, when I was supposed to get some sleep after a long flight, Chelsea insisted that I went on a night out with her and her friends. She couldn't understand why I wanted to stay in bed, alone, on a Friday night.

"Let me show you what Lagos really looks like, not the version the British media shows on TV," she said.

To be honest, she didn't have to tell me, because I could see things for myself – her parents' compound was as big as the whole of my street in the UK. Within the compound was a self-contained bungalow with a swimming pool, a gym, two living rooms, a massive bedroom and a spotless kitchen, all of which belonged to Chelsea. There were hundreds of staff on her parents' payroll, ranging from butlers, chauffeurs, soldiers who guarded the house, cleaners, gardeners, cooks – you name it, they had it.

True to her words, Lagos nightlife was second to none. The weather was great, the nights as warm as a summer day in the UK, so night crawlers were happy to come out in their thousands, ready to be entertained and unwind after the week's hustle and bustle. We had danced, chatted and laughed until the small hours, and I had thoroughly enjoyed the company of Chelsea and her friends.

The following morning, before I travelled to my grandma's and true to her other promises, she had taken me to various radio stations and television houses to tell my story. As people dialled in to ask questions about my father, I felt like a mini celebrity.

She had also invited me to a red-carpet event at Africa Independent Television (AIT), this was where I met Ramsey Noah, Richard Mofe-Damijo, Omotola Jalade Ekeinde, Genevieve Nnaji, Kate Henshaw, Stella Damasus and Desmond Elliot – all in one day. I was over the moon and couldn't wait to tell all my Nollywood-loving friends in the UK about my Naija experience.

As my starry-eyed thoughts drifted to my friends in the UK, I realised as much as I would have been happy to swan around in my role as celebrity and prospective queen, I missed my home. I wasn't ready to disappoint my family, especially my mother, who had come all this way to save me. 'Yes Grace, save you from yourself!' I chided myself, silently, secretly wanting Adetoro to persuade me. As if to prompt him, I repeated, "Oh Adetoro, I do want to, but I don't know…"

Just as he was about to reply, we heard a knock on the door. It was Olori Simi.

"Olori Simi, is everything ok? How are the children… and Olori Remi?" Adetoro asked.

"We are all doing fine, there is no need to worry, Kabeyesi," Olori Simi said reassuringly, as she eyed me suspiciously.

"Then what brings you here at this time of the night?" he asked.

"I need to discuss something important with you, can I speak to you in private?" she whispered.

"Ok, give me a minute to change into something decent. Wait for me outside," he replied, as he hopped out of bed and headed in the direction of his closet.

"Adetoro, you heard her, there is no need to panic. You seem frazzled, breathe," I said, but my words seemed to fall on deaf ears as he grabbed his phone and shut the door behind him.

Adetoro didn't come back until at least an hour later, just as I was dozing off.

"Is everything ok dear, you seem subdued," I asked, as I yanked the blanket off my body to welcome him back into the room, back into the bed and back into my arms.

"Everything is ok, but I must attend to some critical family issues at the old quarters," he said, as he scanned the room for nothing in particular. "Don't wait up for me, you can sleep here or go back to your room, but my preference is for you to stay here. It will be nice to see you first thing in the morning."

He leaned forward to place a kiss on my cheek. Instead of welcoming it, I bristled. Furthermore, I felt jealous and angry about this invasion on the little time we had left together.

"What must be so urgent that would make a whole King of Ikoko vacate his bedroom for another?" I snapped, before he had the chance to avoid eye contact with me and just dash out of the room. "Whose bed are you going to warm tonight, it's certainly not mine?"

"Listen woman, I have no time to answer unnecessary questions, I will see you in the morning," he said defensively, before placing another peck on my lips; and off he went.

This turnaround in his manner and attention had happened so fast and I was frustrated that I didn't know what had caused it. I felt foolish for my jealous outburst, but within minutes of returning from his long conversation with Simi, all our plans had to be dropped for something more important – even though we had planned to go for a walk after dinner. Although I didn't know Oba Adetoro as well as I would have liked to, it was apparent that something was up. He looked intimidated and anxious, almost like all his power had just been stripped off him. Suddenly, instead of feeling affronted, I felt curious. 'What could these people have on him,' I wondered, 'There's only one way to find out…'

'Here comes Detective Grace!' I thought, as I slid out of bed and quickly threw on some clothes. I certainly wasn't just going to lie there, alone in the king's bed, while he was up to god knows what elsewhere. I stepped out of the king's suite, to find guards Adewale and Olalekan watching football in the living room. As soon as they saw me, they stood up to ask me how they could help.

"I am just going to lie in my room, when Kabeyesi returns, let him know where I am," I said. On second thoughts, I added, "Can either of you get me some fruits? I am really hungry but don't fancy anything heavy."

"We have a varied selection of fruits in the kitchen," Olalekan said, as he began to list all of them, without taking his eyes off the TV.

"Do you have papayas?" I queried.

"What is that Ma'am?" Olalekan asked, looking at Adewale for help, but he also looked as confused as the other guard.

"I don't know what it's called in Yoruba, I saw a tree full of ripe ones in the garden when I was out with Kabeyesi yesterday. It's similar to a watermelon, but it's not as big or juicy." I explained.

"Oh, I know what she means! Ma'am, you mean pawpaw?" Adewale nodded, as I watched them continue to steal glances at the television.

"Yes, that's it," I agreed.

"In Yoruba language, it is called "Ibepe". I don't think we have any in the kitchen but we can go and pluck some for you if you want," Olalekan offered.

"No, don't worry, that can wait until tomorrow. Carry on watching your football. I will help myself to some fruits in the kitchen," I said and, without further discussion, they both returned to their seats to continue watching their game. They probably thought I was doing them a favour, little did they know that I was a woman on a mission.

When I got downstairs I looked in the study first, then the throne room, downstairs living room, reception room and, finally, the kitchen; I was pleasantly surprised to find all rooms were empty. I had no time to fiddle around with fruit-cutting, so I opened the backyard door and started a journey to the old quarters. I had no idea what I was doing, or how to get there without being spotted by the night guards, but something kept telling me to go for it no matter what, so I did.

It wasn't as pitch-black as I had envisaged, the sky was covered with bright and shining stars and the street lights planted strategically along the roads made it feel safe. As the gentle evening breeze caressed my skin, I wondered what I would tell people I was looking for if I got bitten by a poisonous snake or scorpion; or worse, someone jumping out of the bushes to attack me. But I knew if I dwelled on the negatives, I wouldn't be able to accomplish the mission which was uppermost in my mind. So I continued walking until I met a couple of guards minding the front door of the women's apartment; one of them was asleep, whilst the other was reading a newspaper.

"Hi," I said, immediately jolting him back to reality.

"Hello Olori. What are you doing here at this time of the night," he asked.

"I am here to see Mama Soji, is she here?"

"Does she know you are coming?" he asked.

"No, but I'm sure she will be pleasantly surprised to see me," I said, convincingly. So he led the way to Mama Soji's room. Luckily, she was still awake.

"What! Olori, what are you doing here; is everything ok? The guards, where are they?" Mama Soji asked, as she sat me down on her bed.

"I'm fine ma," I reassured her, "I was just bored, so I decided to take a stroll and get some fresh air and, before I knew it, I was here."

"What about Adewale and Olalekan? Neither of them volunteered to come with you?" she queried, raising a cross eyebrow.

"Please don't blame them, I didn't even tell them I was coming here – like I said, I didn't plan to come this far. They are probably wondering where I am now..." I said, as I suddenly realised the consequence of my little wander.

Mama Soji's face softened. "What brings you here, my dear?" she asked, looking ever so sure of herself, as always.

"I don't know if you know, but Kabeyesi and I are...I mean, we are kind of..." I stuttered, as I tried my best to avoid Mama Soji's 'I told you so' look.

"Tell me something I don't already know! I'm not surprised by what you are trying to tell me. Kabeyesi is a charmer, all the girls in this town have been praying for years to be in your shoes. I'd say, hold him tight," she advised.

"I don't know about holding him tight if he decides to bail out on me whenever he pleases," I harrumphed, knowing too well that a question would follow.

"What do you mean by that?" sniffed Mama Soji, "You've only been here for two days, you can't jump to conclusions just like that."

"I'm not making any hasty judgement ma, I'm talking about what has already happened. From what I've seen so far, I have a feeling something weird is going on in this palace," I said candidly, before adding, "I know you are not supposed to say anything to me, but if you had seen how a whole King of Ikoko dropped everything the moment he saw Simi, you'll understand why I'm flabbergasted. I know it's none of my business as I'm supposed to be leaving tomorrow, but I think it's only fair to know what I'm getting myself into if I do decide to stay. He wants me to stay, or at least I thought he did, but unless I know what is going on around here I will be off in the morning like planned."

"Hmmmm," she sighed, "You must promise not to say a word if I tell you what I know."

"Not a word, I swear!" I agreed, as I put my index finger on my mouth and pointed it in the air, just like we did when I used to live in Nigeria.

"Ok, let's go back to the new quarters, we can't talk here. Also, the guards are probably on their way to notify the king of your disappearance, we must head back right now. We can talk safely in your room when everyone is asleep," Mama Soji whispered.

It turned out that Adewale and Olalekan were so engrossed in the Arsenal vs Manchester United game, they hadn't noticed I left the building at all, let alone walking to and from the old quarters. They weren't surprised to see Mama Soji either, so we just walked past them and into my bedroom.

"Would you like me to get you a drink or something to snack on?" Mama Soji asked, but I was more interested in what she had to say, so I shook my head and urged her to tell me the story.

"Before Oba Adetoro became king, his brother, Oba Oyekan was on the throne for a few years before he passed away. I don't know if he has told you about this?"

"Yes, he has," I confirmed.

"Then you would have been told that Oba Oyekan wasn't himself after Olori Toke died and, when he couldn't take it any longer, he killed himself. But that's far from the truth," she explained, as she threw a blanket over me and got another for herself, and we settled down on the animal print settee.

Mama Soji continued, "For some strange reasons, Oba Oyekan didn't love his first wife, Olori Simi, and he made no attempt to disguise it. He was constantly belittling her in public without an ounce of remorse, it was as if he deliberately wanted to hurt her. Not only was he disrespecting her, he constantly cheated on her with other women until he eventually married Olori Remi – that was when the real problem started.

"The two wives always had something to fight about, and I don't mean little quarrels or bickering, we are talking life-threating hostility between two women who gave as good as they got. As Oba Adetoro might have told you, things died down when Olori Toke came on board, until she eventually passed away.

"Oba Oyekan was severely depressed for months, so the chief councils organised a mandatory short vacation for him, they felt the change of environment would do him some good. The king eventually agreed to go, but on the condition that he chose his destination.

"He announced he was going to pay his brother a surprise visit in Lagos and asked me to go with him. He thought I was doing him a favour when I accepted to go with him, but it was a win-win situation for both of us because it was an opportunity for me to see my son, Soji, at Lagos States University.

"When we arrived at Adetoro's flat, he wasn't in, but the gateman assured us that he and his girlfriend would be back pretty soon, as they only went to the supermarket around the corner. He showed us the stairwell to his flat and we stood there, observing people walking along the street.

"True to the gateman's words, it wasn't long before we spotted Adetoro and his so-called girlfriend, strolling contentedly as they held hands and kissed each other playfully on the street – in broad daylight.

I had to squint to confirm who this female companion was, because she looked just like our Olori Simi.

"As the couple walked through the gate, unaware of our arrival, Oba Oyekan spoke up, "Hurry up lovebirds, we've been waiting all day for you. Come and let us in!" At the sound of the king's voice, Adetoro and Simi froze in their tracks, before looking up at the balcony to confirm what they just heard. Disbelief and shame were written all over their faces and, when I caught Adetoro's gaze, he had horror in his eyes. Then they turned their backs and walked away as fast as they could, without actually breaking into a run. Neither of them spoke, but the looks on their faces said it all.

"Just before we left, Oba Oyekan approached the gateman and asked him how long he had worked there. The gateman said he had been there for over eight years, so Oba Oyekan asked how long the girlfriend had been coming to visit. And do you know what he said? Five years! Also, that she was the only girlfriend and he thought they should get married!

"To date, I have no idea how Olori Simi managed to travel such long distance to Lagos without the king or anyone else noticing. One could argue, however, that she did what she had to do as Oba Oyekan paid her no attention, but how do you explain sleeping with his younger brother?

"To my dismay, it was going to be a very short trip as Oba Oyekan ordered Olaitan to head back to Ikoko. If I had reminded the king about stopping by at Soji's university, I was sure he would have let me go, but I didn't have the guts to ask, unless I wanted to be an insensitive and selfish woman. It turned out we were only about thirty minutes into our journey when Oba Oyekan remembered himself. He asked driver Olaitan to park the car and excuse us for a few minutes.

"He apologised for putting me through it all, and said he had almost forgotten about Soji. He said we should go back to get him and ask if he wanted to join us at the palace. They could continue their chess game.

He also offered to give me time off so I could spend more time with my son, either at the campus, or at the palace.

"I told him not to worry about me, and it was I who was worried about him, after the shock of seeing his first wife with his very own brother. I said I would accept his kind offer another time, and take a holiday to visit my son, but right now I must look after him.

"Oba Oyekan told me he was not surprised by Simi's behaviour, as she had done it before, sleeping with his best friend from University, just before their wedding. He said he thought he could forgive her, but it had haunted him. He said she was only in his life because of their children, and he couldn't risk throwing her out as he feared they would suffer. However, he said that, after what we had seen today, she wasn't fit to be the mother of their children any longer.

"He was angry at Simi, but he was most upset and felt betrayed by the actions of his brother. Oba Oyekan said if Adetoro loved her that much, he should have just confessed like a man, instead of sneaking around behind his brother's back like that. He was so shocked and shaken by the whole thing, he told me he actually feared for his life now they knew he knew. And he implored me to keep our secret while he worked out what to do.

"I gave him my word and we agreed to speak no longer on the matter. Instead, we drove back to the campus to collect Soji and bring him back to Ikoko for a few days. That night they played their chess game and Oba Oyekan even seemed in slightly better spirits, despite the events of the day. In a way, it seemed the experience had switched his depression into a new-found sense of purpose.

"However, the following morning, we found King Oyekan hanging from the ceiling fan in his bedroom. It looked like suicide and that's what everyone thought, but I knew it was not and it made my blood run cold. It just didn't add up, the Kabeyesi I spoke to the previous day wasn't suicidal, he wasn't even seeking revenge. He just wanted what was best for his children and himself and was determined to make plans to guarantee their wellbeing.

"I became really scared for my life as well, because if Oba Oyekan's death was staged, it wouldn't be long before mine came knocking. My suspicions rang true when Oba Adetoro and Olori Simi called me to join them in a meeting, on the very same day the king was found dead.

"They told me they had called me to discuss "a matter of life and death." They said they knew Oba Oyekan's ego would have been crushed after seeing them together, but they didn't think he would react so badly. They said that, now he had gone, there would be no point in me running my mouth about what we had seen and open old wounds and, anyway, they had decided to put a stop to their relationship to honour Kabeyesi's memory.

"I still remember the sinister look in Oba Adetoro's eye, but it was Olori Simi who really scared me. She smirked at me and reassured her lover that I wouldn't say a word for two reasons – one that he would be crowned the next King of Ikoko, and I knew what that meant, and two, I only have one living child who I would kill for, and I wouldn't risk losing him for something that doesn't concern me."

"It wasn't just Olori Simi's threat that scared the living daylights out of me, it was her evil stare too – they were like needles piercing through my entire body. So I promised them I wouldn't say a word. To gain their trust I added that I am a woman myself, and seeing the way Kabeyesi had treated Simi in the past few years, I had no right to judge."

Mama Soji finished her story and shivered, despite the hot climate, pulling the blanket tighter around her body. "Abosede," she said, taking my hands in her own, "I'm putting my neck on the line by telling you all of these, please DO NOT tell anyone. I'm only doing this because I warmed towards you from the moment I met you, and I believe Olori

Simi is devilish and would do everything within her power to eliminate whoever she considers a rival."

I had been transfixed throughout her tale, sharing her shock at seeing the adulterous lovers together, her horror at Oba Oyekan's murder, and her fear at Simi's threats. My mind was reeling and, in my heart, I knew it was true. 'Well,' I told myself, 'You did ask…'

I smiled at Mama Soji. "Thank you for telling me, I won't say a word. You have been so kind to me since I got here, which has made it easy to warm towards you too. Actually, I think it's your Moi Moi that really won me over," I said with a wink, which made her giggle. I continued, "But, jokes apart, you have just done me a huge favour by telling me all of this, now I can see clearly."

"What are you going to do now?" she asked.

"I will go with my mum tomorrow. I still can't get my head around the hold Simi has on Adetoro, you need to have seen how his mood changed when she was around."

"I saw her practically dragging Kabeyesi into her bedroom tonight, in fact I see them 'together' all the time," Mama Soji whispered. "There is no doubt about it, he likes you but Olori Simi is his menace; he made the gravest mistake of his life when he slept with a woman who is by far stronger than him, mentally and spiritually. So, my dear pearl, I am going to sneak back to the old quarters and tomorrow, I suggest you leave with your mum as planned. This kind of love is not worth dying for." And I agreed with her every word.

Everything Mama Soji said shed a whole lot of light on how Adetoro behaved at lunch the previous day. Ignoring me like a plague was probably his own way of disguising his feelings for me in the presence of his lover. I kind of felt sorry for him, because he was clearly in a very dangerous situation which could cost him his life. From the look of things, Snake Simi wasn't ready to let go of him, and any woman who attempted to come between her and her toy boy would taste her venom.

As I tossed and turned in bed after Mama Soji had left, I wondered what Simi was hatching in her evil mind when she pretended to be the friendliest and most welcoming of the wives when we met. I just wanted the day to break so that I could get the hell away from the cursed town of Ikoko.

The next time I opened my eyes it was morning. I quickly got myself out of bed, into the shower and, within minutes, I was ready to flee for my life. As I contemplated on whether to go to Adetoro's room acting like we were ok, or head to the dining hall for breakfast, I heard a tap on the door. Before I could get it, Adetoro opened the door and allowed himself in.

"Hey my angel, how are you doing?" he asked, as he leaned in to give me a kiss. "I hope you had a good night's sleep, although you didn't sleep in my room as promised. I was a bit surprised to find an empty bed late last night."

"What do you mean?" I asked, as I busied myself tucking the edges of my bed in, so I wouldn't have to look at him. "I was in your room all night, I only came in here this morning to change my clothes. Besides, you already told me not to wait up. Where were you anyway?"

"I'm so sorry my angel, I shouldn't have left you by yourself. One of the kids wasn't feeling well and, when he begged me to stay, I was left with no choice. It's no wonder my bones ache so badly this morning; his bed was too small for both of us," he said, as he placed both of his hands on his hips.

'Your bones hurt alright, you were in my bed during the day and in Simi's bed all night!' I thought, 'You pair of murderous snakes! You make my skin crawl now, so crawl back to your snake pit with your snake lover, I am out of here!"

However, as I didn't want anything to get in the way of leaving the palace peacefully, I managed to keep my sentiments to myself. I played along and followed him to breakfast.

I was quiet over breakfast, but he just assumed I was pensive about leaving and left me be. I was sure he also valued not being questioned further about his antics. He had that guilty air about him, that slightly smug, slightly sheepish look that men have after cheating. I have only ever seen 'that look' on the faces of men and dogs. I would have expected the old Adetoro to try and persuade me to change my mind at the last minute and stay with him, but he was not the man I wanted him to be. Anyway, none of it mattered anymore, soon it would all be ancient history.

We were only half way through our meal when I heard my dad's voice, and my heart swelled with love for the man who raised me knowing all too well I wasn't his. Even though we didn't get along that well (to be fair, I wouldn't have gotten along with my real father either), it was apparent that he loved me as his own. I jumped from my seat without excusing myself and ran into his welcoming arms, as he covered my face with kisses whilst my mum looked on with admiration. You could tell from her expression that she perfectly understood what was going on between Dad and I in that moment– we had finally found each other, we had finally connected. The real father I was looking for was there all along, but it took finding my biological dad to recognise the fact.

Now my family was here, they were all I cared about. Their very presence eclipsed anything I may have felt for the adulterous snake who called himself a king. My mum had been right to be concerned and I just wanted to go home.

I knew I still had to say goodbye to Adetoro and a part of me wanted to advise him to free himself of the bondage he was in, but I knew that would only put Mama Soji in danger. As much as I would have loved to have said goodbye to Mama Soji too, and thank her for all she did for me, I also knew I wouldn't have been able to look her in the face without one or both of us accidentally giving something away with our body language or facial expressions. I could be a good actress when I needed to be, but I didn't want to take the risk. So I had to act as calm as possible, and get out of there as fast as possible.

So I simply walked up to Adetoro, gave him a peck on the cheek and said, "Thank you for your hospitality. I am sorry I am not staying, I wish you all the best, goodbye!" Then, before he could even respond, I turned on my heel and walked away, back into the loving arms of my family.

I didn't look back, not once and Adetoro didn't say a word, not one. Whilst my goodbye was simple, it was clear it was a final farewell, never to return again. Not to see him and not to see my biological father either. On my way out, I placed the book he had loaned me on a table and, as I did so, I thought 'And she walked away, towards a happy future. The End.'

Little did I know what was to come.

CHAPTER ELEVEN

London, No Place Like Home

FOR the first time in my life, I was grateful for waking up in my small double room, it suddenly looked so beautiful and enough. I wasn't ready to get out of my cosy bed, even though I could hear my mum calling my name and urging me to get up as soon as possible.

"Grace, are you still in bed?" Femi said, as he barged into my room, "Mum wants you, she says you should hurry up, there's a thanksgiving service dedicated to thank God for your safe arrival home. I'm going to have my breakfast now, I don't want it to get cold."

"What's for breakfast, glutton?" I shouted after Femi, who was already hurrying down the stairs.

"Pancakes and omelette, can't you smell it?" he replied.

Returning to the UK and reuniting with family and friends felt a little strange, as I was no longer the girl they used to know. At times I was extraordinarily quiet and reserved, and people who were used to seeing my bubbly side couldn't comprehend my sudden change in behaviour. My bittersweet experience in Nigeria had made me wise beyond my years, the two weeks I spent in there felt like two years, as I was exposed to the good, the bad and the ugly, which changed my mentality forever.

Even after a couple of weeks of returning to the UK and back to my everyday life, I found it difficult to settle in fully. I became withdrawn, stopped going out with my friends on Friday nights, the afternoon run with my work colleagues no longer seemed interesting, and worse of all, I stopped calling my mum for our normal evening gossip.

Most times I just wanted to be cuddled up in bed with my teddy bear, watch rubbish TV and allow my mind to drift back to my Nigeria experience, especially the short time I spent with Oba Adetoro. Despite finding out about his little secret, I kept thinking of how my life would have been if I had stayed with him. I had tried to fight my feelings for him and, to be honest, the natural passion I felt for him had been one of the reasons I fled the palace. The truth was, he set off my alarm bells in all ways and, to my frustration, it seemed I couldn't just forget him so easily. I was sure my confused feelings for him weren't just an infatuation, they were definitely more, but there was no way of finding out.

Friends continually complained about my new 'party pooper' attitude, especially Tiwa, who kept nagging me for either turning down her invite to a night out, or refusing to pick up her calls and return them. It wasn't long before she called my mum to notify her that there was something wrong with me. At first my parents dismissed my friend's observation and put it down to me finally being mature in my thinking, but when I went home four weeks after our return from Nigeria and made an unexpected announcement during dinner, they changed their mind.

"Mummy and Daddy, I have handed in my resignation at work. And before you say anything, I am starting a new one next week Monday," I said, as I watched my parents digest what I was saying. It was Dad who first spoke, "How is that possible? Aren't you going to work off your notice period?"

"My boss understands what it means to be traumatised, so he was happy for me to use up the rest of my holidays," I said, as I turned to mum for her verdict.

"Where is the new job?" Mum asked.

"It's at National Rail here in London, just four stops away from home on the Northern line. I hope they extend my contract after my first six months," I said, but if I had foreseen my mum's reaction to my last sentence, I wouldn't have added it.

"What! You left you reputable and well-paid permanent job at BMW for a contract job? Are you crazy?" she asked, as she dropped her fork and knife on her plate such that some rice scattered on the dining table.

"Take it easy," Dad advised.

"Have you forgotten how hard you worked to get that job at BMW?" Mum added, ignoring Dad's advice completely.

"I just want to be closer to home Mum, is that such a bad thing?" I asked, defensively.

"Since when did you care about being close to home, you have always wanted to be as far away as possible, what changed?" Mum retorted.

"Can you both stop raising your voices, I really don't see what the problem is here," Dad intervened.

"Thanks Dad. I don't know why mum is freaking out, I know what I'm doing. Not only do I need to be closer to home, I also need a hands-on job where I can pick up new skills. My mind is made up and there is no turning back…so let's move on." I said, before clearing the plates from the dining table.

"There is more to this than meets the eye, we are definitely going to see the therapist as suggested by Tiwa's mum. Make sure you are ready by 8am tomorrow morning," Mum said, turning to Dad for support, but he was busy scrolling through his phone.

"Mummy, I DO NOT need a therapist. I am ok. I just fancied a job change," I said, as I filled my glass with some water. "This is a positive thing, stop making it sound like it's the end of the world. I will now be able to save better, like you keep advising me to. My contract job pays threefold what I was earning in my permanent job, and moving back home will mean saving my monthly rent of £675 towards a mortgage of my own. What's there not to like?" I asked.

Despite laying out all the advantages to my mum, she didn't seem convinced, but she knew not to push further because, when my mind is made up, no one was able to change it.

The weekend before I started my new job, I decided it was the perfect time to finally go out, let my hair down and have a good time. Tiwa was right, it was time to stop hiding away and moping, and I knew the only way I could have a splendid night was to invite my best friends, Tiwa, Funke and Bolu. I had no idea where to go, but I was sure that Tiwa would already have something lined up for the weekend, so I called her first. To say she was over the moon is an understatement.

"Thank goodness, I finally got my babe back!" she screamed, almost splitting my eardrum.

"I have always been here Tee," I replied.

"I was beginning to worry, Gracie, I thought we've lost you for good. Now that you are back, let's hit Coko Lounge for Tobi's 25th birthday."

"It's been a while since I heard from Tobi, how is she doing?" I asked.

"She's good, she was even asking after you the other day. And guess what, Funke and Bolu are also coming out tonight, you know what that means? The four Sinclair Sisters will turn up tonight and groove the night away, in style. I am so excited, let me go and find a suitable outfit to wear," Tiwa said as she blurted out her words, a hundred words per second.

Tiwa already talked really fast, but when she was excited, or angry, words escaped her mouth uncontrollably. Before she hung up the phone, to probably ransack her wardrobe, I quickly got a word in.

"Tiwa, whose turn is it to pay the cab fare? You or me?" I asked.

"It's your turn, but it's my treat tonight, so the cab fare, the drinks, and food are on me…The good-looking men, however, are all mine."

"What! Remember, it's my night, don't go and start snatching all the hot men with your Coca-Cola body and charms. Remember the rules, I see him first…"

"I take him home!"

"Tiwa, stop playing, I see him first…"

"I take him home, what's wrong with what I just said, that's the rule. Whoever sees the hot guy first takes him home. So why are you tripping?"

"You should have said, 'you, i.e. I take him home!'

"Ok, Grace Abosede Olokose, you see him first, you take him home. Happy?"

"Yes Tiwatayo, I'm happy now," I said.

"Silly girl, as if we will actually take a guy home, our mums would kill us," Tiwa said and we both laughed about what our mums, especially hers, would do should she even think of bringing a man that wasn't a fiancé home.

"See you at 9pm. Funke and Bolu will already be at the venue because they'll be doing Tobi's makeup," Tiwa added, before hanging up the phone.

As soon as we entered Coko Lounge, I knew it was going to be an entertaining night – waiters and waitresses carrying different colours of cocktails to punters who awaited their drinks eagerly; Toni Tetuila's 'My Car' on full blast; disco lights pulsing to the beat and giving the entire hall an electrifying effect.

The bar was filling up quite quickly but we were lucky enough to find a vacant booth, and I wasn't going to let anyone steal it from us. So I asked Tiwa to find the celebrant to inform her of our arrival and look for Funke and Bolu. Knowing those two, they were probably in the bathroom doing each other's makeup! They never did their own makeup until their clients were looking like glamorous divas. Funke, Bolu, Tiwa and I all went to the same secondary school together and, without one another, school would have been hell on earth. After secondary school, Funke and Bolu went to fashion school and pursued their dreams of becoming professional makeup artists. Tiwa and I, however, went down the science route – Tiwa studied dentistry and I engineering. But one thing the four of us had in common was our love of food, dancing and partying.

As we sipped our drinks, I looked at my friends and silently thanked God for sparing my life whilst in Nigeria and for blessing me with such amazing friends, who were already making me forget my sorrows as we danced and drank the night away. At some point, the girls were so glad to finally have me back in the groove, that they asked the DJ to play our favourite song. As we busted our moves to JLo's 'Love Don't Cost a Thing' with Tobi, the celebrant, all eyes were on us...but there was one pair of eyes transfixed on me in particular, as he pushed his way through the crowd to get a better view.

At first I couldn't believe my own eyes. Surely it couldn't be...could it? I squinted through the flashing lights and dry ice and recognised a familiar face, one who I wouldn't have expected to be there in a million years. My heart started to pound like the beat of the music, as I remembered the sensation of his kiss on my lips, back there, so far away in Lagos...and I let the memory wash over me as I moved my body to the music...

As we smashed the dance floor with our mastered choreography, the crowd started cheering and we kept giving them more, but I wasn't trying to impress anyone other than the man whose eyes were locked with mine. DJ Tee, a childhood friend, must have been on the same wavelength as us, because he kept chanting "Go Sinclair Sisters, Go Birthday Girl!", encouraging us to give the dance performance of a lifetime. And we did.

Our three minutes of fame came to an end too soon, and we were swamped with the other club goers, giving us high fives and thumbs up, wanting more. Hot and sweaty after our exertions, we excused ourselves from our fans and headed to the bar to get cold drinks. I, however, had more than a cold drink on my mind. As we made our way through the crowds, my radar was set to scan the room for the man who had been watching me…the man I had not seen since my adventures in Lagos… and there he was, grinning at me, and I ran into Felix's waiting arms. Unlike the last time I saw him, he was well groomed and appeared taller and happier.

"I never thought I'll see you again. What happened to you?" he asked, as he led the way to an open window.

"It's a long story bro," I replied, as the cool air blew on our faces. I was happy to see Felix, but my nose was still out of joint that he had seemingly abandoned me to the attackers that day. I added. "Anyway, you can't have cared that much as you didn't make much of an effort to rescue me, as I recall. It's a good job I landed in the care of someone who did!"

Felix looked affronted. "Sunday, Morolake, and I looked for you well into the night that day, we even involved the authorities, but you know the Nigerian Police, they were bribed by the masquerade handlers and that was the end of that. I hung around for another day to interrogate some of the younger men, but they said you stopped breathing so they left before the authorities pinned your demise on them, how mean? The fact that you were nowhere to be found gave me the consolation that you probably weren't dead, so I retrieved my passport from Sunday and left Nigeria the following day. If not for my mum and sister, I don't think I will ever consider returning to that country. And when I do, I will make sure I am completely prepared," he explained.

I laughed. Felix didn't know the half of it. "That makes the two of us," I said, 'All the fun I had in Nigeria was ruined by the nasty experience towards the end of my trip. Let's just say we were unlucky. I know I will return, but I will make sure I am financially capable to hire the best security agencies in town next time!"

"You call that nasty? That was life-threatening. You still haven't told me what happened to you. Don't tell me the masquerades and their handlers had you all that time?" Felix asked.

'Oh Felix,' I thought, 'The masquerades were nothing compared to the dangers which could have awaited me if I had stayed!', but instead I told him a version of events, which omitted the fact that I fell in love with the King of Ikoko and discovered his murderous secret, thus putting my life even further at risk.

Felix listened to my story with interest and encouragement, his eyes wide at my descriptions of the palace. "Wow Abosede, that sounds like a fantastic adventure, I am so happy you fell into the right hands and are returned safe to the UK!"

At the mention of 'falling into hands', I had a sudden flashback of Adetoro's hands on my body and felt my heart quicken and my body started to throb. Felix must have noticed the sudden change in my body language and thought it was because I was still attracted to him. Standing there in front of him, I realised this was true. Whilst the memory of Adetoro was like a decadent temptation which was ultimately bad for you, my attraction to Felix felt natural and comfortable – he felt safe.

He grinned at me. "Let's get out of here, should we go to mine? I live just a couple of stops away from here," he asked, as he made way for one of the bouncers who wanted to open the top window to let more air in.

His place was the only place we could go, as we couldn't go to mine, so I agreed. I wanted to spend some more time with him and catch up, after all, we had been through a lot together. When Tiwa and I were joking about finding a hot man and taking him home, I had no idea it was going to happen literally. I briefly introduced Felix to my friends, before excusing myself from the party so we could leave together. Having heard my story and knowing who Felix was, my friends were most approving of this turn of events. Tiwa had winked at me in approval, "You go girl!" she cheered, as Felix and I slunk out hand in hand, a little embarrassed, but mostly feeling excited to have found each other again.

I noticed that he smelled good. His aftershave was deep, rich and spicy, and his ridiculous beard had long since been shaved off. We chatted as we walked to the tube station, but once on the train our conversation came to a natural pause. When the silence was getting a little awkward, he put his arms around me and I rested my head on his shoulder. I don't know what was going through Felix's mind, but I was just thinking how lucky we were for fate to have reunited us. The more I settled into his embrace, he reassured me by pulling me closer. The feeling I had was different, there were no butterflies at the bottom of my belly, it was just pure and simple contentment.

This was a new emotion for me to experience with a man, and I discovered I liked it. I especially liked it because of the new secret I was carrying, a secret not even my best friends or my parents knew. In fact, I had only just found out myself and it had shaken me to the core. Then, just as I had been wondering what to do and had decided to just go out and dance and let fate sort itself out, Felix had walked right into my story. I decided his appearance was, indeed, a gift from fate and, being a resourceful woman, I welcomed this serendipitous event with open arms.

Chapter Twelve

The Clay Pot

"WELCOME to my royal palace," Felix said, as we arrived at his house. His choice of words immediately jolted my memory back to Ikoko palace, but I quickly wiped the thought off my mind as it wasn't the time or place to think of such things. As much as I liked Felix and rather against my will, I knew my heart was still with someone else. It would have been easier if my heart was free to fall in love with Felix, but I was betrayed by my body and the baby in my tummy – King of Ikoko's baby, my deepest secret. I shook my head, as if to shake off the thought because I just wanted to have fun and feel loved So I forced my mind to travel back to the room where Felix and I were held captive, and of course our kiss.

"A penny for your thought," Felix said as he gestured for me to sit down on his sofa and handed me a cup of tea.

"I'm just thinking of how lucky we are to have found each other tonight. I never envisaged this reunion," I said, as I sipped my tea.

"Are you happy about it?" he asked.

"No, I'm not happy, I am ecstatic," I said, and we both laughed.

"A day hasn't gone by without thinking about you and our little kiss; aggressive and unexpected, like we see in Nollywood movies. I am so glad I found you tonight and no matter where this goes, I will never forget you; we are friends for life, Grace," he said, before refilling my cup of tea. "But…but, I will love it more if we can take this to the next level. We aren't getting any younger, I don't know about you, I'm not willing to mess around any longer," he added, as he pushed my hair behind my ear.

And there it was. I was being wooed right there and then, by someone who already knew everything…well, almost everything about me. I knew I had no choice but to accept his proposal. I had never really had a mature relationship and he was offering me one – at a time when I needed it the most. So I dropped my cup on the centre table, drew closer to him, and gave him a hug which consequently led to a kiss, followed by an entwined walk to his bedroom, unto his bed…and the rest they say is history…

We both fell into a deep sleep and I did not wake up until the early hours of the morning, to visit the ladies' room. I had been using the bathroom more often than usual lately, which I assumed was one of the early symptoms of pregnancy. When I got back to the bedroom, Felix was still sleeping ever so peacefully. As I watched him take each breath, I wondered if I was able to carry out the plan I had started to hatch in my mind the moment I set eyes on him at the club.

I had always been more of a romantic than a cunning woman in love, and what I was doing felt out of character. I loved Felix in a way, but I wasn't in love with him. I wondered if this would be enough, for either of us. I also wondered what Adetoro would think, if he could see me in the bed of another man, whilst carrying his baby. In my mind a battle raged between the moral me, who felt ashamed for my deceit, and the warrior me, who would do whatever it took for survival.

Again, my mind drifted back to Ikoko, and my conversation with Mama Soji about the history of Ikoko Town:

"His clay pot was going pear-shaped, he had to do something to bring it back to life, so he did what he had to do."; "You've mapped your life out perfectly, along the line, something threatens to ruin it, wouldn't you do something to put your life back on track?"

'Is it time to follow in the footsteps of my forefathers, or more precisely, my mother, by reshaping my life?' I wondered. History has it that many women before me had done it. In fact, I was the result of such deceit myself, but I wasn't sure I had it in me to pin another man's baby on an innocent man? More so, to do this to a man who had suffered heartbreak from his first love? I wondered if it would be wiser to just walk away at that moment, or wake him up and tell him the truth and bear the consequences? The worse that could happen would be him wanting nothing to do with me ever again. As my mind played out different scenarios and their potential outcomes, I prayed to God to direct and help me with my decision, but I needed to act fast because time wasn't on my side. I was already seven weeks pregnant.

It wasn't long before Felix's alarm clock beeped and he jumped out of bed to turn it off.

"Why is your alarm clock far away from your bedside, it's hazardous to jump out of bed like that you know?" I said, and he looked to my side of the bed as if he had forgotten I was there.

"Oh, my goodness, it wasn't a dream, you are actually here?" Felix said, as he pulled me closer to him. I could see his love for me in his eyes, and feel it in his embrace. I let my worries fade away and allowed myself to melt into his embrace.

I left Felix's house that day without coming clean about my situation, and whilst I promised myself to tell him soon, I knew I actually wouldn't. The fact that I couldn't bring myself to be honest from the start had set a precedent and formed a plan. One day turned into one week, and before I knew it we had been seeing each other for over a month. My new job and pregnancy symptoms took most of my concentration, but I still had a lot of time left for our relationship. In fact, things were moving so fast that Felix had met my parents and brother. I had spoken to his mum and sister in Nigeria and we had visited his uncle's family. After visiting his uncle, I thought it was the best time to break the news.

Never one for subtlety, I dropped the bombshell while we were driving home. "Felix, I am pregnant," I declared, as I scrutinised his face for any sign of disappointment, however slight.

"You know I am driving, this is not the best time for one of your silly jokes," he said, as he kept his eyes on the road.

"I took a pregnancy test yesterday, and it was positive…I am serious," I continued.

"This is really important Grace, tell me you are not joking," he said, before pulling up in the nearest roadside parking.

"I am serious honey, I am six weeks pregnant," I said, without blinking once. As I said, I can be an excellent actress when I want to be, and I reckoned I could just about get away with telling this little white lie about how far gone I was.

At first, Felix just sat there, still gripping the steering wheel so tight. Then his shoulders relaxed and he turned to face me, with a huge smile and a look of happy disbelief in his eyes. "This is great news, I am going to be a father, someone is going to call me 'Daddy' soon. Oh, my mother will be so happy when I tell her. Congratulations to us, we made a life," he said, before leaning in to give me a kiss.

His reaction was so wonderful, it made me feel utterly wretched and unworthy of such care. I wondered what he would have said if I had told him the truth. 'Come on now Grace!' I told myself, 'You are just feeling all emotional because of the hormones, hold it together, the plan is working just fine.' However, for all of my pep talk, I found big fat tears rolling down my cheeks.

"Why are you crying, don't you want the baby?" he asked, looking confused and concerned at the same time.

"I do," I reassured him, "I just wasn't sure how you would take the news. I'm glad you are mature and responsible enough to want the baby," I said, but I knew my tears were of guilt.

Felix was a good man and didn't deserve what I was doing to him, but he hadn't made it so easy. The more I spent time with him, the more I realised I couldn't let him go. He was reliable, focused, handsome, and ready for a serious relationship. My love for him grew day by day, almost at the same rate the baby inside of me was growing, and I knew our love was exponential; it could only increase. I kept telling myself I made the right decision, if not, why else did fate bring us together on that fateful night? Even my parents and friends confirmed how good Felix and I were together.

"You've bagged yourself a good man, make sure you do all you can to keep him," were my mother's exact words.

"Gracie, have you seen the way he looks at you, you are so lucky. From what I see, he will pop the question very soon. If you didn't tell me the story, I would have thought you've known each other for years. I am so happy for you, girlfriend," was what Tiwa sent to me in a private message when she saw a picture of the two of us on Friends Reunited.

And they were all right, Felix was a natural husband material. As soon as he heard about the pregnancy, things moved even quicker than I ever imagined. Before I knew it, my twelve-week scan was due. Even though the appointment was about three weeks late, I still couldn't tell Felix because the numbers wouldn't add up. Instead, I told him I was on my way to check things out at the doctors, just an extra monitoring appointment due to my diabetes. And when he insisted on going with me, I told him I didn't want any fuss, especially as Mum was friends with all the admins at our doctor's surgery.

"I don't want her finding out just yet," I said, which was partially true – I didn't want Mum to find out yet.

"Ok, let me know the outcome of your appointment, ok. If everything goes well, let's hook up this evening at Coko Lounge to celebrate the end of the week. Is that a deal?" he asked.

"Of course, we can," I said, as I walked through the automatic glass doors of the hospital.

The scan went well and I was given a picture of my unborn child after my twenty-minute session with the sonographer. As I stared at the picture on my way home, I was so sure in my mind that the baby was a boy and he had Oba Adetoro's shape of head. Fear engulfed me, I started sweating profusely as I hurriedly walked to the nearest reception area for a seat. Before I knew it, I was hyperventilating and the whole hospital became blurry.

"Ma'am, are you alright? Someone call A&E!" called a male voice and, within minutes, I was being wheeled back into the hospital.

"Who can we call? Are there any health conditions we should know about?" asked a voice.

"Type 1 Diabetes…call my mum please," I said, as I called out my mum's mobile number.

When I opened my eyes, my mum was by my side and the moment she noticed I was awake, the questions started, and kept coming.

"How are you feeling sweetheart? What happened to you? What were you doing in the hospital anyway? Your dad is on his way, I should call Felix to let him know too," Mum kept going and if I didn't stop her, she would have carried on.

"No! You don't have to call Felix, I will see him later tonight. I am feeling better now. Besides, I don't want to bother him with my diabetes issues," I said.

"Grace, he needs to know what he is up against, this is not something you can hide from your future husband."

"Mum, he is not yet my fiancé, he is just my boyfriend," I said.

"If you say so," Mum said, with a little mischief in her eyes which made me wonder if she was hiding something from me.

When the doctor returned, he advised me to keep an eye on my blood sugar levels and return for another scan in two weeks' time. Apparently, my glucose skyrocketed, the reason for my symptoms.

"Grace, you are pregnant and you didn't tell me? What have I done to deserve this?" Mum asked when the doctor left us.

"I'm sorry Mummy, we wanted to wait until after our twelve-week scan before telling you."

"How far are you gone?" she asked, so I did a quick calculation in my head to back up my lies – true number of weeks minus five weeks.

"Ten weeks," I said.

"Oh, thank God! My baby is carrying one of her own. I'll be the youngest grandma amongst my friends," she said, as she fussed around me, tucking in my bra strap. "But you should have told me before now, considering your underlining medical condition and the fact that we live under the same roof."

Mum took me home and, later that evening, I went to meet Felix at Coko Lounge as planned. The moment I walked in, I recognised a lot of faces, including my dad, mum, friends, Felix's friends, his uncle and wife – it was quite obvious, even before they all shouted, "Surprise!"

Felix pushed his way through the crowd, went down on one knee and asked me to marry him. If I was an outsider watching from afar, I would have said things were moving too fast; we've only known each other for less than three months and he was already asking for my hand in marriage in front of our entire family and friends. I would have loved it better if he had proposed in private, but the deed was already done, and Felix was a good man who loved me just the way I was. So nothing was too fast or elaborate, it was just perfect. It was too perfect. I silently congratulated myself on the fulfilment of my plan, but something deep inside niggled at me. I ignored it.

"Grace?" Felix repeated, promoting me from my silence.

"Yes!" I said, burying my nagging doubts once and for all. "Yes, I will marry you!"

The entire hall screamed and started taking pictures of us on their mobile phones. It was like being surrounded by paparazzi, and I had a brief flashback to being treated like a celebrity in Lagos, when I was out with Chelsea.

"I thought we should do this before you start showing," Felix said, as he cradled me in his arms. "We can fix a wedding date for after the baby is born but, in the meantime, I think we should move in together. Here is the key to our three-bedroom house in Chelmsford, I just completed the mortgage process yesterday."

"You bought us a house?" I asked, as my jaw dropped.

"Yes, I did. Anything for you baby girl! I read somewhere that getting 'busy' aids easy delivery, so we better hurry home after this to bless our new home." Felix said.

"Felix, frequent sex is advised for safe delivery, but that's in the third trimester," I explained, laughing.

"Well, nothing stops us from starting earlier, considering your sex drive lately," Felix whispered in my ear, which made me giggle even more, and others looked on in admiration. 'If only they knew!' I thought.

As friends and family congratulated us, I couldn't help but wonder what it would have felt like if I was actually marrying Felix without such a huge secret hanging between us – my happiness would have known no bounds. Even though it was such a happy day, I couldn't bring myself to being a hundred percent happy, as I didn't think I deserved him.

A day didn't go by without thinking about my decision to rob the one I loved, in order to be with another, for the sake of convenience. I never thought I would end up doing exactly what I loathed my mother for. 'Is this a generational curse?' I wondered. 'If yes, that would mean my child is destined to hate me when he is older and would go looking for his biological father?'

Sometimes I wondered if I should seek my mum's opinion on the matter, but I dismissed the idea every time because I couldn't bring myself to tell her we were cut from the same cloth after all; especially as I had blamed her for years. Another option that kept playing on my mind was to inform Oba Adetoro I was carrying his child, but I couldn't justify what good that would do for any of us. Neither I nor my child could move to Nigeria, as I didn't think we would be safe in his palace. He on the other hand was a king and wouldn't just up and leave his people and family to relocate to the UK. I could not have a child out of wedlock, or be married to a man living abroad, so my thoughts always cycled back to Felix – he was a good husband and father material, there was no way my decision could be wrong. Could it?

So, as we took our first dance in the presence of our friends and family on our engagement night, I made the decision of my life, justified using my own interpretation of the greater good theory. I had to, because keeping my mouth shut would guarantee my unborn child a better life, so I was going to leave everything to fate and enjoy the moment. After all, my mum and dad were happy enough together, even though he knew I was not his biological daughter. They had made it work, I was sure I could too. 'All you have to do Grace,' I told myself, time and time again, as if a mantra, 'Is to keep your mouth shut and keep your secret to yourself! How hard can that be?'

CHAPTER THIRTEEN

Out In The Open

I had been working at National Rail for about four months when Trisha, my boss, called me into her office just before I left for the day.

"Grace, although you haven't announced your good news, we can all see that you have a bun in the oven…it's a joyful thing so there is no need to hide it," she said, as she scrolled down her computer for no apparent reason. I waited for her to look in my direction before I spoke. Even though her tone was congratulatory, I wanted to see her face properly to judge how she really felt.

"You are right Trisha, I am so sorry for the unnecessary secrecy. I just felt bad for withholding the truth before I started the job, I didn't tell anyone because I thought you might pull the offer," I blurted out, in all honesty.

Trisha smiled at me and I relaxed a little. "You are right, we probably wouldn't have employed you but that would have been our loss; you have been an exceptional colleague so you have nothing to worry about. Moreover, you were employed as a temp, so there is no reason to be guilty," Trisha explained, "And now you are here, we certainly cannot discriminate against you for being pregnant."

"Thanks for your understanding, Trisha," I said swiftly, as I sensed she still had more to say.

"I have invited you to my office to discuss your career plans. You've only been here for four months now and have fit in nicely with the rest of the team. Depending on what plans you have after the baby, we were thinking of making you a permanent member of staff. What do you think?" she asked, as she forced a tight-lipped smile, as if scared of what my response would be. "When are you due by the way?"

"I am due in June...I honestly didn't see that coming, that's such great news," I replied, noticing the look of surprise on her face.

"Really, that far gone? I would have sworn you were still in your first trimester, not four months to go. Congratulations!" Trisha said with a chuckle. "I know it's too early to say, but do you think you will return after the baby, if yes, when might that be?"

"We haven't projected that far, but I reckon I will be back when the baby is about seven months."

"Ok, that sounds like a plan. When are you going on maternity leave?"

"I plan to work until my contract finishes in two months' time. If possible, I will work until about two weeks before the baby arrives," I said.

"Fantastic! This might come out a little selfish, but I need you to promise me you'll return, because we are trying to cut down on cost. Whilst you are away, the plan is to get Sarah and Louise to share your job, seven months is a bearable amount of time for us to manage without you, but more than that would start to pinch. When you return we'd be glad to offer you a permanent job, that way we save cost and you get job security," Trish said.

"You have just made my day Trisha. All things being equal, I hope to return to work mid-January after our wedding in December," I said, and she pencilled down the dates on her huge calendar on the wall.

When I left her office, I got my bag and hurried to the tube station, as I couldn't wait to break the news to Felix. As soon as I opened the door, I blurted out my good news to Felix in excitement, dates and all, without thinking. He just sat there, looking at me as if I had just stabbed him in the chest. The expression on his face made my blood run cold and, with horror, I realised what I had done.

"Hang on a minute, did I just hear you say you plan to work until end of May, meaning two weeks before the baby arrives?" Felix asked, as he sat up in the sofa and dropped the remote control on the centre table – my initial excitement had evaporated and was replaced by fear. I felt sick.

"No, I mean…" I stuttered, as I tried to cover my tracks even though it was obvious I had been found out in my lies, "Felix, I am not feeling very well, I need to lie down…"

"No, that's exactly what you meant, don't bother with the lies!" he snapped, "Of course you feel sick, sick with guilt! I have had my suspicions for quite a while now; you always found an excuse to go to scans on your own, you convinced me not to find out the sex of the baby, then you stock up on blue outfits only?" Felix asked as he wiggled his finger at me – hand, body and voice shaking. "Grace Abosede Olokoshe, why are you telling me our baby is due second week in June when you previously said it's 15 July?"

I had imagined this confrontation so many times but, despite my fear, I never thought I would be so calm and collected. I settled myself down on the sofa opposite Felix and stared into the air, partly to keep calm and partly so I didn't have to look at him.

"Grace, I am talking to you, please say something. What is going on? When is our baby due?" Felix asked, again.

I bit my lip, suddenly trying not to cry. All the lies and deceit came bubbling up, to be released in a huge stream of tears. "It's not our baby Felix, it's mine," I said, as the tears rolled down my cheeks. "I am so sorry, I was going to tell you…but things were happening too fast, I couldn't bring myself to ruin our happiness. I'm not blaming anyone, I know I should have come clean months ago."

"Ruin our happiness?" spat Felix, "You lie to me because you don't want to ruin our happiness? If the baby is not mine, whose is it then?"

"It's mine," I answered, as I watched Felix start to pace back and forth across the living room, whilst taking off his shirt even though it was a cold February evening. My heart started pounding because it was difficult to predict his next move.

"Grace! I will only ask you one more time, whose baby are you carrying?" he yelled, tensing his muscles and clenching his fists. I doubted he would hit me, but he looked as though he may punch a hole in the wall if he didn't calm down.

"Ok, have a seat, I'll tell you everything," I cajoled, hating how he hovered over me, coiled like a spring ready to explode.

"I told you about the palace I was taken to in Ikoko?" I started, tentatively, "Well, the only bit I left out was the fact that I was sexually involved with the king," I said, as I cleared my throat for no particular reason. "He is the father. Luckily, it wasn't anything serious, so when I heard he was sleeping with one of his brother's widows it was easy for me to leave. I didn't know I was pregnant until I got back to the UK and I had no idea I was going to reunite with you either. When we hooked up, it felt so good and right that I couldn't bring myself to ruin what we had. I swear to God, I haven't been in contact with Adetoro ever since I left, he doesn't even know I am carrying his baby," I explained through my tears. Even to my own ears, my story didn't sound good.

"Let's get this right. You found out you were pregnant, the father doesn't know, I turned up and you pinned someone else's child on me? How convenient?" Felix retorted. "When were you going to tell me? Who else knows about this? And don't tell me your mum doesn't know.

What am I even saying, isn't that exactly how she pinned you on her husband?" he asked, as he flapped his hands around and mistakenly knocked off the glass of water on the centre table.

"Please do not disrespect my mother, she knows nothing about this," I replied, ignoring the water that had splashed across my lap and onto the carpet. "I am the one to blame here, do not direct your anger at my mum. If anything, I am worse than her, at least she told my father about me, he knew what he was signing up for."

"Tell that to the dogs, I can bet my last dollar she just sprung it up on him just like you just did. You are exactly like your mother!!!" he snarled.

"Felix, for the last time, do not mention my mother again! She has nothing to do with any of this. I made my bed, so let me lie in it without you involving or disrespecting her." I stood up and started to make my way to the bedroom, "Give me a few minutes to get my things and I'll be out of your way. To be honest, I'm actually relieved. Although I'm sorry for hurting you like this, I'm glad it's all out in the open."

"Of course, you are," Felix retorted, looking at me as though he hated me. "It's always all about you Grace, isn't it? Poor little rich girl, carrying the baby of a king and thinking you are better than me. Now your conscience can be at peace from your lies, while my heart lies bleeding and you stamp on it with your wicked feet and tell me you are sorry for hurting me!"

"Felix," I cajoled, "My time with you has been a blast, I love you and always will but it's time to call it quits…and clean up that mess if you don't want a smelly house," I added, gesturing to the spilled water.

I stomped into the bedroom and started to dump my belongings into my suitcase. 'That went well – not!' I told myself, realising I had now opened Pandora's box. I was going to have to tell my mum and dad, and soon everyone would know. No longer could I act like a respectable wife and mother, my dirty secret would soon be out and all would know I was the mistress of a polygamous king, carrying his illegitimate son. I felt small, silly and ashamed.

I was so lost in my thoughts, I did not hear Felix follow me into the bedroom and I jumped when I felt his hand on my waist.

"Baby, you don't have to go, I was just so angry that you kept such a huge secret from me," he said, as he set aside my suitcase. He had put his shirt back on and the angry edge was gone from his voice. He sounded calm and resigned, but there was something else in his tone too as he said, "Sit down, let's talk. I also have a secret of my own."

"What secret?" I asked, as I searched his face for clues. He was struggling to look me in the eye. "Go on, I'm listening!"

"Just like you," Felix began, twiddling his thumbs, "I've been meaning to tell you, but I wanted to wait until after the wedding. Since we are sharing and letting the cat out of the bag, I decided there is no better time than the present..."

"Felix, just spit it out. Are you in love with someone else? Are you already married to someone else? Did you get someone pregnant?" I interrupted, "Nothing would surprise me Felix, not after what I have been through. I have not told you everything about my time at the palace and I never will, some things are a matter of life and death. So, promise on your own life that you will tell me the truth now. I have had enough of lies." I realised the hypocrisy in my speech, so I quickly added, "I am sick of all the lies, including my own. If you want to step up as a man and be better than the rest, then tell me the truth."

Felix nodded, "Yes, it is time for truth. When I returned to the UK after our kidnap, I got a call from Uncle Richard summoning me to his house. When I got there, Funmi, my first girlfriend was there; through her crocodile tears, she told me her child had been diagnosed with Autism Spectrum Disorder.

"At first, I wondered why any of that was my business, then she said her husband had demanded a DNA test, because he couldn't accept the fact that he fathered a child with such 'abnormal' behaviours.

"His logic was, no one in his family was ever diagnosed with autism, no biological child of his would refuse to be held by him, laugh only when he thought someone was hurt, and be severely destructive. Although his theory was wrong, he was right about one fact – Samson wasn't his. The DNA test came back negative. According to Funmi, only then did she realise that Samson was mine."

I let his story sink in. In a way, it made me feel better, as though we were now more equal. It also worried me. If Felix already had a biological child, he surely wouldn't want to act as father to my own baby, at least not after finding out the truth. "So, what does she want from you?" I asked, keeping my tone calm and even.

"Nothing," he replied, as he watched my face for a reaction, but I kept my expression blank. I wanted him to finish talking before I gave him any signs as to what I was thinking or feeling. This now felt like a game of spies in the house of love, and I couldn't decide which one of us was the deadliest secret keeper.

"She and her husband are separated, she wants nothing from me apart from being part of Samson's life. I met the boy, he's not as bad as described by Funmi, all he need is structure and routine in his life," he added.

The casual way he told me made my hackles rise. He had been so angry at me, then calm as you like and smiling, he throws his own spanner into the works as though it was nothing. Worse, he didn't even have the decency to acknowledge his own hypocrisy. At least I had the decency to be aware of it and to feel remorse. I felt I had the upper hand again, and span to face him. This time I looked him right in the eyes, so he could see how incredulous I was. "Ok, let me summarise what you've just said; you found out you have a son and you were waiting to tell me after the wedding. So why the hell were you acting all self-righteously and throwing insults at my mother and I?" I ranted, realising I was trembling as I do when I feel emotionally exhausted, confused, and helpless. "We have been living a lie all this while, please let me continue packing my bag, I am off to my parent's house. It is over between us!"

"You better sit your ass down! You don't get to say it's over when we've already set things in motion for our wedding. Do we just throw away what we have, or was I just a meal ticket and eligible father for your unborn child?" he shouted, but I was now too angry to reason, let alone respond to his stupid question.

"Well, I can only speak for myself; you are the best woman for me and I'm not ready to let go just because we have children with other people. If anything, it's the reason we should be together – Grace, say something," Felix said.

"I don't know what to say, Felix. Our relationship is built on mutual captivity and lies, it's hardly a healthy basis for a marriage. Do you really think we can get over this? I asked. "A marriage without trust is an accident waiting to happen."

"I don't foresee any accidents, we are good," Felix encouraged me, as he waved his hand in the air as if to blow my fear away. "The only thing I want you to do for me is call the King of Ikoko and tell him that the child is his," Felix said, as he cupped my face in his hands. I flinched, but I didn't move away. Felix continued, "I know the pain I felt when I found out I had missed out on the first four years of my son's life, even worse the confusion on Samson's face when I was introduced as his dad. You should be familiar with the feeling too. Please don't go Grace"

Felix was right on a few counts. I did know what it felt like, I should let Adetoro know, and we had already come a long way. Within all the drama, we probably knew each other better than anyone else, which could be a strong basis for a marriage. He was also right that there would be no point in calling it quits now. It might not have been a fairy tale, but it was certainly a thriller. Where in the world would I have found a man with such compatibility and understanding? We were both products of broken homes, kidnapped by the same culprits, and each had a child with an ex-partner. I realised, all in all, he was my best option. I relaxed and rested my cheek against his hand.

"Put my clothes back in my wardrobe, then," I replied, smiling sheepishly, as you do when you make friends again after an argument.

"Yes, madam!" he said and we both laughed.

And just like that, our secrets were out in the open and we both felt lighter for it. In fact, we felt giddy for it, and turned on too. This experience had brought us closer together, not pushed us further away. With a sigh of relief, I fell into Felix's arms. He clung to me like a man drowning and, scooping me up, he masterfully ripped off my clothes as he carried me to the bed. "We are destined to be, Grace," he growled in my ear, and brought me to ecstasy with the best make-up sex I have ever had.

Lying together in the afterglow, Felix asked, "Tell me, when is the baby really due? Bring out all the pictures you've been hiding and confirm the sex of the baby right now!"

"You've already guessed it right, it's a boy and he is due on 12 June 2005," I replied, as I played with his hairy chest. "But they say boys cling to their mothers for a little longer so he might come third week in June. Are we going to tell our parents about this?" I asked, as I snuggled up closely to Felix.

"I don't know, let's think about it," he whispered in my ear.

"It's one thing forgiving each other, but how do you think our families will take the news? Nobody likes a bastard as a grandson," I said.

"My mum already knows about my Samson, we might as well tell her everything. We must notify both parents, there is no point in hiding anything from them," Felix said, and that was what we did.

When we went to inform my parents, especially my mum, they didn't take it well. Mum kept crying as if I had just opened old wounds.

"Despite all my prayers, our family curse didn't end with me. My mother, her mother and my great-grandmother made the same mistake, now you?" she cried, and all we could do was console her.

Dad was silent at first, but when we were leaving, he asked to see me in private.

"Grace, I know we haven't always seen eye to eye, but you must know I love you as my daughter, right?" Dad said.

"I love you too, Dad!"

"I applaud your courage in informing your fiancé about this before the baby's born. And I must say, Felix is super bold for accepting another man's child as his own. I wouldn't have accepted you if we weren't already married; your mum didn't come clean until you were born," Dad said, as he struggled to keep a firm voice.

"Dad, I'm so sorry to have opened old wounds," I apologised, as I watched him wipe away a tear that managed to escape from his eye.

"Apparently, your mum was seeing me and your real dad at the same time. I was really hurt and it took me a very long time to heal; we almost didn't make it. But, because like Felix, I was heads over heels in love so I had no choice than to bring you up as my own. I must say, I have never regretted that decision, you've been a delight…apart from your occasional stubbornness."

"Thanks Dad!" I said, as I tapped his shoulder playfully.

"But, you must tell the real father about the child's existence; it's very important. It will only cause resentment and bitterness from him and your child in future if you don't. I needn't say much as we both know how you reacted when you found out I wasn't your biological father and how bitter your father still is. Promise me you will tell him," Dad encouraged.

"I will tell Adetoro very soon," I said, as I gave him a big hug, "I love you Dad! See you soon!"

When we got home we called Felix's mum. Because we didn't discuss with her face to face, it was difficult to judge her reaction, but from her voice and words, she seemed ok with the news.

"You will give us our own son very soon; four boys and four girls," she joked. "Don't worry our wife, mistakes do happen, the good thing is you didn't hide it from your husband for too long," Felix's mum said.

'Husband?' I thought. Felix and I weren't married yet, but she was already addressing me as her daughter-in-law. Whilst a little odd, I found that heart-warming more than anything.

A few weeks later, Felix brought Samson to our place. He was such a handsome boy and the spitting image of his dad. I struggled a bit with his hyperactivity and destructive behaviour, but I was willing to learn and understand him because I knew he couldn't help the way he was. Felix and I had both read a lot about how to deal with autistic children, but there was no 'one size fits all' technique, we just had to be patient with him and shower him with abundant love.

By 5 June 2005, exactly a week before the baby's due date, Felix and I were completely ready for his arrival. He would come back early from work just to make sure everything was ok, he did almost all the house chores and ran around with Tiwa to put things in place for the wedding. The two of them were such great organisers, and my surprise baby shower was proof that it was ok to leave almost everything to them, especially Tiwa.

Every time I watched Tiwa going out of her way for me, I prayed for the strength to be able to reciprocate all her efforts, especially as her first love, Tunji, proposed to her a month before my baby shower. I had no idea they had reunited after their nasty breakup in university. I was so happy for her and couldn't wait to help her with her own wedding preparation and baby shower when the time came.

By 12 June, there was no sign of the baby. Even though I read about the myth of boys coming late, I couldn't help but feel disappointed when there was no sign of the much-dreaded contractions the midwives had warned me about. By June 26, there was still no sign of labour, so the doctor decided to induce me. Nothing could ever prepare a woman for the kind of pain I experienced, it came on so fast and was one excruciating contraction after another. Even though I wasn't fully dilated, the contractions were so spontaneous and unbearable, that I passed out a couple of times. Anyone watching from afar would have thought Felix and I were both in labour; as he cried his eyes out as he watched me suffer, knowing that he couldn't render any help. When his presence wasn't doing anyone any good, my mum and the midwives asked him to take a break.

For the rest of my lengthy labour, it was just Mummy and I. When I wasn't listening to the midwives, she screamed at me, and when I did, she cheered me on until my boy, her grandson, Jason, was placed in my arms on the 26th day of June. The first thing I did was look at his little face, his fingers and toes, there was no mistake whose son he was. Even just born, he looked just like Adetoro. The only difference was he had my eyes.

When Felix saw him, he held him in his arms and sighed.

"God works in mysterious ways, this child is a splitting image of Oba Adetoro," he said. My heart missed a beat to hear Felix say his name and, more so, discover he knew what he looked like. As if Felix read my mind, he quickly added, "I looked him up on Google, of course. They have the same shape of head, nose, and mouth – I know it's too early to tell, but I think it's safe to say that this boy looks nothing like you right now. It's the same with my Samson, any fool will know he is mine.”

"It's nature," I said, "All babies look like their fathers, it's so the father will know they are his and accept them. I still can't get my head around how Funmi and her ex-husband didn't realise Samson's paternity from the day he was born. Perhaps they did, and just didn't want to…Anyway, I do think Jason looks a little like me, you can see it in his eyes…"

Felix leaned forwards and planted a kiss on Jason's head, "It doesn't matter who he looks like. Welcome to the world, son. I am here for you and, by the grace of God, I promise to love you as my own!" he cooed, which brought tears of joy to my eyes as mum and I exchanged glances. I felt so lucky and thankful to be blessed with the cutest bundle of joy, a great husband in Felix, and my mother. The three best things that ever happened to me all in one room, I felt like the luckiest girl on earth.

CHAPTER FOURTEEN

The Explosive Nuptial

AS the saying goes, time flies when one's having fun. Our wedding day, 17 December 2005, sprung upon us like a visitor. Felix and I originally wanted a small wedding of about 150 guests, but our parents weren't having any it, they insisted on 150 guests each from the groom and bride's sides. Catering for 300 guests and having a tasteful wedding would have been impossible based on our budget, but members of our families all chipped in one way or the other. Even guests from Nigeria, Felix's mum, his sister, and my maternal grandparents, did their bit to ensure that we had the glamourous wedding we felt we deserved.

As I sat in the bridal car with my dad, watching people flocking into the church in anticipation of the wedding ceremony, I wondered what it would have felt like if I hadn't complicated my life.

"Are you ok, sweetheart?" Dad asked.

"Yes, I am, I'm just wondering if Jason is ok," I replied, trying to calm myself.

"Don't worry about Jason today, he is in good hands, we both know your mum would have spoilt him rotten by now. Today is about you, Felix will be astonished by your beauty," Dad said, which made me blush.

"Thanks Dad, I'm just a bit nervous!"

"Don't be, I should be the one nervous, walking someone else's child down the aisle, I feel like I don't deserve this privilege."

"You don't feel like I'm your daughter?" I asked, disappointed, as I searched his face for confirmation. Once upon a time I would have believed it, but our relationship had come along in leaps and bounds since then.

"You are my daughter, there's no doubt about it, it's just that, you and your mum should have invited Otunba, he should be here," Dad said, like the honourable man that he was. Otunba would never have suggested such a gesture of goodwill.

"The one who nurtures a child is the true father, no one better deserves the honour of walking me down the aisle than you!" I said, as I watched a smile form on his face. I knew exactly where Dad was coming from, I should have insisted on inviting my father over, but it felt like too much hassle for him and for us. Besides, I didn't really like him and I didn't want the king's spy sniffing around my new life.

Just like Dad, I didn't really think I was worthy of walking up to the aisle to happiness, knowing too well that I had robbed someone else of the joy of raising their son. My mind travelled back to the day I called Adetoro to tell him about Jason.

After months of putting off the call under the guise of adjusting to motherhood, Felix literarily dialled Adetoro's number, waited until he heard a male voice, then put the phone on speaker and shoved it in my hand.

"Hello, may I speak to his royal highness Oba Adetoro Ajagbe please?" I said, as soon as the receiver repeated his greetings.

"Abosede, is that you?" Adetoro asked. For some reason, I expected one of his servants to answer the phone before passing it over to him; but then, I was calling his mobile phone so it made sense.

"Yes, it is me. How have you been?"

"It's been a year since you left here without looking back, why should my wellbeing concern you?" he replied. "The number you jotted down before you left was a fake one, your mum refused to give me or Otunba any of your contact details, so I had no avenue to be in touch. Why did you neglect me like that, I thought we agreed I was going to visit the UK?"

His arrogant attitude annoyed me, reminding me that he wasn't the man I had initially thought he was, the man I couldn't help but fall for. But then, he was notorious for his charm, and I wasn't the only woman he had tricked. "I left you a fake number because I saw you with Olori Simi," I snapped, "I thought you said you weren't sleeping with your brother's widows. I couldn't be with a liar, so I left without looking back." I felt spiteful, because the way he victimised himself was just too much for me to bear. 'A typical narcissist!' I said to myself, 'Blaming everyone else for his own shortcomings!'

Adetoro snorted down the phone. "Because of Simi? You foolish woman, why didn't you say anything before you left? If you were so upset I could have broken it off with her." Then, as if on second thoughts, he added, "So you left because you were jealous? You didn't really expect me to abandon sexually active women who needed servicing from yours truly, did you? I am the king after all!"

I don't know how I managed to stay calm and not rise to the bait, but I did. In my head I was calling him every name under the sun, but I remained composed. "Adetoro, I really don't care what you do with your sisters-in-law, or should I say, wives. I am calling to inform you that I am getting married in three months' time and I had a baby three months ago." I said, as I paused for it to sink in. "The baby is a boy, he is yours, but you don't have to worry yourself with anything, my husband and I are capable and happy to bring him up without any assistance from you. However, you are welcome to see him anytime you are in the UK or when we are in Nigeria. Just be aware, we have full custody of him and I am only letting you know as it is the correct thing to do.”

Adetoro snarled, “So, baby snatching runs in the family! Do you realise you've just done exactly what your mother did to Otunba? Only difference here is I am not as soft as your father. I am King of Ikoko and no one snatches my child from me!”

“Adetoro, I'm going to put the phone down if you don't lower your voice,” I warned. I could picture him pacing around whilst on the phone, he sounded breathless and angry.

“No, you listen to me!” he bellowed, “Royal blood runs in that boy's veins, which means he belongs here in Ikoko. Get yourself a good lawyer because I am going to fight for my heir until my very last breath! I already have a UK visa, all I need to do now is to get a ticket and get on the plane in time for your wedding. If you're not looking forward to seeing me, you better dig a hole in the ground to hide yourself, my son, and your coward husband!”

When I didn't reply, he continued, “Are you there? You can only run, you cannot hide, the UK is a very small place. I WILL FIND YOU! What a travesty, you carried him for nine months, gave birth to him three months ago, and you are only just telling me? Who does that? When did you say you are getting married again, December? Expect an additional guest at your wedding, you and your husband can go for your honeymoon, I'll be taking my son back with me!”

“Don't respond to his threats, let him continue ranting,” Felix mouthed, as he caressed my hands, comforting me and giving me strength.

“Are you still there?” Oba Adetoro shouted again.

“I'm here, just waiting for you to finish ranting.”

“I am not ranting you snake, I am demanding my child, my first fruit,” he shouted.

"You call me a snake?" I laughed out loud, "You are the snake and your cursed palace a snake pit! That's why I left! For the record, I didn't find out about the baby until I returned to the UK and, when I did, there was no way I was going to come back to Ikoko to live with you and your wives and uncountable children. Who lives like that? In addition to it being a style of merry hell I don't care for, I also can't risk being killed or putting my child in harm's way for someone who thinks women are just motor cars that need servicing."

Felix nodded in agreement and gave me a thumbs up, before jotting down additional points to add to my speech and waving the paper in my face. Adetoro was now just huffing and puffing down the phone like an angry bull, clearly rendered speechless by my home truths.

Emboldened, I continued, "Yes, if you want to see your son, you are welcome to visit anytime. But my child is not coming to live in Nigeria knowing what I went through when I was there. Also, let me enlighten you, my child is a British citizen, no lawyer would take him away from his mother or his country. Like I said, you are welcome to visit him when you are here – under our supervision." I expected more ranting, but all I could hear was heavy breathing before the line went dead.

Later that evening, I called my mum to give her an update on the matter, and she said my biological dad had been calling her and leaving spiteful text messages, but she had ignored them all and eventually blocked his number. And that was the last we had heard from either Oba Adetoro or my biological father.

"Knock, knock!" called the catechist as he tapped Dad's side of the window on the wedding car, startling me back into reality. "It's time to join your husband at the altar!"

As I walked in, the first thing I noticed, apart from everyone turning around to admire my dress, was the contrasting decoration colours that complemented the bridesmaids' dresses and colourful headgear. As Dad and I got closer to the altar, through my veil, I noticed Felix's eyes fixated on me, but his expression was difficult to read until he whispered in my ear, "I never imagined such an angelic look, you are full of surprises, wifey!"

I had been to so many weddings and read numerous articles about them, and I can categorically say that our W-Day was as classy as they get – from the picturesque St Pancras Old COE church, Kings Cross, to the beautifully adorned reception venue, to my elegant wedding dress and glamourous makeup. And I haven't even mentioned Felix and Jason's matching Hugo Boss suits and ultimately, the wide variety of food available for our guests.

It was indeed a beautiful day and one I will remember for the rest of my life. It was the day my world got turned upside down, halfway through what was supposed to be the happiest day of my life.

My mum, Tiwa and my sister-in-law, Tomi, were meant to take turns in babysitting Jason. They were instructed not to hand him over to anyone except from me or Felix. As Felix and I looked on proudly from the high table as people enjoyed themselves, I noticed Mum was running helter-skelter around the room, whispering into people's ears. Tiwa and Tomi were also doing the same thing. Alarm bells started ringing. Something was definitely wrong, so I left Felix's side to ask Mum where my baby was. At first, she ignored my question as she continued whispering in people's ears, until I yanked her over and looked directly into her eyes.

"Mother, where is my son?" I demanded, my heart sinking.

"I don't know…but we will find him," she wailed.

In that instant, I realised what had happened. I had thought it unusual that Adetoro and Otunba had gone so quiet after all their vitriol, but had been too caught up in our wedding plans to give it too much attention. And that was my fateful mistake. A busy event such as a wedding presented the perfect opportunity for a snake to strike unnoticed.

'There is fire on the mountain,' I said to myself, as I strode to the front of the hall to snatch the microphone off the MC.

My voice echoed in my own head as I spoke. "Hello everybody, my son is missing, has anyone seen him? My gut instinct tells me he has been kidnapped…scrap that, I have reasons to believe he has been snatched. Please keep looking! Felix, call the police, our son is missing!" I cried, before dropping the microphone on the floor, lifted my huge wedding gown and running outside.

As I stepped out of the reception hall, I was met by a gust of winter air, but it wasn't enough to stop me. I made my way to the car park where our limousine driver was waiting.

"Take me to the nearest police station!" I cried, and he looked at me like I was from a strange land.

"Where is the groom?" he asked, but when he saw the fire in my eyes, he put the key in the ignition.

As we drove out of the venue, we saw Felix, Mum and others venturing to stop the driver, but my stern voice made sure the driver listened to me only.

"My son has just been kidnapped, don't you dare stop the car without my say so!" I commanded.

As I ran to the police station reception, barefoot in my ivory wedding dress, people stopped to stare in bewilderment, but they were the least of my concerns.

"Officer, my name is Grace, my six-month-old baby has just been kidnapped by his real father; I know he did it because he threatened to. My husband, who is not the biological father, and I have custody of Jason. but the king wants to punish me by taking my baby away from me…" As the words left my mouth, I realised I wasn't making any sense, so I wasn't surprised when the police officer called me out sternly.

"Ma'am, I need you to calm down and speak a bit more coherently," he said, as he positioned the tip of his pen point on a notepad. "I gather that your son has allegedly been kidnapped by his father, who isn't the man you are marrying today?"

"Yes, that's correct," I replied, but I needed to get him to understand the gravity and urgency of the matter. "Officer Brandon, we are wasting time talking about this, by now my child is probably being crossed over the border…Once he gets to Nigeria, I will never see him again. You don't want to be the one responsible for not doing your job, do you? Do something fast, like close the borders and send your men after the culprit!"

"Ma'am, I'm here to help you but you need to answer some questions first. You can start by telling us where your husband is right now, your full names, address including the biological father's, and your child's name and description. Do you have a picture of him on you?" he asked.

"As you can see, I am in my wedding dress, I don't have anything on me. My husband is at the wedding venue, just about five minutes' drive away from here. His name is Felix Ajao, my child's name is Jason Ajagbe and my name is Grace Olokoshe. The biological father of my baby is Adetoro Ajagbe, King of Ikoko town, a small town on the outskirt of Lagos State, Nigeria. I am no longer with him but he is Jason father, ever since I told him, he vowed to take him away from me. I thought it was just a threat until now," I garbled, as I impatiently watched Officer Brandon jot stuff down on his notepad.

I was aware my story sounded outlandish and that a wedding dress wasn't the usual attire seen in police stations. I must have appeared quite mad to some, but the policeman remained unfazed. At least, he believed me, even if he was taking way too long to do anything about it.

"I am a terrible mother to have put my six-month-old baby through this, I should have been extra cautious, especially today! Officer Brandon, please do something fast, Jason will need a feed anytime from now," I wept, before collapsing on the floor in a heap of ivory fabric.

By this time, I was no longer interested in my wedding dress. In fact, I wanted to rip it off. I was in the middle of fiddling with the flimsiest hem of the dress, when I felt Felix's hand under my chin and could hear him saying my name, although he sounded very far away, or as though he was speaking through water or glass…the next thing I knew was when I opened my eyes to find myself in a hospital room, with mum and Felix by the side of my bed.

"Have they found Jason?" I asked, as I turned to Mum and back to Felix. I felt a bit woozy and my head was pounding.

"Nurse, she is awake, please get us a doctor right away. Grace, we will find him, calm down," Mum pleaded, but I wasn't ready for anyone to patronise me.

"You are telling me my son is still missing, how many hours have I been out? And what are you doing here? Why are you not out there looking for my Jason? You are his grandmother for heaven's sakes, why are you just sitting here doing nothing?" I ranted, as I attempted to get myself out of the bed.

"You are my daughter, I'm here to look after you to ensure you are strong for when Jason comes home. First thing is to get your blood pressure down, and the only sure way of doing that is calming your nerves. The authorities are doing their job and I'm sure he will be found, very soon," Mum tried to reassure me, but I wasn't convinced.

"No," I protested, swinging my legs out of the bed and wincing at the pain in my head as I moved. "You don't understand, it will be too late if we don't act right away…." I trailed off as my feet hit the floor and my legs collapsed beneath me.

"Now will you listen to your mother, Grace?" asked Mum, helping me to my feet and back into bed. "You must rest now, all will be fine, you'll see."

As the doctor entered the room with a syringe aimed right at me, I realised I was fighting a losing battle. The doctor pierced my skin with his needle, all my pain melted away, and I fell into a deep and dreamless sleep.

It had been five days without my son, exactly three days before Christmas, and I was still stuck in the hospital. I knew I had to think of something quickly, something that wouldn't involve talking to the doctors because, whether I raised or lowered my voice, the result was always the same – I was drugged and sent into slumber. Mum seemed to be there every time I woke up, whether it was day or night, and Felix drifted in and out.

"Mum, how are you doing this morning?" I asked, upon waking from my latest drugged sleep and studying her countenance for clues during my moments of lucidity, before I was drugged again.

"Oh, my baby is awake, how are you feeling?" she asked.

If I was to say what really was on my mind, I would have questioned her appearance, as she seemed too dressed up and adorned for someone whose grandson had been missing for five days. But I bit my tongue to avoid being drugged again.

"I feel much better, my head isn't pounding anymore…I have seen this dress before, is it the one you wore for my graduation?" I asked, making sure I looked as genuine as possible. I may have still been feeling a little fuzzy around the edges, but I was no fool. I also had a new plan forming.

"Wow, you've got great attention to detail, it is the one," she replied, "Our CEO is visiting today, so I thought I should make an effort, I'll be off in a few minutes."

"Mummy, I 've been thinking," I started, mock innocently, "Have you asked Otunba if he's willing to help us find Jason?" Inside I was seething with anger and frustration, but I camouflaged it with a smile.

"Yes, my love. He is aware of the situation and has promised to help us locate Jason. His exact words were, "He is my grandson, so it is my responsibility to find him!". He asked for some run around money and we have sent it to him. We are on top of it my dear, you just get some rest," Mum said.

"I haven't seen Felix in two days, was he here today?"

"No, he is certain that Oba Adetoro abducted Jason, so he flew to Nigeria to see things for himself. As we speak he is on his way to Ikoko," Mum replied.

"Great, well done Felix! He is a rare gem. I appreciate you all for your support," I said, with a broader smile that was guaranteed to melt her heart.

I wasn't sure if my plan had worked, because she got up right away and returned with Doctor Emmanuel. My heart fluttered at the sight of him because, ever since I was admitted to the hospital, he always seemed like he found pleasure injecting me with the sleeping potion.

"Ms Olokoshe, how are you feeling today?" Doctor Emmanuel asked.

"I am ok, thank you?" I said and, by this time, my cheeks were already aching due to the prolonged fake smile.

"Your mother thinks your anxiety is improving, is that right?" he asked.

"I think so, I feel better than yesterday. It's must be the winter sun shining through my window this morning," I said.

"It could be, or knowing that your husband has gone to bring your son home."

"I think it's both. I am lucky to have Felix, he is my hero."

"We'll keep an eye on your blood pressure for an extra day, if all is well, we will discharge you tomorrow, in time for Christmas. How about that?" he asked, as he watched my reaction.

I wasn't prepared to stay in the hospital any longer than I was supposed to, so even though my heart skipped a beat when I thought of the possibility that my son would spend his first Christmas at some stranger's home, I just smiled and nodded in response.

The following day, I was discharged from the hospital and Mum took me to her house. The first thing I did after a well-deserved shower was to call Felix, who confirmed he had arrived in Ikoko. He said he could bet his last dollar that Oba Adetoro didn't know anything about Jason's disappearance.

"Felix, have they cast a spell on you? He has our son! Have you checked the old quarters, that's where his mother and sisters-in-law turned wives live?" I asked.

"Grace, the police and I checked everywhere. Oba Adetoro just got his UK visa two days ago, so there is no way he could have travelled. He is as perplexed as we are," Felix reiterated.

"Don't be fooled by their tricks, his wives could have done the trip. Check their passports too," I shouted into the phone.

"Baby, we've checked everything. I hate to admit it, but Adetoro and his wives are innocent."

"Until I prove you are all guilty!" I retorted.

"Babe, calm down, Jason is definitely in the UK. In fact, Adetoro and I are both coming back there to find him. Your father asked to come too, but we insisted that he stayed behind and keep looking here. I will be home on Christmas day love, hang in there," Felix said.

Hearing Felix speak as if he and Adetoro were pals infuriated me, but I kept quiet because my plan was forming in my mind. Felix may have fallen for the lies of the snakes, but I was wiser.

CHAPTER FIFTEEN

Flight of Necessity

AS usual, Christmas day was dry in the UK, but it was more noticeable because of the situation on the ground. Even seventeen-year-old Femi, who was still excited about Christmas, stayed in his room until I went to drag him out.

"Everybody, get out of bed and let's celebrate the birth of our saviour Jesus Christ!" I cheered and when the whole family joined me downstairs, I added, "If all of you are acting gloomy and miserable, how am I supposed to react?"

"Yes, it's a trying period in our lives, but must we wallow in self-pity on Jesus' birthday? I am certain that my boy will be home very soon," I said, as I strode to the kitchen, ignoring the weird looks I got from Mama and my mum.

When I opened the fridge, there wasn't anything interesting in it except from some yogurt and sweetcorn, so I went to check the pantry. I was surprised to find that there was no turkey, chicken, or goat meat in the freezer.

"Mummy, how come you didn't do any Christmas shopping this year, you hardly have any foodstuff in this house," I said.

"Remember we were coming to yours for Christmas this year, so I didn't bother with shopping," she replied.

"You are right. I, on the other hand have too much food in the house.

I had done all my Christmas shopping before the wedding. Let me have your car keys, I will be back in a jiffy. Femi, you'll have to come with me, I can't have a grown man like you in the house and be seen struggling to carry a 15kg turkey and other foodstuff on my own," I said.

Femi left, probably to change into something decent, while Grandma and Mum looked at me with confusion written all over their faces.

"Felix and Adetoro will be back this afternoon, I don't want them feeling hungry on Christmas day," I added.

Femi hopped in the car with me and off we went. When we got home, I asked Femi to get the turkey and other food condiments from the pantry, while I went to my room to pack a few light clothes, my passport, credit and debit card, insulin kit, Jason's clothes, his feeding bottles, sterilisers, my breast pump, and nappies. I put everything in a suitcase and called for a cab to take me to the airport.

When the cab arrived, I put all my stuff into the boot, went back in to make sure Femi had all he needed, and handed him the car keys. "Tell Mum, Dad, Mama, Felix and Adetoro that my instinct tells me my child isn't in the UK, I am off to Nigeria," I said.

I didn't buy the argument that Jason was in the UK, because no one wanted my child in the UK; Adetoro was the one who threatened to snatch my son on my wedding day. As far as I was concerned, his coming to the UK was just a diversion tactic.

Femi wasn't able to stop me because I hopped in the cab before he could protest and headed straight towards Heathrow. I couldn't spend another day in the UK knowing that my child had been missing for over a week.

I had read that Christmas day was the best day to buy cheap spontaneous tickets to random holiday destinations, but this wasn't anything like that. There was only one place I wanted to be in exactly seven hours – Ikoko, Nigeria. As I watched the flight attendant scroll through her computer, I prayed that there will be space available on the next available flight to Murtala Muhammed Airport.

"You are lucky, there's a Business Class British Airways at 10.25am, but you will need to check in as soon as possible, boarding gate closes in forty-five minutes!" the flight attendant said.

"That's perfect, I only have a bag to check in, if you book it right now, I should be fine," I said, and I was right, within forty minutes of booking the ticket, I was on the plane. Before take-off, the first thing I did was dial Chelsea's number. Thankfully, she picked up her phone.

"Hey Chelsea, Merry Christmas darling, how are you doing. This is Grace…I am so sorry I haven't been in touch since my last visit to Lagos," I said.

"Grace, it's good to hear your voice. Why did you behave like that, leaving without saying goodbye? One would think we didn't treat you well during your visit," Chelsea said.

"No, not at all; you were a fantastic host, I have no excuse, but you have to believe me when I say a lot has happened since the last time I visited," I said, expecting Chelsea to ask me what happened, but she didn't say anything so I continued. "I appreciated everything you and your BBC co-workers did to help me; I found my father in the end but then I ended up being the one everyone was hunting for. I was kidnapped and almost lost my life."

"What?"

"It's a long story, Chelsea, I will explain everything when I see you. Now, what I need more than ever is your help. My six-month-old baby has been kidnapped and I believe he has been taken to Nigeria. I land at Murtala Muhammed Airport in six hours' time, so I need someone to pick me up. Chelsea, I know it's Christmas day so I don't expect you to leave your family for me, I don't deserve it anyway. All I need is a car, a driver and two of your security escorts. I am ready to pay whatever; can you do this for me?" I asked, as I held back tears to prevent me from choking on my words. Especially as the countenance of my fellow passengers indicated that they've been listening to my conversation.

"Poor you, what a sad news! Don't you worry, I will be waiting for you, with my driver and two army officers at the airport. What time do you arrive?" she asked.

"5:45pm your time. Honestly, I don't deserve you, Chelsea, thank you very much. This time, I promise not to disappear on you ever again," I said, before hanging up the phone.

Probably because I was coming from the UK, where the streets were dead on Christmas day, I was surprised to see the airport buzzing with lots of people trying to sell stuff to me. Some were almost forcing me to use their phones to make a call, but I refused because I knew it was at a cost. Besides, I had no naira on me. Freelance bureau de change officers also went about doing their business like it was a weekday; they kept bugging me to change dollars or pounds with them, but I had been warned not to because it's difficult to separate the good ones from the fraudulent ones.

When Chelsea didn't show up after I had waited for almost an hour, I began to panic. As I paced up and down, wondering if I should go back into the airport to check if any of the legitimate bureau de change offices were opened, I saw Chelsea running in my direction.

"I am sorry we are late; the traffic was on another level today. How long have you been waiting?" she asked.

"About fifty minutes," I said.

"Thank your lucky stars, we could have kept you waiting for up to two hours if I hadn't listened to Adamu, my driver," she said, as she pointed to a man who stood next to a black jeep in the distance. "There is a driver and two army officers in the silver jeep behind the black one, let me introduce you to them."

When we got to the jeeps, Chelsea climbed into the black jeep and said, "Sorry dear, I won't be able to go with you because I have guests waiting at home. In fact, my parents only let me out because I told them it was you and the circumstances in which you are here. But you have my number, just call me if you need anything."

"Madam, where are we going?" the driver, Taju, asked.

"We are going to Ikoko town, on the outskirts of Lagos state," I said.

"That's far o, with this traffic?" Taju moaned.

"Taju, have you ever lost a child? This woman has just lost a six-month-old baby, I don't think anywhere is far for her. Move the car my friend!" one of the army officers commanded.

"Thank you, sir. What's your name?" I asked.

"Yusuf, and this is my partner, Benjamin," he answered.

Chelsea wasn't exaggerating when she said traffic was outrageous; it took us thirty minutes just to drive out of the airport. Although music was playing on the car stereo, I was bored of sitting in the car with no one to talk to, even though I wasn't in the mood to chat. I just wanted to get to Ikoko, catch them unaware, and ransack the whole palace until I found my son. Boredom slowly turned into sleepiness and I found myself dozing off, I fought it for a while but eventually gave in.

The next time I opened my eyes, we were on the Lagos Oshodi-Apapa Expressway. I suddenly became alert and started searching through the crowd of roadside hawkers to see if I could find little Sola, the bread seller.

"Madam, do you want to buy something?" Benjamin asked, when he noticed me looking out the window.

"No sir, I am just looking for a small boy, the bread seller who connived with a gang of criminals to kidnap me last year – I met him on this road. He looked like he needed help and, when I lent him my helping hand, he repaid me with evil. This is partially what formed the genesis of my current problem," I explained.

"Point him out when you see him!" Yusuf hadn't completed his sentence when I spotted Sola amongst a group of bread sellers. My heart skipped a beat. I hadn't thought I would ever set eyes on him, but there he was, trying to overtake the other hawkers. I thought I would be angry if I saw him again, but I wasn't; all I felt was love and pity for him.

"That's him in the yellow jumper and black jeans," I said.

As soon as Yusuf was given the word, he rolled down his side of the windscreen enthusiastically, like a lion ready to pounce on his prey.

"Oni bread!" he called in his baritone voice.

As usual, all the other bread sellers crowded around our jeep.

"All of you, disappear! I only want to buy from the boy in yellow," he said.

The moment the other bread sellers saw Yusuf's uniform, they fled, but Sola stayed looking so sure of himself.

"Why are you selling bread on Christmas day, don't you have parents?" Yusuf asked and when Sola didn't reply, he added. "You should be at home with your parents eating jollof rice and chicken with a bottle of chilled coke. I am going to take you home now, put your tray in the boot and hop in. I will pay for all the bread you haven't sold."

When Sola heard that Yusuf was prepared to buy the remaining bread, his eyes almost popped out of their sockets. He did as he was told, and we got him.

"Hello Sola, how are you doing? Do you recognise this face?" I asked when he was in our car.

"No o, I have never met you before," he said, with his 'butter wouldn't melt' look.

"So why does it look like you've just seen a ghost? Today is Christmas day, I don't think you fancy a sleepover in the police station, do you?" I asked.

"Police station? No ma, I don't know you!" Sola said, still insisting that he had never set eyes on me.

"You are sure about that? This is your final answer? Sola, we are trying to help you here. You are just a child so we cannot hold you responsible for what you did to me. But if you don't cooperate, you will be the only one to pay. Now, I am going to ask you again, for the last time – do you know me?"

Sola dropped his eyes and twisted his hands together in his lap. He looked so small and sorry, I wanted to lean across and give him a hug, despite what he had done to me. "Yes, ma! I am so sorry, it's the devil's work," he admitted, "What do you want me to do? I will do whatever you ask me, I am hardworking ma! Whatever you say, I will make it up to you."

"My dear, the devil has nothing to do with this," I said, patting him on the shoulder, "Every bad decision has consequences, but there is a way for you to make amends." I paused for effect and he looked up at me with those big eyes, "Yes ma'am, anything you say, just tell me."

I smiled, my plan was working better than I had hoped. "Sola, the only way out is for you to take us to the men who kidnapped me last year, it's time for them to pay for their sins," I said, solemnly, in my best 'good cop' voice. Knowing he had no choice and, I sensed, genuinely wanting to help fix things, Sola nodded in agreement.

When we neared Sola's neighbourhood, I suggested seeking the help of roadside policemen, but Yusuf and Benjamin disapproved until I told them the kidnappers were heavily armed. Realising we may be up against greater firepower, the army officers relented and Yusuf went over to talk to the policemen while Benjamin waited in the car with me.

We were an imposing fleet by the time we pulled up at the house, to find all four men smoking and drinking on the veranda. Suddenly, being back in that place shook me to the core. I think I had been in a state of shock since Jason was taken, drugged whilst in hospital, and on autopilot the rest of the time. It had felt as though I was watching myself in a movie, or in a dream, there but not there. Being back at the house, however, brought me crashing right back into the present, as though waking to find a nightmare was real.

I froze, unable to do anything other than watch the scene unfold around me. It all happened so fast. As the police and army officers leaped from the cars and descended on the kidnappers, the men were so shocked it took a moment for it to sink in and, by that time, it was too late. One of them attempted to run, but judging from the empty bottles on the table, they were also drunk and so he did not get very far before apprehended with the others.

Seeing my kidnappers arrested and carted off to prison, to be further interrogated by the police, gave me a little peace in my soul. As emotionally intense as it had been for me to be back there, the experience had proven cathartic.

I had also insisted Sola had to be arrested with the rogues. Not because I was bitter towards him, but to both teach him a lesson, so he understood every action in life had consequences, and so he didn't look like a grass to the rogues. However, before we left Lagos, I made sure I jotted down details of the police station Sola was taken to, plus his aunty's contact details, as well as his father's in the UK. "When I find my own son, Sola will be my next project," I muttered to myself, as we continued our journey to Ikoko.

Due to our little diversion, it was very dark when we arrived in Ikoko, but it worked to our advantage; everyone would be relaxed and getting ready to retire to their bedrooms. It was so late that the gateman wasn't going to let us in, until Benjamin and Yusuf got out of the jeep to address him and let him know who they were driving.

"Sorry Oga, I didn't know you were in the car," he stuttered. Please drive in, the gate is opened."

As soon as we were in the compound, my heart started beating ever so fast as I directed Taju to the old quarters. If my son was here he would be with Adetoro's mum, Mama Soji, Olori Simi, or Olori Remi.

"You are driving too slowly Taju, please move it!" I commanded. This time, I didn't feel as though I was watching myself in a movie. Adrenaline was coursing through my veins like fire and I felt like a mother lion ready to fight for her cub. Of course it helped that I had my own little army with me.

We pulled over in front of the massive building and stomped in like we owned the place, including Taju the driver. I suddenly felt very powerful knowing very well that the three men behind me had my back, two of which were sufficiently armed.

"Everything that has breath in this house, report here right now," Yusuf commanded, as he and Benjamin corked their rifles. "Like I said, if you are a living being, and want to keep it that way, bring your ass down here at the count of three – 1…2…"

Before he could finish counting, there was a great commotion. All the women and children started crying as they rushed down the stairs, guarding their heads with their hands, some covering their eyes with their hands. Even the night guards looked scared for their lives at the sight of Yusuf and Benjamin.

Emboldened, I instructed Benjamin to go search the old quarters and stepped forwards, commanding the room. "Which one of you women has my son? Talk now before you witness the wrath of a woman whose child has been taken off her!" I growled, authoritatively.

"Your husband was here; we don't have your child. You are scaring our children, please let them go, it is us you need," Olori Simi pleaded.

'Ha,' I thought to myself, enjoying the fear in her voice, 'Not so big and clever now are you, Queen Snake!' I glared at her, "How can I trust

YOU?" I interrogated her, "After everything…"

In my state of heightened emotions, I was about to blurt out that I knew her murderous secret, but was fortunately stopped in my tracks by Benjamin reappearing in the room. "Clear, there is no one upstairs" he reported.

I nodded to Benjamin and, in that pause, I saw the look on Mama Soji's face, so I bit my tongue and turned my attention away from Simi and towards her instead.

"Mama Soji, you were like a mother to me during my stay here. You looked after me like you would your own. Please, if my son, Jason, is here please let me know. I don't know where else to look," I said, my voice starting to break and tears forming in my eyes as I said my son's name.

Whilst I didn't trust Simi the snake, I knew Mama Soji would tell me the truth. She owed me, in a way, as I had kept her secret. "I would have told you if your son was here, but he isn't. I swear on my husband's grave. I already told your husband, Kabeyesi was here all that time, he only just travelled to the UK with your husband this morning," Mama Soji said, before adding, "I suggest checking your father's house, he recently got a new car and has been gallivanting around town as if he has just won the lottery, not like someone whose grandson has been reported missing. I can take you to his house if you want."

I wanted to hug her. Her words resurrected all hopes that had been shattered by not finding Jason at the old quarters. We had a new lead and I was desperate to follow it.

"Take me to his house right away," I commanded, rallying my little army and dragging Mama Soji with us.

My father's road wasn't as privileged as that of the palace. There was no light, the road was untarred, and had several potholes. We bounced along uncomfortably in the dark, with only our headlamps casting pools of light and shadow in the night. I was thankful Taju was such a good driver and that I had armed protection with me, this was not the sort of place one would want to get lost at night. I was sure there were bandits hiding in the bushes, ready to jump out and ambush any car which stalled on the bumpy path.

"I didn't think my father's house would be this far away from the palace," I said, as Taju swerved to escape another deep pothole.

"It is my dear, and he walks to the palace every day; I don't know how he does it," Mama Soji explained. She tapped Taju on the shoulder, "Stop here, we have to park the car here and walk to the bungalow up on the hill. It's about ten minutes' walk from here."

We scrambled out of the jeep, grabbed some torches, and headed towards the bungalow in the distance. If we had gone at Mama Soji's pace, it probably would have taken us ten minutes to get to the house, but I was a woman on a mission and, leading the charge, I ensured we were at the door to my father's house in half that time. Yusuf and Benjamin used the end of their guns to knock at the door vigorously, but no one showed up.

"If you don't open this door, we'll be forced to bring it down and I promise, it won't be just the door that will need fixing. We are not armed robbers; we are armed army officers. Open the door this minute!" Yusuf commanded.

There was a scuffling sound from within the house. "We can hear you in there! Open this door NOW!" bellowed Yusuf, and the door slowly creaked open.

My father peeked out into the night, squinting in the light of our torches. When he saw me, he looked as though he had seen a ghost and reeled back in shock, like a man caught red-handed at a crime.

"Father, where is my son?" I demanded, before commanding Benjamin to search all the rooms. "My mother sent you a lump sum of money to help find my son, your grandson, and I hear you've splashed out on a new Toyota Camry – the one parked outside? You see why my mother left you?"

"I don't have your son, he is not here," he said, calmly, "Your husband and Kabeyesi have gone to look for him in the UK where he is...where they believe he is." He knelt down in surrender, guarding his head just like the women at the palace did. For a split second, this made me wonder if it was a Nigerian thing to shield one's head at the sight of a gun; even in Nigerian movies, people's priorities were their heads, not their hearts, it seemed.

"You sound so sure he is in the UK, where exactly is your grandson?" Yusuf asked, as he corked his rifle for effect. "Is that why Kabeyesi is in the UK, to bring Jason back here? Start talking now before I paralyse your right leg with one of these bullets!" he added, to my horror.

I realised I hadn't really thought about what would happen if the army officers had to use the weapons they carried and I hoped I didn't find out. Still, I realised I had to play along. If my father saw I was nervous about the guns, he might use it against me.

"I don't know where your son is, ask Kabeyesi," Otunba said, with a slight smirk on his lips. I realised he had seen the expression on my face when Yusuf threatened to shoot him.

I pulled my best poker face. "Father, I have no feelings for you, it costs me nothing to ask Yusuf or Benjamin to pull the trigger," I said, "And if you keep lying, you will find out for yourself."

"But, I don't have him," Otunba reiterated, this time sounding a little more convincing. However, I had more reasons to doubt him than to trust him.

"I have reasons to believe you know something about this, because you diverted the funds given to you into purchasing the car parked outside. Rumour also has it that you've shown zero concern about Jason's whereabouts, now you are trying to pin it on the king who you vowed to serve," I challenged him, before turning to Lieutenant Yusuf, "I agree with you sir, please shoot his leg if he doesn't talk!"

Otunba was finally listening. "Please don't shoot. Abosede, I am your father, tell them to put the gun down!"

"If you were any sort of real or decent father, we wouldn't be in this position now," I argued, "With you on your knees at my feet and with guns pointing at you. If you were any sort of father you would understand my heart is bleeding, because I haven't seen my son in eight days. You are only doing this to me because of what mum did to you. I am not going to stand here and be punished for the sins of my parents, especially NOT when you bring my own son into your sick games!"

"You are now being punished for what your mother did, she got away with it but you will not!" Otunba spat back, slowly standing up, but still with his hands behind his head, "You had the guts to give a royal blood to an ordinary man, you are ten times more malicious than your mother. Unlike you, she gave you to a higher bidder; your husband is a nobody!"

When nobody shot him, Otunba strode back into his living room and sat down on his sofa. We followed him, guns still pointing at him, but he no longer seemed to see them as a threat.

"You are all hot air and drama, just like your wicked mother. She stole my first daughter away from me, now my first grandson, tomorrow's king? I wasn't going to let that happen again!" He laughed like a man man, "Now put your stupid guns down in my house if you are not going to use them. If you shoot me I might bleed out on the floor, right here, and you will never find out where the boy is."

"Just try me and find out!" snarled Yusuf, "I know exactly how to shoot a man to give him the maximum pain and a slow death…maybe we should aim for your belly instead…"

I spontaneously flinched again at the prospect of a bloodbath and, again, Otunba spotted it and smirked. The smile did not stay on his face for very long though, as Benjamin strode over to him quick as a flash and pistol whipped around the head. Now it was Otunba's turn to flinch.

Benjamin loomed over him, "You heard the lady, now TALK!"

"Ok, ok" he said Otunba, waving his hands in the air, "You got me. You are right. Kabeyesi knows nothing about this, I did it to teach you and your mother a lesson. Happy now?"

Benjamin raised his gun again and cocked his eyebrow, ready to land another blow.

"You can do what you like to me," Otunba said, "But I am not the criminal here – she is, this whore and her whore of a mother! Officers, this girl and her mother are the ones who need to be beaten and locked up for good!" He turned to me and the look on his face was one of sheer hatred. "I should have left you to the masquerade bandits when I had the chance. You may be my blood, but you arc no daughter of mine!"

As the venomous words left his mouth, it took all my self-control to not snatch one of the guns and beat him with it myself. "How dare you?" I hissed, "You are not worthy to even be in the same room as me and my mother, much less have any claim on my son!"

Otunba stood up and turned his attention to Yusuf and Benjamin instead. "You are men. Put yourselves in my shoes. If your woman gave your child to another man, wouldn't you want to punish her, even kill her? I bet you would, at least beat her. Shouldn't we teach this whore a lesson? I think we should…"

His sentence was cut short by the sound of a sudden bang which left my ears ringing, followed by a wailing noise and the smell of hot metal. Otunba was on the floor, writhing and holding his foot, from which blood was now pouring. Yusuf had shot him and was standing over him, spitting down on him.

"What kind of father derives pleasure in hurting or even killing his own daughter?" snarled Yusuf, "You are lucky I only took your foot. One more word of disrespect and I will take your knees next."

"Yusuf!" I interrupted, "Please don't kill him, if you do we will never find Jason! We need to let him talk!" As much as I hated Otunba, I didn't want him to die.

Otunba just kept writhing on the carpet and screaming with pain. He looked so pathetic I felt sorry for him, despite all he had done. "I am diabetic, this wound won't heal, you shouldn't have shot me," he moaned, "I was going to tell you where the baby is…now you can't make me."

"Tell us where he is before I shoot away your other foot. Wicked man! As you can see, I don't talk too much, but I believe in action. My bullet is not as weightless as Yusuf's; your foot would have been in pieces if I pulled the trigger," Benjamin said, in a voice that sounded even thicker than Yusuf's.

The pool of blood thickened and grew darker around my father's injured foot and he tried to stem the flow with his hands. His fear for his life was starting to grow larger than his bad attitude. "Ok, ok," said Otunba, "Don't shoot me again. Please, get me a doctor and I will tell you…"

"Speak first, doctor later!" commanded Yusuf, "Or I will let Benjamin loose on you!"

Knowing he was beaten, Otunba gave up. "He is with my niece in Scotland. When Kabeyesi wasn't going to do anything about your evil deed, I vowed to serve justice by contacting my niece in Scotland to help with the abduction. She snatched the baby right under your mother's nose, on your wedding day. Your son is in Scotland with Sade, she was going to come with him to Nigeria, where he rightly belongs, in the new year," he explained, matter of factly.

"Give me your niece's full name?" I commanded, as I got my phone out ready to type his response.

"I don't have her address," he mumbled.

"Father, that's not the question. What is her first, middle and surname? We can talk about her address later," I snapped.

"Her name is Folasade Helen Omotosho," he replied, as he groaned again in pain.

"Does she have a maiden name?" I asked, making sure I got everything I needed out of him before he passed out. He wasn't looking good at all.

"Tijani," he replied.

"Good, now what's her address? You better tell me quickly so we can take you to the hospital before you bleed to death or have a heart attack from the shock and pain." Then I added, "For all it's worth, I wouldn't want to watch that – you are still my father," and that was my mistake.

Jumping on my moment of sentimentality, Otunba became cocky again. "I don't have her address, I don't live in London, you stupid witch!" he retorted. But Benjamin stamped on his injured foot, and he squealed like a pig to the slaughter, before passing out cold.

As soon as I hit send on the message I had been typing on my mobile phone, I instructed the men to carry Otunba into his car and drive him to the nearest hospital. Then I asked Mama Soji to ride with me and Taju to the nearest police station. Even though my father was already in pain, it wasn't enough. When he recovered from his wound, I was going to press charges and have him locked up for a very long time. The only reason I would consider releasing him would be if we found Jason in one piece – hale and hearty, safe and sound. Once I had my son back in my arms, I might find some compassion in my heart again. Until that time, however, I was a woman on a mission and I would take no prisoners along the way.

We left my father at the hospital with a couple of policemen, before embarking on the journey back to Lagos.

"It's too late, why don't you stay the night at the palace and leave first thing tomorrow morning?" Mama Soji suggested, but I just wanted to get the hell out of Ikoko; apart from my Jason, nothing good came out of stepping foot in that town. As I said my goodbyes to Mama Soji at the hospital, I knew we'd probably not see again, so I gave her the £500 in my wallet and asked for her phone number so we could keep in touch.

On our way back to Lagos, I called Felix and Mum to give them the news, but all they did was start a blame party over the phone. It was as if everyone in the room were competing to tell me how unreasonable I had been to have flown to Nigeria on my own and ignored all of their calls all day. I let them rant to their heart's content and, only when they were silent, did I finally talk.

"Felix, are you on speaker?" I asked.

"Not anymore, I am on my way to your room," he said.

"Great, I need you to be alone, I don't want Adetoro to hear what I'm about say. You can tell Mum and Dad later," I said.

"Go on, spill! Have you found him?" Felix asked.

"Jason is in Scotland, we just forced it out of my father. Long story but in the meantime, listen to me carefully. Call the police, tell them a lady called Folasade Helen Omotosho, nee Tijani, has my child. I don't have an address, but I already texted you her landline number and full name. I want only you and Mum to go to the police, as I'm not a hundred percent sure of Adetoro's innocence. Felix, I am trusting you to bring my baby home, keep me updated. I will take the next available flight back home tomorrow," I said, as all the emotion of the day caught up with me and tears started to roll down my cheeks. This time, they were tears of relief and joy in hearing Felix's voice, along with hope that we were now so close to bringing my baby boy home where he belonged.

After giving Felix the necessary details, I called Chelsea to inform her of the developments and, of course, ask if I could pass the night at her parents' house. She agreed, so I asked Taju to drive us there.

As we navigated our way through the bad roads of Ikoko, with our car's headlight as the only source of light, I closed my eyes to say a quick prayer to God for a safe journey back to Lagos. I had just opened my eyes when I noticed a trailer driving at top speed in our direction. Taju also saw it, because he immediately swerved to the right of the road in order to avoid the danger coming our way. Yusuf, Benjamin and I shouted at the top of our voices to warn Taju of the huge obstruction we were running into, but it was too late, as the jeep had a head-on collision with the tree, violently jolting us all in our seats

"Are we all ok?" Taju enquired.

"Apart from the fact that we are now stuck here, yes, we are all ok," Yusuf replied. "Why didn't you listen to us?"

I wasn't ok, as my neck had been sprained and I noticed blood dripping from my chin. As I held my chin in place, I closed my eyes again to say another prayer to God for sparing my life. Yes, as Yusuf rightly said, we were stuck on a very dangerous road with no money on us, but there was a solution.

As Yusuf and Benjamin helped me out of the jeep, I asked if either of them had money on them to take us to Lagos, but of course, no one planned for an accident so the answer was 'no'.

"Why don't you call the woman you gave all of your money to, she should be able to help," Taju suggested.

And he was right, if I had foreseen an accident, I wouldn't have given Mama Soji all my money. As suggested, I called Mama Soji, and she and the palace driver were with us within the hour.

"You could have died for nothing, I told you to stay the night but you didn't listen," she scolded.

When we returned to the palace, Mama Soji walked me to the same room I stayed in during my first visit to Ikoko, while the men crashed in one of the guest rooms downstairs. She stitched up my injured chin, gave me some aspirin, and put me to bed. As soon as my head hit the pillow, I was out like a light. My last thought was that it was a shame I had no time to reminisce about my previous time at the palace, and I had a burning desire to peek into Adetoro's room.

By the time I woke up in the morning, I already had a total of sixty-nine missed calls from Felix, Dad and Mum. I couldn't decide who to call first, without getting an earful about the latest dramas in the proceedings. In the end I opted for Felix, because only he could tell me what I wanted to hear.

"Where have you been? You've got us so worried. Why haven't you picked up your phone?" he garbled when he heard my voice.

"Felix, yesterday was a long day, I am so sorry. I managed to close my eyes around twelve midnight and didn't open them until two mins ago. Did I forget to add that I was involved in an accident? Anyway, have you found our son?"

"Accident, where are you?" Felix lamented, which probably alarmed my mum because I could hear her voice in the background.

"Give me the phone!" I heard, as I imagined her snatching the phone from Felix.

"Mum, I'm ok, where is Jason?" I asked.

"Your lead was spot on, that heartless father of yours should be locked up for good!" she said.

"Mum, you are right, but please let's try and be the bigger people here! Otunba is being punished and hurting physically and emotionally, because of what we did to him. First his daughter, now his grandson. Not to mention the fact he's been shot and arrested too. We are not exactly better than him, are we. Don't you think we should be locked up too?" I asked, in need of her comfort and reassurance. "What is the update on Jason please?"

"We are at a police station in Scotland as we speak, we've written a statement but, before we leave, the Child Protection officials need to examine Jason. You did it baby, you found my grandson! Come home quickly, he needs you, we all need you!" Mum said. In that moment, the world stood still and butterflies fluttered in my chest until I thought my heart would burst.

I couldn't wait to get home to feed my baby until my nipples were sore. I knew from then onwards that no other child or human being would ever have my heart the way Jason did. Even though he wasn't yet in my arms, I felt as though I had just given birth to him all over again. I had moved heaven and earth for us to be together again, and I would do it all over in an instant if I had to. If I had ever wondered what kind of mother I would be to my child, I now knew. I would gather an army and return to the scenes of the crimes, to fight my own blood father in battle, and confront the Snake King and Snake Queen of Ikoko in their own palace – all to be reunited with my baby. 'Grace,' I congratulated myself, 'Looks like you would make a worthy queen after all, a warrior queen!'

Later that day, as I sat on the plane back to London, I closed my eyes and prayed for us to fly a little faster.

CHAPTER SIXTEEN

Breaking Point

OUR entire family and close friends were waiting for me at Heathrow Airport. Unexpectedly, behind them was a crew of paparazzi and reporters taking pictures and throwing questions at me as I emerged from the arrival hallway.

"Grace the superhero, Grace a true mother! How does it make you feel knowing your son is alive? Would you ever forgive your cousin and biological father?" they chanted, but I wasn't in any mood to speak to anyone until I've seen my son. The flashlights were blinding, but I was determined to find my husband, mother, or Adetoro, who would most probably be carrying Jason. The crowd of media vultures just blurred into white noise around me and I kept my head down and ignored them, I only had one thing on my mind.

Luckily, my mum had been smart enough to stand back with Jason, keeping him away from the crowd. The reporters were all concentrating on me, they didn't think to look around for my baby. Felix, Adetoro, and my little brother, Femi, however, came towards me as soon as they saw me, and shielded me with their masculine physiques as we pushed our way through the crowd. When Mum noticed we were coming closer and the paparazzi were still following us, she ran with the baby out of the airport and into Dad's waiting car. I had only just hopped into the passenger seat and hadn't even finished securing my seatbelt, before Dad put his foot on the accelerator and off we drove out of the airport and away from the eagle eye of the British media.

Jason was oblivious to what was going on around him, because he was fast asleep in his car seat in the back with Mum. Seeing his face made my heart feel as though it would explode with joy, and I wanted nothing more than to pick him up and hold him to my breast, to feel his little heartbeat against mine, back safe, where he belongs.

"Dad, when you find a safe place to pull over I need to swap places with Mummy, I need to sit next to my baby," I said.

"Of course, darling," Dad said, as he pulled up on the hard shoulder of M25. "You deserve to sit next to your son, supermom!"

As I slid into the back seat, next to my baby, I could hear his breathing and smell that delicious baby smell. My body ached to hold him again.

"She is indeed! Look at your handsome and adorable son sleeping peacefully, isn't he gorgeous? Well done, Grace, you have done well. If not for you, we would have lost him for good. You are the queen of all mothers," Mum said, as she watched me from the front seat as I caressed Jason's little face just like I did on the day he was born.

"He missed his first Christmas in his home thanks to…erm, all the drama…anyway, when you have both settled in, we would like to throw you a party to celebrate the second half of your wedding and a belated Christmas party for Jason. What do you think?" Mum asked.

"No, not anytime soon," I sighed, "Sorry Mum, but I don't see myself going to or hosting a party in the near future. As from today onwards, nobody will look after my child apart from me. As it stands, I'm not returning to work as planned, Jason has been through enough in his young life, I will do everything within my power to protect him, even if it means giving up my own life." My eyes remained fixed on my son, as I willed him to wake up so we could have a cuddle.

"It's early days yet. You will have to let go at some point Grace, if not you will end up smothering him unintentionally, and I'm sure that's not what you want," Dad advised.

I tutted, "Come on, give some peace Dad. After what Jason and I have both been through, it's right we should have some bonding time together." Dad opened his mouth to respond, but thought better of it and remained silent for the rest of the journey.

When we got to my house, it was empty, just the way I wanted it to be.

"Dad and Mum, I just want to be alone with Jason. I am not in the mood to see anyone, the only person who is welcome to stay is Felix because it's his house too. Please send my love and apologies to anyone who might take offense, but this is my decision," I said, as I waited at the door for them to leave.

I noticed how Mum and Dad exchanged glances, but they didn't say anything, they just got up from the sofa and headed towards the door as requested.

"Let me stay to help you with Jason at least, just for tonight?" Mum suggested.

"No!" I snapped, "I don't want anyone to touch my baby ever again. I almost lost him due to your negligence, I almost lost my own life on a number of occasions because of your bad decisions. Nobody holds my baby but me!" As the words left my mouth, I knew I was being cruel and wounding my mother deep in her heart. I also knew I was being a hypocrite, as I had made equally bad decisions myself. At that point, though, I was just so exhausted and emotionally overwhelmed, and it all came spilling out.

Mum gasped, her hand flying to her mouth, and she wept as though I had just struck her across the face. She grasped at Dad for support and, even though I could see I was the exact definition of 'the kettle calling the pot black', at that moment, I had no sympathy for her. I just wanted her and Dad to leave us alone.

"Let's go honey, let's give her some space," Dad said, as he comforted Mum and led her out of the front door, "She will come around as always."

When they left, it felt like all my shackles had just been taken off. If not for the fact that Jason was still sleeping, I would have played some danceable Nigerian gospel music to thank God for his mercies. When Jason still didn't wake up twenty minutes after we arrived, impatience started to set in, especially as I had been wasting my breast milk for a week and a half, and I was dying to nurse him – so, I woke him up.

'Are you sure this is a good idea Grace?' I asked myself, as I leaned over Jason, 'You know what they say about waking a sleeping baby!' I just couldn't help myself, so I stroked his cheek and spoke softly to him. Slowly, slowly, his little eyelids fluttered and his eyes began to open... and the first thing my baby did when he saw me, was to kick his legs in the air and give me a great big smile – my heart melted.

"You remember your mummy Jae-Jae, you haven't forgotten me!" I cooed, which made him giggle just like I remembered.

My greatest fear had been for him not to recognise me when we finally found him, which would have ripped my heart into pieces. As it was, he was home safe and sound and we were together again. After his feed, I played his favourite music and danced around the living room with him, happily lost in our own little world. However, that bliss was short-lived, as Felix suddenly turned up with his mother and sister in tow.

"Felix, didn't Mum convey my message to you? I don't want anyone in this house apart from you," I hissed, annoyed at being interrupted and without worrying that his mum and sister could hear. "Can you ask them to stay at your uncle's house for a bit please? I feel claustrophobic when too many people are around."

"It's been a long day for all of us, let them stay the night," Felix tried to cajole me, "I will drive them to uncle Richard's tomorrow morning."

"NO! They can't stay here tonight, they have to go right now!" I snarled, holding Jason close, "I said NO visitors!"

My mother-in-law touched her son's arm, "It's ok, take us to your uncle's house…in fact, call us a cab so you can attend to Grace and the baby. She is still in shock. Shock does weird things to people, she is obviously not herself."

Felix did as he was told and wished them goodbye. Once we were alone, he turned to me and said, "Grace, my one and only wife! I admire your bravery so much! Well done for bringing our son home. I am so sorry the wedding ended the way it did, but we thank God that everything is back to normal, thanks to you."

I looked at my husband and realised how much I loved him. I also noticed his beard was overgrown and it reminded me of when we first met. I smiled and ran my hand through the bristly hair. "You did a lot too, baby, I am equally proud of you," I said, "Although your tastes in facial hair are still as dubious as the day we first met!" We both laughed. "Felix, in all seriousness, I thank you for everything. Your effort affirmed that I made the best decision when I said 'I do'" I paused, tentative about bringing up the subject, the 'elephant in the room', but knowing I had to, "Where is Adetoro now?"

Felix smiled and I relaxed. "He is in a hotel in Hyde Park. He is actually an ok guy, you know; I see how you fell for him. He did all he could to help us find Jason despite being bitter towards you."

"Did he see Jason?" I asked, feeling my blood boil. Adetoro was his father, of course he would have seen his son. Still, Adetoro hanging around made me feel uncomfortable.

"Yes, he did," confirmed Felix, "He took several pictures with him. According to him, Jason looks just like him when he was six months old." Felix chuckled and I didn't like it.

'Oh great,' I said to myself, 'Turn my back for five minutes, off on a superwoman mission to confront my villainous blood father and hunt down my son, and my husband falls in brotherly love with the Snake King!'

"Did he say when he is going back?" I asked, hoping the tone of my voice didn't betray how I was really feeling. I wasn't sure I had enough energy left for another emotional outburst just yet.

"No…why?" said Felix, but his tone certainly spoke volumes, he had clearly fallen under Adetoro's spell.

So I blurted it out, "I don't want him hanging around for too long. Jason is ours not his!"

"Biology says otherwise babe, Jason is his son and Adetoro understands the boundaries, so there is no need to feel intimated or agitated."

"Don't you 'babe' me!" I snapped, "I am not agitated, I am just pointing out the facts. You do not know Adetoro, you do not understand what kind of man he is and what he is capable of. You have only known him for five minutes and you are best friends. Whose side are you on, actually?" I was so irritated by his new-found closeness with Adetoro, it made me want to scream.

I knew, away from the cursed palace and back in the suburban and domestic safety of our own home, I was being over the top in my outburst, but I couldn't help it. Everyone apart from Felix felt like a threat to me when it came to Jason. I just wanted it to be the three of us.

★★★

It was New Year's Eve and I thought we were just going to have a quiet evening after church, but Felix had other plans. When we got back home, the house was full to the brim with our friends and relatives; I wanted the floor to open so it could swallow me and Jason, and I held him protectively to my bosom.

"What is going on here?" I asked, but no one seemed to understand what I was saying, probably because of the music. People were walking around my house like they owned the place, the ones who I knew congratulated me on finding Jason, some wished me a prosperous 2006, and the rest of them, who I didn't recognise, did as they pleased. Small chops and alcoholic drinks were strategically arranged on the living room centre table, with delicious looking food placed on my dining table – one wouldn't be blamed for mistaking my home for a buffet restaurant, from the way people helped themselves to food and drinks. Even though my tummy rumbled, I wanted to ask everyone to leave before descending on my favourite food.

Suddenly Funke appeared right in front of us. "Wow, who have we got here? It's only the lucky boy and his superhero mother," she said, as she tried to take Jason from me to give him a cuddle.

"Leave my child alone, stupid girl!" I shouted. "Did you even ask before you tried snatching him off me?"

Funke, Bolu and Tiwa exchanged glances, and wondered where my aggression came from as they had never seen me like that since we were toddlers. I couldn't blame them for their confusion, because I was also surprised by my display of madness, but it was the least of my worries. All that mattered to me was protecting Jason.

"Funke, I am so sorry I shouted at you like that. My anger wasn't directed at you in particular, you don't deserve it…unlike the one who calls herself my best friend," I said, as I gave Tiwa the evil eye. "I trusted her with my son and she let us down, she didn't even have the guts to inform me as soon as she realised that Jason was missing. Who does that?"

"I'm so sorry Gracie. I still don't know how they managed to take him right from under our noses. Now that we've found him, let bygones be bygones; please forgive us daring," Tiwa pleaded, but I just walked past her as if she wasn't talking to me.

I continued walking until I reached the stereo which was playing the light music. I turned it off and turned off the muted television too. That got everybody's attention.

"Hi everyone," I said, as I secured Jason on my hip, "It's good to see you all and I appreciate your presence here this evening. I don't want you to take this the wrong way, but I need all of you to clear off because I don't know who invited you. Make sure you pick up all of your belongings and leave my premises. I wish you all a happy and prosperous 2006."

I then turned on my heel and stalked off towards the bedroom, but Felix stopped me at the bottom of the staircase.

"Are you out of your mind…I mean, are you crazy?" he asked, as he yanked my arm, almost making me lose my balance.

"Felix, you are hurting me, get your hands off me and don't you ever manhandle me in front of my son!" I snapped, as I switched Jason to my left hip. "Especially grabbing me whilst I am holding my baby, I could have lost my footing and fallen, taking Jason down with me. What's wrong with you?"

"I should be asking you that question," Felix retaliated, "You're the one behaving like a lunatic and disrespecting me in front of our friends and family. Are you the first one to lose a child?" He paused to point to one of the guests in the direction of the downstairs toilet. "At least you were lucky enough to get him back after a week, some people, like that woman there, haven't been reunited with theirs for many years, so what's your problem? This is getting way out of hand, I don't think I can take it anymore."

"What I don't understand is why you decided to host a party without discussing it with me first!" I yelled, which must have frightened Jason because he started to cry.

"I'm so sorry honey, your daddy's insensitivity is out of this world," I cooed, as I transferred Jason to my back and started to rock him.

"I didn't tell you because I knew you'd say no, but we can't live in isolation forever. Besides the people we've invited are our friends and family, what' wrong with that?" asked Felix, defending his decision.

"What's wrong is that I feel uncomfortable when we have many people around, can't you see it? Ask them all to go, please!" I begged, but he didn't seem to be concerned by what I was saying.

"If you've developed a phobia to people, then you must face your fear by having them around. You had no problem in church or at the supermarket, so what's the problem now?" said Felix, pompously, "And just so you know, my mum and sister are going back to Nigeria next week and they are going to spend the rest of their holiday here – in my house. Whether you like it or not."

If that wasn't annoying enough, he then stalked off up the stairs. 'How dare he?' I ranted to myself, 'That was supposed to be my exit, and now he has not only manhandled and disrespected me, he is also stealing my dramatic exit!'

"No, that's not going to happen," I hissed, with a double meaning, as I followed him up the stairs, "Either your family leaves, or I will… and I will, of course, take Jason with me!"

"The choice is yours then," smirked Felix, "My family are staying here, period…and Samson is staying too!"

"Samson?" I asked, with a sick feeling in my belly.

"Yes, Samson, my son. If not for what happened, he was meant to spend Christmas day with us, it's high time the boys started bonding," Felix said as a matter of fact, before storming out of our bedroom.

I had never seen Felix so blunt and inconsiderate and, for all my pride and indignation, I was shocked he had behaved in such a terrible way towards me. I had no choice than to believe he meant what he was saying and, unfortunately, I was also going to stand by my words. I followed him to the living room – the conversation wasn't over. To my surprise, most of our guests had already left, leaving my parents, Mama, Adetoro, and Felix's mum and sister. Mama was holding her forehead the way she did when she was worried about something.

"Mama, I didn't know you were here too," I said, ignoring every other person in the room.

"How would you know when your eyes were on top of your head when you came in? Abeke, I'm worried about you. Tell me what is going on? Hand me my great-grandson," she said, as she peered into my eyes questioningly.

"Mama, he is tired, he needs some rest, you will carry him later," I responded, trying to avert my gaze. Mama knew me too well, I swear she sometimes read my mind.

"Then can I hold my son?" Adetoro interjected, and the sound of his voice wound me up to the point of madness. 'He is doing it on purpose, Grace,' I said to myself, 'He is trying to make it seem like you are crazy, Felix too, they are both snakes!'

I turned at Adetoro like a mother bear. "Never! You think I don't know that you connived with my father to snatch my baby away from me? And now you also try to turn my husband against me? Why else did you come to the UK, if not to finish what you started?" I snarled, spitefully.

"I know nothing about his kidnap," said Adetoro, in his charming voice, "Calm yourself, I was as surprised as you were to find out that Otunba did such a thing to his own daughter; he shall be removed from my cabinet when I return to Nigeria. You know I would never do anything to hurt you or my Prince Adelanke."

"Who is Adelanke?" I asked, raising my eyebrow and glaring at him.

"That's the name I gave my son; he is a prince so he deserves a royal name. I was going to discuss this with you," Adetoro said, smoothly, "If you had given me a chance to…"

"His name is Jason, period," I retorted, cutting him short. In interrupting Adetoro, I knew I would have angered his king's ego. I suppressed a little smile.

"And you don't think I should have a say in naming my own child, my first offspring? In the Yoruba culture, I should have named him, not you," Adetoro said, trying to mask the anger in his voice; but I could still hear it and he could tell, by the look on my face, that I had him sussed.

"Everybody calm down, there is no point in getting agitated," Dad butted in, in a bid to quench the fire before it got out of control. He waved his hands in the air, as though he was a referee in a boxing ring and was waving us back to our respective corners. However, I was still up for a fight, or at least to say my piece.

"My child's name is Jason Ajagbe," I informed Adetoro, firmly, "He has your surname, you should be thankful. Ask my mother, she didn't even bother to give me my father's surname – although, that's not such a bad thing now."

Then it was Felix's turn to step into the ring. "This is not the right time to discuss baby names, it's too late for that anyway. Jason already has a birth certificate with his official names on it, so let's leave it for now…please?" I saw Adetoro's nostrils flare like a bull at the words 'birth certificate' and 'official names', but he remained silent. I noticed my mother looking relieved and mouthing 'thank you' to Felix.

"Grace, let me see you in private," Mum said, as she excused us from the living room.

"Have you seen the way your mother and-sister-in-law are looking at you?" Mum began, in her 'serious voice', "Look, you have incredibly understanding in-laws, but there is only so much they can take. Even your husband is starting to lose it with you. So, listen to what I'm about to tell you."

I nodded my agreement and put Jason in his cot, then sat down next to her.

"I have researched your symptoms, it's called Post-Traumatic Stress Disorder (PTSD). It's a mental condition triggered by a terrifying event, in your case, you've developed a kind of phobia of having people around and the fear that someone will snatch your baby again. It's ok, there is nothing to be ashamed of, we just need to seek the help of a mental health specialist. When you are ready," Mum explained, gently, and she was right. I needed help because my behaviour had been irrational and scary lately, so I had no choice than to accept my mum's help.

"Now, I want you to go back to the living room and apologise to everyone, including Felix," Mum said, so I did as I was told.

After apologising for my rude behaviour, I added, "Mummy and Tomi, you are welcome to stay, but you are not allowed to go anywhere near Jason. I am not ready to hand him over to anyone."

"Grace, you are exhausted, let them help you; let us help you," Felix tried to reason with me, "You don't even let me carry him anymore, he sleeps in our bed, is that even healthy? In a week's time Tomi and mummy will be gone, is that how you want to be remembered?" I just ignored him and went back to my bedroom to be with Jason.

As I lay in bed, I heard my mum speaking to the guests, probably apologising on my behalf and giving them a lecture on PTSD. I was also curious about the mental condition, as what Mum told me had resonated with me on some level, so I turned on my laptop to read more about it. 'Are you sure about this?' my inner critic warned me, 'Do you really want to go to those places in your head again? Maybe better to just try and forget all about it, just keep people away and keep Jason safe.'

Indeed, the first few reports about PTSD made me feel so uncomfortable, it was like having an army of ants crawl around inside my body and my head, as I recognised myself and my symptoms more and more. For some reason, I thought of Samson, Felix's son, and had a new empathy for how he might feel, 'wired differently' from everyone else, slightly separated from reality, as I felt right then. However, as I read the treatment for PTSD on Google, I bumped into something called 'watchful waiting' and it made my heart skip a hopeful beat.

According to the article, if one's symptoms are less than four weeks, it was recommended to monitor the symptoms to see whether they will improve or get worse, because two in every three people who develop problems after a traumatic experience get better within a few weeks without treatment – so, watchful waiting it is was. I was determined to monitor my emotional health as closely as I was attuned to my physical health, so I could manage my diabetes. 'You can do this Grace,' I told myself, 'You can get through this. You have already fought the battle and won, now you just have to heal from your battle wounds.'

Chapter Seventeen

Happy Birthday

IT was the first day of June 2006, which meant Jason would turn one in twenty-five days. I was so excited about my baby's birthday party, especially because I saw it as an opportunity to thank God for his life and all that we've been through in the last six months. My PTSD had improved, in fact, I liked to think that it had disappeared by February, because I was able to leave Jason with Felix, my mum, and even let him play with his big brother, Samson, whenever he was around. Samson was older, so most of his autistic behaviour was more toned down. I found that I was more understanding of his differences too, more appreciative of his endearing quirks, and more aware of his triggers and how to avoid them. Samson loved playing with his little brother and Jason brought out a very sweet and caring side in him. Even his mum, Funmi, noticed it too.

However, even though I felt my mental condition was stable, I still didn't want a huge party for Jason; I only wanted a little get together with close friends and families. This was much to Felix's delight, as he had been complaining about funds lately and I could see the financial stress was getting to him. Every argument we had circled back to my decision of not returning to work after Jason's first birthday.

"Sweetheart, I think you need to see a mental health specialist, because you are still showing signs of someone who hasn't gotten over the trauma," he said, when we were arguing about the increased gas and electricity bills. Of course it was all my fault, as I was now at home all day, according to Felix.

"Can you stop saying that? I'm fine and I don't need a psychiatrist to tell me that," I snapped, "Stop blaming me for everything Felix. You are hardly Mr Cool Calm and Collected of late, maybe you need to see a specialist!"

He ignored my spiteful attack and deflected it back at me again. "So why won't you go back to work? Jason is old enough to go to nursery and nobody will steal him from under their noses."

"They stole my baby from under the noses of our families and closest friends Felix, a nursery is not a stronghold with armed guards. Anyway, I think I'm woman enough to make my own decisions when it comes to what I want to do with my baby – I choose to stay with him until he is old enough to go to school. Besides, it will save us cost in the long run, we've already discussed this."

"I can't do everything you know?" sighed Felix, knowing his argument fell on deaf ears, "We have two children to consider here, your help, however little, will go a long way and would be much appreciated." He waved the paper bill in my face and I batted it away.

"Why are you always taking your frustration out on me?" I shouted, "Why don't you ask Funmi, Samson's actual mother, to find a job too? Isn't she in a better position to work? Samson is six years old and in full-time education for goodness sakes, what's stopping her?" I paused to take a breath, "However, my baby, Jason, is still an infant. I don't know why you are pressurising me into going back to work so soon. If not for the money you give Funmi on a monthly basis for Samson's upkeep, we would be ok…you earn enough for the three of us."

"Are you asking me not to support my own child?" asked Felix, his eyes wide and a vein throbbing in his temple, "Samson is my blood, as

Jason is yours!"

"Oh, it's like that now?" I sulked.

"Yes, it is!" retaliated Felix, "And you? You might want to give your baby's father a ring and accept that offer he keeps begging you to accept – to support his child! Let the poor man support his child and let me support mine. It's bad enough that you deprive men of their own flesh and blood in your family, but not letting a father support his own child either…wow Grace, I don't even know who you are anymore. You say you are better, and maybe you are, but you are still being unreasonable."

Felix's behaviour at home had completely changed over the months. To be fair, I wouldn't say mine hadn't changed either, but I was doing everything within my power to make our marriage work. Whereas, every chance he got, he made me feel as if Jason and I were a liability to him. Sometimes I even wondered why I married him and not Adetoro; despite Adetoro's lapses, he cared and would go out of his way to check on me and his son. He still insisted on sending us money for our monthly upkeep, but I always rejected it because I didn't want to hurt Felix's ego. It was ironic that Felix was throwing my good gesture in my face with his cruel words. Still, they didn't hurt me as much as they once would have. Our marriage was crumbling before my eyes and I didn't really care. All I cared about was Jason and there was no space left in my heart for another man.

On the eve of Jason's birthday, I heard a knock on the door at around 9pm. Felix had just left with his friends to go to the club. That was his new thing – he would go out every Friday and Saturday night, come back on Sunday and sleep until noon, watch football, and call his mum and sister in Nigeria. Before we knew it, it was Monday morning. We were living in the same house, but we hardly saw each other. Just the way I liked it.

I went to the window to peep through the curtains and was surprised to see who was at the door. It was Adetoro. My anger at him had long since faded, and sometimes, in my dying-if-not-already-dead marriage to Felix, I fantasised about what might have been if I stayed in Ikoko.

"Surprise!!!" Adetoro exclaimed, as soon as I opened the door, with a grin so wide he looked like the Cheshire Cat from Alice in Wonderland.

"What a pleasant surprise!" I cheered, unable to contain the surprising flood of joy I had to see him, before giving him a big hug… which immediately brought back the good old memories I shared with him in the past…

"Jason, guess who is here? It's your…erm, come and see who is here," I called, as I struggled to find the appropriate title without confusing my boy.

"Come here son," Adetoro said, simply, as he bent his knees whilst opening his arms in anticipation of a hug from Jason, who had just got up from his play mat. I was amazed by what I saw.

Ever since Jason turned nine months old, he developed a weird separation anxiety that Felix blamed me for. He wouldn't let anyone hold him, not even Felix. If I dared leave a room without him, he would scream the house down. When we had visitors he would be fine until they tried to hold him, then would have a meltdown. I tried explaining to Felix that it was a perfectly normal developmental phase for most babies, but he wasn't having it.

However, with a smile on his face, Jason toddled happily into his father's arms. If I had anticipated such a reunion, I would have had a camera ready to capture the moment, but it was ok because the sight was already ingrained in my mind for life. More so, the moment shook me to the core because I realised, there and then, that I felt ok with Adetoro embracing Jason. Adetoro held him ever so closely, as if he was never going to let him go.

"He doesn't let anyone carry him apart from me," I stammered, as I picked a little fluff from Jason's hair and, in the process, inhaled Adetoro's aftershave which immediately jolted me back to Ikoko.

"Blood is thicker than water, he knows who his real daddy is," Adetoro said, his eyes glowing with pride. And for the first time in a long time, I felt a flutter of something in my heart for someone other than Jason.

After putting Jason to bed together, Adetoro and I sat down together and discussed a range of topics. These included, Jason's wellbeing after the kidnap, how my father was coping in jail and recuperating after his gunshot and, of course, Adetoro's 'wives' and 'children'. To me the best news he shared with me was about Mama Soji, who had just won an American visa with her son so he could go and work as a doctor. The duo had relocated without wasting any time. I was so happy for her, because everything the woman did, she did for her son, so it was about time she sat back, relaxed, and let him look after her with the medical degree she worked so hard for him to acquire.

Remi, Adetoro's brother's second wife, or should I say his second wife, met a High Chief in Ogun State who was happy to marry her as his fifth wife, and was willing to accept her four children. The only person he didn't say much about was Simi, and I wasn't going to ask him. We had been talking for over two hours before I even offered him anything to eat.

"I shouldn't be eating heavy carbs this late, but since I've never tasted your cooking, yes, I will like some amala and egusi Soup," he said. "Anyway," he continued, as he followed me into the kitchen, "Where is your husband, it's almost twelve midnight and he isn't home? Is everything ok with you two?"

"Yes, everything is ok between us. He just went out with his friends for a birthday do," I lied, as I laid out his food on the table, hoping it would distract him from his line of questioning.

"Oh my goodness, the aroma of this food is something else – I didn't have you down as such a good cook!" Adetoro exclaimed, washing his hands in the bowl of water I had placed in front of him. It had worked, a man, even a king, can always be distracted with food.

"But, you haven't even tasted it yet," I joked, as I watched him bite into the goat meat, close his eyes in delight, and smack his lips with gusto.

"Trust me, Mama Soji has nothing on you!" he mumbled, his mouth full of food.

"Now that is full on flattery. No one can come close to Mama Soji's cooking. She is a goddess in that department. If I close my eyes really tightly, I can still taste her Moi Moi from over a year ago, it was divine," I said, and we both laughed.

Adetoro devoured his meal like a starving man and wiped his mouth with a napkin, before throwing it down on the table like a knight's glove. "Thanks for your hospitality," he said, standing, "I better start getting on. What time is the party tomorrow?"

"12 noon," I replied, my heart suddenly sinking at the prospect of him leaving, I had enjoyed his company. "You don't have to go, you can crash in the guest room, it's just there gathering dust. I can fix it up for you in a few minutes," I suggested.

Adetoro faltered for a moment, clearly tempted, but then he straightened himself up and headed for the door. "No, it's not proper, call me a cab please, I will wait downstairs. And I will see you tomorrow," he said.

When he left, I couldn't bring myself to sleep, as I replayed the later part of my evening, analysing every detail of body language and the exact words Adetoro used. It was obvious that he still liked me, but I couldn't admit even to myself that I had feelings for him too.

On the morning of Jason's birthday, it was as if he knew it was his special day. His mood was exceptionally jolly as I put the finishing touches in place. Felix was still hungover and in bed, so I had all the time and space to do as I wished. As I was sticking the birthday decoration over the front door, a voice startled me. If I hadn't been steady on the ladder I probably would have fallen off it.

"I know I don't have children yet, but there are two buns in this oven, are we ok to attend my godson's first birthday?" called Tiwa's voice.

To say I was happy to see my best friend was an understatement. She was heavily pregnant beyond recognition.

"Tiwa, what happened to you? You are pregnant, with twins, and I had no clue until now?" I cried.

"I'm sorry babe!"

"But it's not your fault, I have been the one behaving like a mentally deranged woman, I'm so sorry for the way I treated you the last time. Congratulations!" I screamed, as I gave my best friend a hug.

"You were 'kolomentally' psychotic, and who wouldn't be if they went through what you had to go through. I haven't given birth to these two yet and I already know if anything happened to them, I would go mental too," Tiwa said, as I gave her another hug.

"Hmmmm, you decided to follow in my footsteps, pop out the babies before tying the knot? Just make sure you give the babies to the right father and ensure they aren't kidnapped at the wedding," I teased, which made us laugh out loud like old times.

"I am glad you're back to your normal self, girlfriend. I bumped into Felix the other day and he seems to think you still have remnants of PTSD, is everything ok with you two?" Tiwa asked, with worry lines forming on her brows.

"Why is everyone asking if we are ok? Honestly, we are fine. We have our normal couple's rows, but we settle it and move on," I said. If I had known my voice would sound screechy, I would have kept my mouth shut because, knowing Tiwa, she would have already picked up on my ingenuity.

"Funke and Bolu told me they see him at the club every weekend, why don't you ever go out with him?" she asked, as she searched my face for answers.

"And where do I put Jason?"

"If you can, I suggest dropping him off at your mum's sometimes, or at mine. I'm always home during the weekend. You must ask for help in order to keep the flame burning between you two – live a little, girl!"

"You are right, I should. But I don't think he wants me to come with him," I said.

"I wonder why!" Tiwa replied, as she rolled her eyes the way she did when she was furious about something.

"Tiwa, spit it out. What do you know? Did Funke and Bolu see him with another woman?" I asked, as I watched Tiwa try and avoid eye contact with me. "Don't go silent on me babe, if you know something just say it. He is still sleeping, he can't hear you, and I wouldn't tell him where I heard it."

"He is back with his baby mama. I hear they are very much an item as they paint London clubs red every weekend…well, according to Funke and Bolu," she said, as she grasped my hands to comfort me. She seemed surprised when I didn't react.

I shrugged, "I'm ok, thanks for telling me, it all adds up. I'm disappointed in Bolu and Funke though, why didn't they tell me?"

"The same thing I told them, what are friends for, right? Their excuse was they didn't want to have a hand in ruining your marriage," Tiwa explained.

To be honest, it didn't come as a shock to me, because it has always been Funmi this, Samson that, for the past six months of our marriage and, whenever I confronted him, he would turn things around on me by accusing me of doing exactly the same with Adetoro.

"Must you call him every weekend? Must you send him pictures of you and Jason via email all the time?" he would say in defence.

Luckily, I didn't have enough time to think about what Tiwa just told me, because our guests were already arriving. Jason was just running around and enjoying himself with the other toddlers, which made me happy because I couldn't be dealing with his clinginess when I had guests to attend to. About an hour into the party, Funmi arrived with Samson, and the first thing Samson did was to run to our bedroom to wake his daddy. If not for Samson, Felix wouldn't have attempted to get out of bed at all.

'Where is Adetoro?' I wondered, as I watched my mum entertain the kids with her party games which I still found interesting, even as a grown up. Femi, my brother, was the paid DJ, whilst Jason was the star of the party as he danced the afternoon away. It was during one of his signature baby dances to Dbanj's 'Tongolo', that Adetoro emerged through the front door. I would be lying if I said my heart didn't skip a beat.

Under the guise of taking pictures, I watched everybody's body language like an undercover detective, including Felix and Funmi's – no one would have believed the pair were involved. As I watched them, I mused over how cheats became automatic actresses/actors when they were around their lovers; it was probably all part of the excitement of sneaking around.

The party went on all day and into the evening and I wanted it to carry on for longer. I wasn't yet prepared to confront Felix, and being alone in the same house as him would inevitably result in that. I also didn't want Adetoro to leave and, still feeling slightly snubbed that he had turned down my invitation to stay the previous night, I became determined to try again when our guests started to leave.

"Adetoro, it doesn't make any sense paying exorbitant fees at the hotel when we have a guest room here. Please stay the night here, Felix wouldn't mind. Right, honey?" I asked, without looking in Felix's direction. I didn't need to see his face to know the reaction this would have – as though I had thrown a baseball straight into his chest, smack bang into his heart. 'Take that Felix, you adulterous pig!' I said to myself.

Felix, realising he couldn't really say no, murmured a begrudging "yes". So Adetoro stayed the night. I spent the night in the nursery with Jason, but I couldn't sleep. I couldn't get the thought of Adetoro out of my mind, so close in my house, just a few rooms away…but so far away. Eventually I drifted into a fitful rest, full of dreams I couldn't quite remember.

The following morning, Felix left without saying a word. Adetoro, however, hung around, confronted me, and started giving me the third degree the moment I set eyes on him. "If I may ask, why aren't you working, Abosede? For some reason, I had you down as an ambitious woman, what's up?"

'How dare he meddle in my affairs?' I thought, but I felt there was no point in going on the defensive. The reason this was such an irritating subject was due to Felix berating me over money, and I shouldn't automatically assume Adetoro was going down that route too. "I'm waiting for Jason to start school before going back to work; childcare is very expensive in the UK," I replied.

"I'm not suggesting this because of the money you'll make, it's more than that," he said earnestly, as though he read my mind, or at least my body language. I relaxed and he must have noticed that too, as he continued, "The fact that you get up early in the morning and come back hours later gives a sense of purposefulness – even if it's a part-time job. Think about it."

"I have thought about it too," I agreed, "But I concluded that it's pointless sending Jason to a childminder when I can look after him myself. I'm trying to give him the best head start in life, a time will come when he'll be too embarrassed to be around me, until then, I want to treasure these moments as I won't be able to get them back."

"I understand what you mean Abosede, but have you thought about the effect on your marriage?" he asked, as he looked around the living room as if to size the place up.

"What do you mean?" I asked, bristling again and hating him for the effect he had on my emotions. One minute he made me feel as though I could trust and confide in him, the next he would make such an arrogant or patronising remark, it made me want to slap him. I was now ready to fight back if he dares say anything belittling.

"From what I see, your husband is not earning a lot, with you not contributing financially, don't you think it would put a strain on your marriage and possibly result in resentment?" he said, casually.

"But wait, who are you to give me marriage advice?" I snapped, "Oh, I have forgotten, you've practically been married to your sisters-in-law for years. Go on then oh great and mighty expert on relationships, keep talking!"

I watched a slow grin form on his face, the way it always did when he knew he was making a point.

"Any fool would notice that things aren't rosy between you and Felix, and I'm pretty sure your lack of financial contribution is one of the reasons. The woman who used to bring something to the table no longer contributes and is now covered in baby puke whenever he returns from work. Oh and the cherry on the cake – the baby isn't even his!"

His words hurt because they were true, but I wasn't going to give him the benefit of showing any emotion. Instead, I stood up from the sofa and pointed to the door, "Adetoro, I think it's high time you left, thanks for the advice, your royal highness."

"Come on angel," he cajoled me, taking my hand and pulling me back down onto the sofa next to him, "I am not saying all this to be hurtful. Deep down in your heart, you must know I'm right. If you decide to go back to work, I am happy to pick up Jason's childcare bills." He moved closer to me. I had nothing else to say and nowhere else to go, so I sat there and let him carry on speaking.

"I'm sorry to be the bearer of bad news here, and I may be wrong, but I think Felix is sleeping with his baby mama. I have played that game long enough to know when lovers are pretending not to be in love. Yesterday, they practically ignored each other throughout the party, how does that happen with someone you have a child with? Unless they aren't on talking terms, and if that was the case, she wouldn't be at your party," Adetoro concluded.

Even though I hated what he was saying, I couldn't debunk his analysis because he was right, so I remained quiet and uninterested.

"I'm going to ask you a personal question, how sexually active are you two?" Adetoro asked.

"You're very right, it's a personal question and is none of your business. Next question!" I snapped.

If I wasn't too ashamed to admit it to Adetoro, I would have told him Felix and I hadn't touched each other in three straight months. Not because I didn't want to – he was always too tired or angry to notice me. And I could no longer be bothered to make the first move.

"Ok, maybe that's too forward of me, but you are the mother of my son, I feel it's my job to look out for you," he said, as he raised his hands defensively, "If you need anything, I am around for another few weeks, I just want you to be watchful, can you do that for me?"

"Yes, your royal highness," I said as I genuflected. "I'll be more observant and if I find something close to home, I might even take your advice on starting a new job," I said and, whilst I was teasing him with my words and gestures, I wasn't joking. In fact I meant every word, as I knew it all already. I just needed Adetoro to wave a couple of home truths in my face to spur me into action.

As soon as Adetoro left, I went on REED to search for jobs in my vicinity. To my dismay, mechanical engineering job adverts weren't jumping off the pages at me. As I scrolled down a little further, one caught my attention – it was a job based in Denmark. 'How do people just drop everything and relocate to a non-English-speaking country?' I wondered, as I shut down my computer with the hope of returning in the afternoon when fresh adverts are usually posted. But one little chore led to another, before I knew it, Felix was back from work.

"Babe, you are back, how was work?" I called from the kitchen, as I sliced some spinach for dinner.

"Work was cool," he answered as he peeped into the kitchen, "How's your guest, hope you were able to catch up on lots of stuff?"

"Yes thanks. I am moving to Denmark," I said, which made him stop in his track, "A job offer came through today."

"With who?" he asked.

"What do you mean?" I queried.

"Who are you going with and how long for?" he asked.

"With Jason of course," I replied. By this time, he was fully in the kitchen so I was able to study his reaction. "It's an initial six months contract with possible extension."

"Ok," said Felix, "How much is the daily rate? What's for dinner?"

I was hardly expecting him to drop to his knees and beg me to stay, but I didn't think he would be quite so cold about it. "You don't mind me going then?"

"Why would I object?" he said nonchalantly, as he picked a piece of freshly boiled meat from the tray, "I see this as a blessing in disguise, we need the money and it's your chance to get back on the job market."

"Is this the only reason you want me to go?" I asked, as I stopped dicing the vegetables and faced him square on, "Seems like you want me out of the picture?"

"What do you mean?" he asked, making sure that he avoided eye contact with me. He knew I had caught him out and he squirmed like a fish on a hook. Rather than being upset about it, I was rather enjoying my little game and opportunity to take the upper ground.

"Felix, cut the crap, you know what I mean – do you want Jason and I out of the picture so you and Funmi can play house together?" I asked, peering into his eyes. "With me out of the way, you won't have to sneak around anymore…wait, have you and Funmi started thinking how to redecorate Jason's room for Samson yet?"

Felix shrugged. "What are you talking about, Grace? Your psychosis is back, right?" he sneered, before walking out of the room.

"Felix, that's low coming from you," I snarled, as I followed him to our bedroom. "Everyone in London knows about your affair with your baby mama, deny it if you can…go on tell me you haven't run back to your first love like a needy child! You didn't even attempt to hide your affair, it's like you've been waiting for me to confront you."

Felix waved his hands in the air, triumphantly, "You know what, this is such a relief! I had no idea you knew. Now that we're both on the same page, there's no further discussion. I see my baby mama; you see your baby daddy, case closed!"

"I'm not like you Felix," I said, solemnly, "My vows meant a lot to me, so I have never cheated on you."

"Maybe not in action, but definitely in thoughts. I saw how you practically begged him to stay last night, but who could blame you, you haven't had a decent fuck in what, six months? Question now is, does he still want you?" Felix smirked, going for another low blow. This was a whole new level of 'nasty Felix' and, by then, I was too cross to respond; so I let him continue showing his true colours.

"You are desperately trying to get even with me, forgetting that I am a man and I can do what the hell I want. At least I had the courtesy not to rub it in your face, unlike you; 'Adetoro, it's too late to go back to the hotel, please sleepover my love,' rubbish!"

I thought I was able to control myself but I couldn't, and tears began to trickle down my cheeks. In a million years I never expected my husband to display such callousness. Even when I predicted what his reaction would be after finding out I had pinned another man's child on him, I didn't picture such coldness. Especially after everything we had been through together. Although our shared dramas had brought us together, the truth is we hadn't really taken enough time to get to know each other before we were married. It was no wonder our love (if it ever existed) wasn't standing the test of time.

"Are you going to Denmark or not? Or was it just a stunt to get me talking?" Felix laughed, not batting an eyelid at the state I was in. Maybe he was even enjoying seeing me upset.

I suddenly felt guilty for enjoying winding him up in our argument earlier, now the tables had turned. "There is no Denmark Felix. Do we still have a chance? I know I don't deserve you after my behaviour in the past few months, but we vowed to stay together for better for worse," I garbled, as an unbroken stream of tears rolled down my cheeks.

"I really don't know…" Felix sighed, his voice a little softer, but with a tone which indicated he still had secrets I had not yet uncovered.

"Tell me," I sniffed, "Whatever it is, we can work through it."

"Funmi is pregnant with our second child," he said.

"What?" I exclaimed. Now it was my turn to feel as though I had been hit in the heart with a baseball bat. "Did you just say she is pregnant?"

"Yes Grace, Funmi is pregnant with our second child. To be honest, I am as confused about the whole situation as you are. For what is worth,

I am really sorry it had to come to this, but like you rightly said, it's partly your fault. When a woman thinks all she need is her child, this is exactly what happens – all your focus and attention has been on Jason since we got married. You wouldn't even let me touch you let alone make love to you – he was in our bed for months. I didn't plan to go back to Funmi, it just happened."

"Nothing just happens, idiot!" I yelled, "In a nutshell, you are telling me you cheated on me with your ex, got her pregnant, and I'm to blame? Have you ever heard of the word 'Protected Sex'? If I hadn't initiated this conversation, how have you and Funmi planned to break the news to me? Felix, what's your exit plan? Tell me!"

"You better don't kill yourself or run mad for something you can't change. It has happened so we all have to find a way forward by dealing with the matter on ground like grown adults," Felix said, all matter of fact.

'That's it,' I said to myself, 'Our marriage has come down to facts, not love, but facts and being 'responsible adults'. Ok then, two can play that game!'

I turned to my soon-to-be-ex-husband, "Felix, do me a favour, give me three months to find myself a job so that my son and I can leave your house. I will also seek legal advice on how to divorce your ass. In the meantime, don't you ever talk to me or my son unless necessary – we are simply flatmates from now on. For the record, you were just a convenient, but stupid, option for me anyway, we were never supposed to happen." I stalked out of the room with my nose in the air, "Now please excuse me while I go and check on my son. Have a good life!"

CHAPTER EIGHTEEN

Tightened Seatbelt

FOR someone who passed the night on the narrow futon in her son's bedroom, I would say I had a good night's sleep. When I woke up, all which had seemed bleak suddenly looked much clearer. It was as though a veil had been lifted from my eyes and a weight lifted from my shoulders. I also had a renewed determination in my spirit, feeling inspired and encouraged to put my mistakes behind me, forgive myself and move on, into a brighter future. Now I just had to work out my next steps.

The first thing that came to mind was to contact my old boss, Trisha. It was the most feasible opportunity to earn a living and empower myself to move on with my life, without Felix, or Adetoro. Within an hour of ending the call with Trisha, Jason and I were out of the door and on our way to speak with her in person.

"Baby boy, it's just you and I from now on, just you and mummy," I said, as I pulled funny faces that guaranteed me loud laughter in return. With Jason strapped in his car seat, happy with his favourite toy and music playing in the background, I made the journey I should have made few months earlier. Still, that didn't matter anymore, all that mattered now was today.

"Hiya! My name's Grace, I'm here to see Trisha," I introduced myself, as I squinted to read the tiny print on the receptionist's badge.

"Is Mrs Crawley expecting you?" she asked. I confirmed I had an appointment and she dialled Trisha's extension. Before long, I heard the familiar sound of Trish's heels clacking rhythmically down the corridor.

"Is this the little terror?" Trisha asked, swooping in on Jason as soon as she caught up with us.

"Yes, that's my superhero, Jason," I retorted, with emphasis on superhero, because I wasn't going to accept negative classification of my child, even if it was meant in banter. "It's so good to see you!" I added.

"Same here, pal," Trisha grinned, as she led the way to her office.

I was surprised to see that nothing had changed in her office, as I made myself comfortable on the same seat I had sat in during my first 'one-to-one' meeting with her. Even the huge wall calendar was similar to the previous year's, and she must have read my mind because she got up to bring the calendar down.

"Grace, look at the placeholder we created before you went on maternity leave. I understand being a mum for the first time is tough, but I was disappointed when you didn't keep in touch, even if you changed your mind about returning, you should have notified us somehow," Trisha said.

"You are right, like I said over the phone, it's a long story," I said, settling Jason down in his car seat carrycot for a nap.

"Yes, you said you would tell me when you saw me. Well here I am and I'm all ears, what happened pal?" she asked.

Trisha's knowledge of current affairs was second to none, so I was sure she would have heard or read about Jason's kidnap on the news, but of course, she wanted to hear it from the horse's mouth. I summarised the incident, making sure I laid more emphasis on my acquired PTSD as an excuse for not keeping in touch as promised.

"I'm glad you're back on your feet," she said, as she got up to close the door. "I couldn't say much over the phone because I had company, that's why I asked you to drop by instead."

"It was a great idea, Jason and I needed some air, anyway," I agreed.

"Left to me, Grace, I would have handed you your old job back, but the contractor who took over from you has been made permanent by my boss. Up until a couple of months ago, I had no idea they even knew each other outside of work, much less that they are related by family. Unfortunately for us, the woman is very unfriendly and pompous; nobody likes her, but we can't touch her as she is good at what she does and, well, protected by the boss."

"Oh wow, I had no idea it happened in the western world too...I thought knowing people in high places only benefitted people living in developing countries, like Nigeria," I said.

"Trust me, it happens everywhere, pal!"

"Wow, catapulting oneself to the top by knowing the right people – good for her," I said.

"Grace, I'm really sorry I had to bring you out here to tell you this, but it's not all bad news; your colleagues made some generous contributions towards beautiful gifts for you and Jason," Trisha said, as she handed me a beautiful handcrafted gift bag, "You and Jason will love these."

As I collected the bag from Trisha, I must admit I felt more than a little deflated, even with the amount of motivation I had woken up with that morning.

"Thank you, Trisha, I better go and thank everyone," I said, as I looked suspiciously at the closed door behind me. "While we still have some privacy, do you know of any good divorce lawyers in town?" I added.

"For you?" she asked, as she drew her chair closer to mine and when she saw my facial expression, "You are getting a divorce? It's not even a year since you got married! Won't you at least fight for it?"

"Felix and I shouldn't have happened Trisha, it doesn't matter how long we've been together for, when it's not meant to be it surely isn't" I explained, as Trisha came around to give me a big hug.

"I feel you, pal. I have been there myself, you know that, right?" she encouraged me, "If you ever want to talk about it, just give me a call."

"That's why I'm talking to you now," I said, hugging her back, "I haven't even spoken to my mum about it yet."

"You know what, I will not only give you my lawyer's number, I will also give you another useful number," she said, as she handed me a notepad, a pen, and her mobile phone. "For custody of your son, you need a good lawyer and a good job. My mate at British Gas told me they are currently recruiting; write his number down after you've saved the lawyer's number. I'll speak to both men on your behalf. In the meantime, if you need help updating your CV, just let me know. Feel free to put me and Mike, my deputy, down as your referees."

"Thanks Trisha!" I said, "I knew there was a reason I came to see you." I gave her a kiss on the cheek, picked up my son, and said goodbye.

Even though my journey wasn't as fruitful as I envisaged, some positive opportunities were emerging and I wasn't going to let anything dampen my spirits, so I drove down to Funke and Bolu's beauty salon in Golders Green.

"Hey girl, let's plan a baby shower!" I cheered in a sing-song voice, as soon as I spotted Funke in the lobby. "Where is Bolu?"

"Let's plan a party, girl! Bolu went out, should be back soon," Funke cheered back, clearly happy to see me, as we did our signature greeting dance. "Give me my baby!" she added, as she unstrapped Jason, who was now awake, from his car seat.

"Jason, is a big boy now, before you know it, he will be out here helping you with your customers," I laughed.

"Unless we open a barber's saloon for him," Funke joined in.

"Who says he can't do women's hair? My best hair stylist till date is a man," I argued, good-naturedly.

"I can't dispute that, babe!" Funke said, before pulling my arm the way she did when she was about to start gossiping. "Have you seen how huge Tiwa is now?"

"I was so surprised. Is she having twins?"

Funke blew raspberries on Jason's tummy, "Young man, you are going to have little friends to play with very soon. The three of you can start off from where your mums left off."

"Speaking of starting from where we left off, Funke, I will be lying if I told you I was completely happy with you," I said. I watched Funke's face drop, she knew exactly what I was talking about.

"Tiwa is such a tale-teller," Funke said, rolling her eyes. "Gracie, you two were barely married for six months and he was already cheating on you... we were angry at him, but we couldn't bring ourselves to break your heart with the news. We were going to leave it for a while with the hope that you'd figure it out yourself – Tiwa obviously thought differently. I am sorry we kept quiet," she added.

Just as I was about to reply, the salon door opened and in walked Bolu and Adetoro, with shopping bags in their hands. Funke looked like she wanted to dig a hole in the ground to hide in. Bolu and Adetoro looked so surprised to see me and Jason, they stopped in their tracks. In seeing Adetoro so unexpectantly, I just felt a rush of heat travel from my feet until it reached my face.

It seemed like the shock of seeing me wore off quicker for Adetoro, because he started walking towards Funke. "Look who is here, it's only my handsome Prince Adelanke!" he chanted as he took Jason off Funke and held him up to admire him.

"I have told you his name is Jason. He is not Adelankeeeey or whatever you just called him," I corrected Adetoro, as I snatched Jason back from him. "I only came here to plan my best friend's baby shower with my other best friends, I didn't know I was interrupting something. I'll see you guys later!" I span on my heel and started to buckle Jason back into his carrying seat.

"Grace chillax, where are you going now?" Bolu cried, "You are not interrupting anything, we were just surprised to see you here. Whatever you think it is, it's not what you think at all."

As she spoke I became increasingly irritated, not only because of what she was saying, but also with the car seat strap that wasn't aligning properly, despite all my effort– I just wanted the damn thing to click into place so I could get the hell out of the beauty shop.

"Adetoro asked Tiwa and I to follow him to Blue Water shopping mall to get you and Jason some stuff. Look…look…look…" Bolu explained, as she littered the shop floor with baby toys, books, clothes, shoes, perfumes, jewellery, and other things I couldn't put a name to. "Oh, look! Tiwa forgot her breast pump!" Bolu added, waving it in the air comically.

I felt all hot again, but this time because I felt foolish for jumping to conclusions. I could tell Adetoro's eyes were on me, willing me to look his way, but I couldn't. I knew he would always find it amusing when I couldn't look him in the eye and took delight in teasing me. This time, he started to sing, "Jealousy, jealousy, na him de worry you…" Bolu and Funke joined in as they laughed at me too.

I was too embarrassed to say a word and felt like a schoolgirl whose secret crush had just been revealed. I realised I could no longer deny the fact that I still had feelings for the father of my child, and it was also obvious to everyone else. To save face and create a distraction, I got Jason out of his car seat again, raised him in the air and asked, "Who wants him?"

As if the traffic light had just turned green, Bolu and Funke ran forward. "I love you Grace, I would never hurt you," Bolu said, as she took Jason off me and kissed my cheek. "He isn't crying," she added, "He always used to cry when anyone other than his mummy held him."

"I am surprised myself. After his birthday party, he has become a little friendlier," I said, as I continued to avoid eye contact with Adetoro, who was still watching from a few yards away. From the corner of my eye, I could tell he was twitching now, desperate to talk to me.

"Can you two watch Prince Jason Adelanke for a while ladies, your friend and I need a walk and talk," Adetoro suddenly requested, clearly unable to contain himself any longer as he practically dragged me out of the door.

As we walked along the row of shops, hand in hand, Adetoro and I remained quiet. I wondered what Felix would say if he saw us walking down the street holding hands. I knew he had no right to challenge me having been sneaky himself, but it didn't stop the guilt I felt, even though Adetoro and I were just having an innocent friendly walk. I guess it was natural to feel that way because technically, Felix and I were still legally married. At least this was what I told myself, because the truth was, my heart had long since left my marriage to Felix and it was now Adetoro who was making my heart flutter. As we entered the gates of Golders Green Hill Park, the butterflies in my chest and belly that I thought had died since my visit to Ikoko, returned with a great vengeance.

"Let me show you our beautiful park; we should have brought Jason with us – he'd love the squirrels and lemurs," I said, leading the way.

"Finally, you get to show me around your own neck of the woods – as planned!" Adetoro said. "We are only a few miles away from the shop, should we go back to get him?"

"No there is no need, I didn't come with his buggy, unless you want to carry him throughout the walk," I said, as we headed for the lake.

"I'd be happy to carry my son," grinned Adetoro, "But it is you I want to talk to. Now that we've both established that you are still in love with me…"

"Adetoro, I'm NOT in love with you," I interjected, before he had a chance to complete his sentence.

"Abosede, (sorry, I don't know why I find it hard to call you Grace like everyone), there is no point in pretending, we are very much in love!" he sighed, his voice thick with emotion, as he sat on a bench before pulling me to his side. "As I've said a thousand times, I fell in love with you the moment I set eyes on your almost-lifeless body, I loved you then and always will. I know we've hurt each other, maybe I hurt you more, but I think it's about time we made amends and moved on with our lives. If not for love, for our son's sake."

Even though his little speech made my heart beat faster and my body long for his touch again, I knew in my heart of hearts that the timing was all wrong and that it would be insane to repeat the same mistake I had made with Felix, and throw myself into love with a man I didn't know well enough.

"Adetoro, it is true I have strong feelings for you, but I am not in the right frame of mind to start another relationship right now," I explained, "I am a mum now and must consider Jason in any decision I make – he comes first! As suggested by you, the first thing I need to do is get myself a job, find Jason and I a suitable house, and begin divorce proceeding with Felix – yes, I'm leaving him. It was hard for me to admit it to you yesterday, especially when I knew you were right all along. He has been cheating on me for months." I paused as he put his hand on mine, as though to comfort and reassure me. I smiled up at him and winked, "If after sorting my life out you are still on the market, who knows what could happen? That's if Simi hasn't dragged you to the alter first."

Adetoro laughed and stroked my cheek, gently, "Take all the time you need, I'll be right here waiting for you."

"But it's not that simple, is it?" I protested, "We both know you are committed to ruling your people for another nine years, and you have

Simi and her children to think about. A relationship needs more than whatever this is, between us, to flourish."

"What 'this' is, between us," grinned Adetoro, "Is love. Simi seems to be your problem, but she is not a threat to us," he reassured me, as he chased away a friendly squirrel.

"Why did you just do that? I like squirrels! Why would you chase such a beautiful creature away?" I scolded.

"Because it was interrupting an important conversation," he explained, "And as beautiful as squirrels are, they are not as lovely as you. Anyway, I don't think being a king should hinder us, because you can always move to Nigeria if you want. I can also buy us a house here and I can shuttle between countries if that suits you better. Contrary to your thinking, all we need is love and we have lots of that…" He paused and gave me one of his most smouldering looks, "…plus we have powerful lust for each another too?"

The butterflies in my belly were going crazy, but I knew I had to keep my cool and not get swept away in the heat of the moment. "I'm not so sure about that, don't think I've forgotten your hideous behaviour when I told you about Jason," I chided him, wagging my finger.

"Don't think I have forgotten how you kept throwing lustful glances at me at Jason's birthday, under the pretence of taking pictures," he laughed.

'Damn, caught!' I said to myself, remembering how, at the time, I had thought I was just like a detective. "You are wrong," I lied, dropping my gaze like a naughty child who had been caught with her hand in the cookie jar, "I wasn't even looking at you like that, not after how you neglected me and hopped into Simi's bed." Speaking her name gave me that awful jealous feeling in the pit of my belly again. "How did you even get yourself involved with her, she's your brother's wife for goodness sake?"

Adetoro sighed, "If I tell you what happened between Simi and I, will you let the subject go?" I nodded, still feeling all hot and jealous, but realising the only way we could get beyond this was if I knew the whole story.

"Good," said Adetoro, "Well, I had just finished National Youth Service Corps (NYSC) and couldn't decide which of the available options was best for me. My mother wanted me to follow my American dream, but Dad and Oyekan wanted me to stay back in Nigeria and join them in the family business. During one of our heated discussion about this, Simi butted in, "The boy is looking for his freedom, let him go. I feel his pain, why keep him when he can do better for himself in the US?" she said. But this made Oyekan angry and he snapped at her, "How dare you open your stinking mouth when men are talking, you are such a rude woman!" I felt bad for her, after all, she was sticking up for me and I hoped he didn't berate her further for it.

"After that incident, Simi and I became closer. She was a good listener and you could have a great conversation with her too – rare characteristics. She would tell me things my brother did to her, most of which were heart-wrenching, and I would find myself comforting her as she cried her eyes out. One day, she came to mine looking tattered and beaten up as if she had been attacked by armed robbers. I asked her what had happened and she told me she had gone to the house of one of Oyekan's girlfriends, to confront her. However, the girl had both her brothers and Oyekan there at the time. The thug brothers had beaten her up and my brother just sat there and watched, doing nothing to stop it. I was horrified by her story, unable to believe my brother could be so callous. For all his faults, this was cruel beyond reason.

"I wanted to go and confront Oyekan, perhaps take a couple of thugs of my own, or maybe punch him square in the face myself. However, Simi wrapped her arms around me, put her head on my chest and begged me to stay with her. She said, "All I ask from him is his love, strong hands to hold me, squeeze me and kiss me…I haven't had sex in months. I am a woman with needs." Before I knew it, her hands were all over me, I tried to push her away but the temptation was too strong. In addition, I kind of felt accountable for the way my brother treated her. It wasn't long before I gave in to her advances and that was the beginning of my relationship with her.

"After making love to her, I felt so angry at myself for sleeping with my brother's wife and, once again, I felt compelled to confront him and to take it out on the person responsible for the mess…or so I thought. I got in the car and drove to my brother's office, luckily, he was there.

"I ranted and raged at him, "Why won't you change? Why do you derive so much pleasure in making your wife cry? You sat back and watched her get beaten by your concubines, and you act like nothing is wrong? When will you start taking responsibility for your actions, without expecting others to clear up your mess?" But my brother just stared at me, incredulous at my outburst.

"After I had finished ranting he said he hoped she hadn't gotten her Jezebel claws into me too and, whatever she had told me was all lies. He warned me she was probably worming her way into my bed, having done it before with Jide, his best friend. He warned me to be careful and said, "You never asked me why I hate her so much. She cheated on me with my friend and I found out a day before our wedding. Guess what, I still married her – foolish me!"

"I challenged him on why he had gone ahead with the wedding, or why he hadn't divorced her already. Whatever the reasons behind the failure of their marriage, it was too cruel to torture her with his own escapades. But he just used their children as an excuse and said she was still good for one thing. "The woman is insatiable in bed and knows exactly how to cater for my sexual needs. The only problem I have with her is her controlling nature in bed. When I need to feel in control, you know, like the man, I sleep with other women," he said. I told him to spare me the detail and walked out of his office, telling him he was twisted and needed to fix his own mess.

"When I got back home, Simi was still in my bed with my shirt on. I asked her what she was still doing there, but she just smiled and started undoing her shirt. Once again I tried to resist her and once again I failed. My brother was right, she was as insatiable Jezebel in bed and would ride you to places you have never been before. Simi became my drug; I knew it was bad for me but I wanted it anyway. What started as a secret sexual affair evolved into a relationship. My father died, my brother became king, and we always found a way to see each other. Everyone believes my brother committed suicide because of Toke, but it was because he found out about Simi and I.

"Just before Mama Soji left for the US, she accused me of colluding with Simi to kill my brother. I couldn't understand why she would think that, until she laid out some facts as to why she thought we did it. Then I realised there was more to my brother's death than met the eye. When I confronted Simi she denied it, of course, but I must admit, Mama Soji's theory had some atom of truth in it and I knew I must do all I could to get to the bottom of what really happened to my brother. Before Mama Soji travelled, she kissed me goodbye and whispered in my ear, "Go and find your true love and make sure you win her back!""

Adetoro ended his story and stood in front of me, with his hands in the air, "Abosede, so, I'm here, if you'll have me."

"Adetoro, thank you for telling me," I said, "I am glad I now know the full story. Although I am still not going to jump into your arms just yet. I'm not sure, please give me some time to think."

"Of course my angel," he said, "As I said before, take all the time you need."

We held hands again on the walk back to the salon to collect Jason, but this time there was nothing heavy hanging in the air between us, in the unspoken words and secrets. This time, the energy felt lighter between us, as though we had finally reached a place of peace and understanding in our hearts.

***

When the weekend came, I was so glad for it – it had been a busy week, both physically and mentally. Felix and I hadn't seen or spoken to each other in a week; Adetoro was waiting for me to give him a decision on our future together before he left for Nigeria; and Jason was going to a two-hour trial run at the nursery down the road, because British Gas had called me in for an interview. As I soaked myself in the bath at my parents' house, in the midst of all these thoughts, I reflected on my life choices thus far and how best to prevent further catastrophes in my life and that of my child. A mistake made twice is called a choice; I couldn't afford to make any more wrong choices.

As far as I was concerned, Felix was history. Surprisingly, just like my previous relationships, I didn't miss a thing about him. The only thing I felt nostalgic for was being married. I loved the respect it demanded from people when I introduced myself as someone's Mrs. I guess it's the same reason why many financially-empowered people stayed in bad marriages; even though they could afford to walk, they loved being respected and sometimes envied by their single friends.

Adetoro, on the other hand, was the one who gave me sleepless nights – there was no doubt in my mind that I was still deeply in love with him, but was it enough? I still couldn't get my head around his explanation of his brother's death, because his story seemed vague and dodgy.

In my opinion, there was no way a woman as frail as Simi could singlehandedly kill her husband, carry him up to the ceiling fan, and hang him with a rope. Every time I thought about it, I hoped and prayed that Mama Soji had truly relocated to the States and not been eliminated by the dubious lovers.

Certainly, the picture Adetoro painted for us sounded appealing to my ears; but certainly not if he was a murderer! I had made a conscious decision never to go into a relationship solely because of the comfort it promised, but trust my gut instinct and my brain as well as listening to the whims of my heart. So, there and then, I decided to do more to find out the truth about Adetoro's little story. 'It's time to be Detective Grace again!' I told myself, as I got out of the bath, wrapped myself in my dressing gown and reached for my phone.

The phone only rang a couple of times before it was answered. "Hi, may I speak to Lieutenant Yusuf please?" I asked.

"Speaking!" barked the male voice.

"This is Grace, the…" I hadn't completed my sentence before he interrupted.

"I know who you are madam, I recognised your number the moment it showed up on my screen. How are you doing? And how is your little bobo?"

"We are both doing fine sir!" I replied.

"I think I already told you that we have released the small boy who kidnapped you, Sola?" he asked.

"Yes, you did…that reminds me, I seem to have lost his father's number. Can you text it to me please?"

"Sure madam, I will ask him for it when next I see him, I check up on him from time to time. After seeing what prison looks like, the boy has turned a new leaf," Lieutenant Yusuf said, chuckling so loud that I had to remove the phone from my ear.

"Ok, thank you sir. Sola isn't the main reason for my call. I would like you to do me a big favour. I know you aren't a police officer or an investigator, but since you are familiar with what has been going on with me and the people of Ikoko, I think you are the best person to help," I said, as I switched my phone onto the speaker and placed it on my dressing.

"Of course, shoot!" he said, as if he was commanding a soldier to pull the trigger.

"Do you remember Mama Soji; the woman who led us to my father's house when I came to Nigeria?" I asked.

"Yes, I know her," he confirmed, before adding, "She left Nigeria, I personally drove her to the airport because she was scared that some people might want to attack her. She insisted that I brought some soldiers along to guard her and her son until they left. She is indeed a lucky woman, ever since I heard of her news, I have asked my son to be on the lookout for the next US Visa Lottery."

"You said you drove her to the airport, who else was there?" I asked.

"No one, only Benjamin, we didn't leave her side until they both waved us goodbye at security," he confirmed. I thanked him for his time and asked him to say hello to Benjamin for me.

After putting the phone down, my heart sank. Whilst I was overjoyed Mama Soji was safe in the USA, Yusuf had said no one else was there. How then, and where then, did Mama Soji whisper in Adetoro's ear as recounted by Adetoro in his story? Even though it hurt, my discussion with Yusuf helped to form my decision; my son and I were going to stay well clear of Adetoro. He was lying and I had caught him out. Whether he had murdered his brother or not, he was lying about something surrounding Oyekan's death, and I wanted no part of it.

Chapter Nineteen

Giving Back

LIFE was, indeed, ironic. When I was hoping for someone to call the previous week, no one bothered. Now that I was expecting an important call, everyone wanted to talk to me. Every time my phone rang, I took a double take to see if I had been successful at the interview, but it was either Felix, Adetoro, friends, or worse, Mum, whose house I was crashing in.

"Get the fish out of the freezer," she would say. Then, before I had time to recover from her previous demands, she would ring back.

"I forgot to mention, blend the peppers, and tomatoes…Don't forget to boil the meat too," she'd say and, because I was a non-paying lodger in her house, I would just say, "ok mummy!" instead of, "why don't you just tell me to cook the stew for you?"

On Friday, when I had given up all hopes of getting my much-anticipated phone call, British Gas HR, filled the screen of my phone and I knew I was at a great turning point – this was moment my independence was finally being handed back to me.

This time, it was me calling my mum back. "Mummy! Mummy!! Can you hear me? I just got the job. I start in two weeks' time," I yelled into the phone, hoping that I hadn't deafened my poor mother. The next person I called was Trisha, to thank her for sowing a great seed in my life in the name of empowerment.

Now that everything was beginning to look rosy, I felt compelled to share some love and compassion with others. There was something I wanted to do and so I picked up my phone again, in a bid to now make a difference in my community. As I waited patiently for the recipient to pick up the call, Jason said "Mama" for the first time, which instantly brought tears to my eyes. It was almost as though he was picking up on the happy vibes and thanking me for it.

"Say it again baby, mama…mama…come on Jason, say mama," I cooed, momentarily forgetting all about the phone call I was making, but Jason just laughed, not quite understanding and thinking I was joking with him.

"Hello, who is this?" said the voice on the other end of the phone.

I was snapped back into reality. "I am so sorry, I had forgotten I dialled your number. My son just called me "Mama", for the first time, so I was encouraging him to say it again," I explained, feeling stupid and wondering what he must think of me.

The man's voice was kind when he said "Ah, that is a moment to cherish. How old is he?"

"He just turned one. Am I speaking with Mr Funsho Olabisi?" I asked.

"Yes, you are. Who is asking, I don't recognise this number?" he said.

"Sorry, I should have introduced myself. My name is Grace…you can call me Abosede, but I prefer Grace," I said and, when he didn't respond, I continued. "I called to speak to you about your son, Sola, in Nigeria. We met…"

However, I hadn't finished my sentence when he interrupted. "Please can we meet up in private? I really can't talk right now. Where do you live, we can meet up halfway?" he said, and I heard the panic in his voice.

"Of course," I agreed and, establishing that we both lived in Golders Green, we set up a meeting for the following afternoon.

The rest of my evening was spent nudging Jason to call me "Mama" so that my parents and brother could hear it, but he had a mind of his own and he only said it when he wanted to. Eventually I gave up and let my thoughts wander. My conversation with Funsho was playing on my mind. His phone voice was intriguing; it had a deep, rich tone to it, which contradicted the gentle persona I detected during our short call. I found myself looking forward to meeting him, wondering what he was like, what he looked like, and what new mysteries I might uncover.

Sure enough, Saturday afternoon came and it was time to meet Mr Baritone, as I had taken to calling him. That night I had found myself fantasising about who he might be and whether I might get pulled off into another adventure. 'You never learn Grace!' I chided myself, 'Don't you think you have had enough adventures to last you a lifetime? You have only just swerved falling back into the pit of snakes in Ikoko! Must you always get excited about meeting a man? This is not about you, it's about the poor child, Sola, who neglect and poverty have put on the wrong path. Get a grip man-eater!'

The aroma of the food hit my nostrils the moment I opened the door to Prezzo, where we had arranged to meet. I did a quick scan of the room to find a huge looking man to match the fantasy description of Mr Baritone, but there were no big handsome heroes to be seen, so I signalled a waiter to ask for a table. Then I felt a tap on my shoulder, "Grace?" the voice said.

"Yes, are you Funsho?" I asked, turning around and surprised to see a tall, lean frame accompanying the voice. He looked just like Femi, my little brother, only older and slightly taller.

"That's me!" he said in a sing-song voice that made me wonder if he had taken singing lessons from Barry White. It was so weird to hear such a large voice coming from such a slim frame, I couldn't help but grin from ear to ear.

"Thanks for calling," he said, as he pulled out a chair for me before getting his.

"I should have called before now, I've just been busy with a lot of things lately," I explained.

"So how is the little man doing? How many times has he said your favourite word?" he asked, as he collected the menu from the waitress.

"Jason has a mind of his own, you can't bully him into doing or saying anything. He only said it twice after the first time," I said, as I rolled my eyes.

"Hmmmm, that reminds me of Sola, he was the same at that age. Too stubborn for his own good, but he's a clever kid, so that balanced things out," he said.

"Clever you say, have you heard of what he got himself into lately?" I asked, as the reserved annoyance I had started slipping back into my mind. As charming and funny as Funsho was, this wasn't going to be another of my inadvisable escapades with a man I hardly knew. I was here for a reason. "Sola is a brilliant kid indeed, but what good would it do if he ends up locked up for the rest of his life?" I asked.

"I have been trying to get him out of that life, Grace, it's just not as easy as I envisaged."

"You obviously haven't tried hard enough. You left the poor boy with your irresponsible sister, who cares even less about him. She leaves him on his own every weekend to be with her man in Ibadan. And when she is around during the week, she sends him to hawk bread on the motorway. Is that what you call trying?" I asked as I attempted to lower my voice in order not to draw attention to our table.

"Your son, as little as he was, singlehandedly lured me to the kidnappers who held me captive for a day, and that's because I was lucky. My ex-husband was held captive for a month as they milked his family dry of their hard-earned money..."

I hadn't finished saying my piece when I noticed Funsho was distracted and scrolling through his phone, clearly looking for something. As soon as he found what it was, up and off he went, before we had even ordered our lunch. Through the window, I could see him pacing up and down the road, shouting into his phone at the top of his voice. I went out to find out who he was talking to.

As I approached him, I realised he was speaking Yoruba, probably to his sister. Unconcerned that passers-by could hear him clamouring, or see tears rolling down his cheeks, he went on and on, in a great emotional state. Up until that day, I had only seen African men cry in movies and my heart went out to him as he bawled his eyes out. I couldn't bear to see his pain, so I took his phone off him, hung up, and gave him a much-needed hug.

"She is a liar, and she calls herself my blood sister. I send her enough money to look after herself and my son and she turns him into a slave? My own son, hawking bread on the streets of Lagos?"

I knew he needed to talk, so I took his hands and led him to the nearest bus stop, where we sat and I listened to him pour out his heart.

"She called me about six or seven months ago to tell me that Sola got mixed up with some street gangs and was taken to the police station. My mum lives in Ondo and is too old to travel to Lagos on her own, so I asked one of my aunties to check out what was going on with Sola. When she got there, she called to tell me that Sola had just been released and neighbours who knew what was going on said Tinu was to blame for everything. My aunty said she heard that Sola was a full-time bread hawker and they weren't surprised that he had mixed up with the wrong crowd.

"I confronted Tinu, but she denied everything, saying that the neighbours were rumour mongers who were just jealous of her. From what you and my aunty have told me, I won't be surprised if my son never set foot in the posh schools I had been paying for," Funsho concluded.

By this time his tears had subsided, so I wasn't going to add more salt to the injury, but I knew Sola wasn't going to any state of the art school.

"That's all in the past now, what plans have you got to bring your son here or return home to be with him? Six years is a long time to be separated from your son. Reuniting with him is all he holds on to?" I said.

"I have tried getting him a visa a couple of times, but I wasn't earning enough to qualify for sponsoring his visit. I have only just secured a good job last year, so the sky is finally blue," he explained, as he allowed himself to smile. "I am so sorry to have broken down like that, it's just too unbearable... and thanks for listening."

"I just got a decent job on Friday too, like you, I am now able to pick up the pieces of my life," I said, which made us giggle like school kids at the bus stop.

"Your story can't be as bad as mine, young lady. You see these eyes of mine," he said, as he touched under his lower eyelid, "They have seen things."

"You may be right, but mine has seen a lot too," I said.

We had been talking for a while and the bus stop was getting a little crowded, so I asked if we could return to Prezzo.

"I'm no longer hungry," he said.

"I am though!" I exclaimed and we both laughed together as we walked back to the restaurant.

Luckily, our table was still available, and just as he did the previous time, he made sure I was comfortable before he took his own seat.

"Excuse my direct question but I've got to ask. You came across really edgy yesterday when I mentioned Sola, like you didn't want someone to hear our conversation," I asked.

"Really, was it that obvious?" he responded with half a smile, as he pushed the table salt shaker to one side.

"Well, not really, I've just been blessed, or cursed, with antennae in my ears," I giggled, which turned his smile into a full one.

"Women are naturally gifted with the ability to detect, interpret and act, no matter how subtle the signs; my girlfriend, Tasha, has a PhD in this department. She was the reason for my hushed voice; I didn't want her to overhear our discussion."

"Tell me more," I encouraged him, sensing he wanted to talk again.

"We've been seeing each other for a year now and I have a feeling she is the one; the only thing I struggle with is her temper. I have never seen a woman so tough, even though she means well most of the time. She had a rough childhood and young adult life, so I understand why she is like that, but I just wish she could be less aggressive. Having said that, she is the kindest and most generous woman I have ever been with," Funsho explained, before adding, "I don't know why I am telling you all this, I just feel so comfortable talking to you."

"But maybe not so comfortable talking to your girlfriend?" I challenged him, "Why haven't you told her about Sola? From what you just told me, she will be able to relate with him based on their similar rough childhoods."

"You may be right, but I can't bring myself to telling her just yet," he said.

"I am sorry, but I don't get it… you've been with a woman for a year and she doesn't know you have a twelve-year-old? Do you think that's wise?" I asked, but he ignored my question. Instead, he turned to the waitress who had just come to take our order.

When she left, I added, "I'm sorry for prying, but I'm talking from experience here. I may not be as old as you are, but I can tell you that keeping secrets in a relationship is a deadly killer. Have you heard the saying, 'Secrecy is the enemy of intimacy'?"

"First you call me foolish, now you call me old and a murderer? Do I look that old?" Funsho asked, with a quizzical look on his face, half teasing me, half serious.

"You have a twelve-year-old, even if you had him at twenty, you are still way older than me," I laughed.

"How old are you?" he asked.

"Twenty–four! And don't you know it is rude to ask a lady her age?"

Now it was his turn to laugh, "The lady who insults me also calls me rude? You had your son at twenty-three then?" When I nodded he added, "Same here, I had Sola at twenty-three. For some reasons, I feel stuck at that age; I don't feel like I am almost forty."

When the waitress brought the bill, Funsho paid for it as most men would, on a first date. What surprised me though, was that he handed the waitress a brand new £50 note.

"Take it!" he said when the waitress hesitated, "Are you a university student?"

"Yes," she said as she accepted the money, still looking in awe of Funsho's generosity.

"Listen, I'm not doing this to impress her," Funsho said as he pointed to me, "She's just a friend. I am only trying to encourage you, because about five years ago, I was you. I worked here during the day, went to lectures in the evenings, and guarded the club next door at night. Hang in there, make yourself proud and make sure you give back, like I just did."

The waitress thanked him profusely, before being called back to her work. When she had left, Funsho turned to me and said, "Shall we?" as he held out his arm for me to take.

"That's very kind of you," I said, "It's not just about the tip you gave her, but the seed of encouragement you've just sown in her life." I didn't admit it to him, but he had seriously impressed me and, whether he had a girlfriend or not, I hoped Funsho was actually real and not just another pretender.

As we were saying our goodbyes at the car park, my phone rang and it was Felix. For some reason, I didn't feel like talking to Felix in the presence of Funsho, so I told him I was going to return his call later.

"Sorry, I had to take that," I said sheepishly.

"Was that your boyfriend, partner or husband?" he asked, smiling knowingly.

"Ex-husband," I said.

"What? How is that even possible, you've been married, had a child and got divorced all under the age of twenty-five?"

"Thanks!" I said, feeling ashamed of myself, even though I knew he was only teasing me.

"I'm only joking," he said, still smiling and enjoying the look on my face. "How long have you been married and why are you splitting up?"

"Just over a year," I said, ignoring the last bit of his question.

"Have you completed the divorce?"

"We haven't even started."

"I can help you, with the proceedings, my firm specialises in divorce so it's well up my street," Funsho said.

"Are you a lawyer?" I asked, astonished by the realisation for a moment, before remembering that Sola had told me his father went to study Law.

God knew I needed all the help I could get, having read all the divorce articles on Google. Even though I had nothing much to lose because our house was solely in Felix's name, neither of us had investments that could cause a feud, and I knew it was very unlikely for him to be interested in custody of Jason, I still wasn't looking forward to the process. Additionally, I had never been a fan of paperwork, so I just wanted it over and done with so I could concentrate on my new job, save enough money to buy my own place, and give all of my love to my son. As much as I enjoyed my flirtations and fantasises, now I had Jason he was my number one priority – no men allowed.

When I got home, Femi told me that Adetoro had been waiting for me for the past hour. I stood at the door entrance watching him play with Jason, who imitated everything he did. As I watched on, I wished that my life was less complicated for the sake of my son. If I thought about the comfort and convenience, Adetoro would have been the best man for me, because he ticked almost all of the boxes – he was the biological father of my son, they had a natural bond, I loved him despite his flaws, and he was even rich enough to buy me a mortgage-free house, but what sort of human being could look away when she knew, or even suspected, her man was a murderer.

"Hi!" I said reluctantly, and as soon as father and son heard my voice, they both ran towards me to give me a welcoming hug.

"Where have you been and why haven't you been picking up my calls?" Adetoro asked.

"I'm so sorry, I've been so busy lately. I start a new job in two weeks' time, so I'm making prior arrangements for Jason and I," I said, as I played with Jason's hair in a bid to avoid eye contact with Adetoro.

"You need a therapy session," I said.

"Me? Why?" he asked, confused, as he searched my face for answers.

"I have been thinking about our last discussion, if you want us to work, you need to seek professional help in the form of psychological therapy – it's the only way out!" I said, as he looked at me in bewilderment.

"Don't look at me like that, you said it yourself, Simi is your weakness…more than your weakness, your addiction, and I don't think that will ever change unless you do something about it. When she is out of sight you might be ok, but what happens when she shows her face? You drop your pants at her command. Your drug, isn't that how you described it?" I asked. "Thankfully, you've passed the first stage of curing an addiction – acceptance. The next phase now is for you to seek help." I picked Jason up and went to leave the room.

"Where are you going?" he asked.

"Give me a minute, let me hand Jason over to mum…then we can have a proper talk."

"Abosede, I'm over Simi, for good. She means nothing to me anymore," he said when I returned to the living room.

"I find that very hard to believe," I sniffed, "I can clearly remember how you left me in your room, waiting for you like an idiot, while you went off to be with her instead. Obviously, I wasn't enough."

"But you are all I need, she was just a distraction. She blackmailed me into sleeping with her that night, I had to keep her happy for your sake."

"For my sake?" I scoffed, incredulous at his pathetic attempt at excuses, "Are you listening to yourself? Anyway, let's put your issues with Simi aside, what about living arrangements – I can't relocate to Nigeria, so that only leaves the option of you shuttling between Lagos and London. I don't see how that can work as we already have trust issues here. Like I said, there is more to a relationship than love. We can't work Adetoro!"

"Don't be a pessimist babe, we are meant to be, even the oracle professed it before you came to Ikoko," he said looking defeated as he realised my mind was made up, "Felix has wormed his way back into your life, right? That weakling is no good for you."

"Listen, I don't need you or Felix to make me feel complete, my son is all I need. Whenever you want to see Jason, just say, I will never prevent you from seeing him as long as you understand that I'm his custodial parent. Erase from your mind that there is a you and I!"

Adetoro sneered at me. "There is no need to confuse the poor boy by dipping in and out of his life, when my Prince is old enough, he will find me – they always do. You travelled miles to find your father, didn't you? I will not set foot in the UK ever again, and if I do, it won't be to see either of you," he said, as he slipped on his shoes and prepared to leave.

For a split second I heaved a sigh of relief, because it meant there would be no child custody battle between us. However, as it sank in, it dawned on me that my baby wouldn't remember how happy he was when he spent time with his father; the bond they shared, even if it was for a very short period of time, had been undeniably pleasing to the eyes.

"Adetoro, think about what you are saying in relation to Jason. When he is older, he will wonder why you never made the effort to see him. My situation was different, my dad didn't know I existed for years, but you are a prominent person in Nigeria, he'll grow to know who you are, or what the papers tell him about you. I am offering you the chance to have a relationship with your son, take it. Or what will you tell him when he comes to find you in future? Like I did and look what happened there!" I said, but he just walked past me and out of the living room.

When he got the front door, he paused and turned back. "And in answer to your question, I'll tell him his mother fell pregnant with my child, ran off with another man and never told me about it until he was three-months-old," he snapped in indignation. When I looked away and he saw he had hit a raw nerve, he walked back to where I was standing, "Isn't that the truth?"

"You want the truth Adetoro?" I asked him, angrily, "This is the truth – I'm shielding my son from you and your toxic relationship with you sister-in-law-turned-wife. From the look of things, you are not keen on having a relationship with Jason because you've already fathered some of Simi's. Everything you told me about your brother's death seems shady and I believe you have a hand in it." When I saw the heart-wrenching look of horror on his face, I wished I could have taken back my words, but it was too late.

"I really don't have anything more to say to you. If you believe I would hurt my own brother, let alone end his life, then I don't know why I'm wasting my time with you? I'm out of here!" he snarled.

"Yes, get out! We are better off without you, do not return," I shouted, as I ordered him out of my mother's house, out of my life, and out of Jason's – for good this time.

Now I had removed some of the cobwebs from my life, it was time to clear the rest in order to pave the way for the next chapter.

CHAPTER TWENTY

Mr Fix-It

I have never been one to worry about a new environment; I'd changed enough schools as a little girl to master my adaptation skills, but working at British Gas was different. I had been working there for three months and I wasn't able to connect with any of my work colleagues, despite their efforts to include me in the team. Work itself was great; I just couldn't be bothered to get to know people, probably because I had too much going on outside of work.

It felt like I left work every day to start another day's job at home. If it wasn't the morning rush to get myself and Jason ready for school, it would be unpacking in our newly-rented two-bedroom flat, laundry, cooking and, just when I thought I had a breather, Jason would wake up in the middle of the night to ask for his milk. In addition, I still had the divorce papers to complete, so one day, I summoned up the courage to give Funsho a call and take him up on his offer.

"Hi, this is Grace," I said, the moment he picked up the phone.

"Oh, wow! What took you so long?" he asked.

"Are you asking me, don't you have my number too? You could have called if you wanted to."

"You are right, I should have, but I have been going through a rough patch lately, it was easier to keep my distance from everyone."

"I can relate, actually," I said, before quickly adding, "Do you want me to call you back another time?”

“No, let's hook up. Although I don't fancy going out,” he replied.

“I actually called to ask for your advice on completing some divorce forms. It's been on my dressing table staring at me every morning, but I don't know where to start,” I said, as I listened for any sound of hesitance in his reply. When I didn't, I added, “You can come to mine, I'll cook.”

“Now, you've given me a reason to drag myself out of bed. Text me your address.” he said.

As soon as I put my phone down I realised I had just made the silliest offer – It was a Saturday morning, I was still in my PJs and, apart from Jason's jar food and baby yogurt, there was hardly any foodstuff to cook. To make matters worse, Funsho was only fifteen minutes' drive away. My only saving grace was that Jason was still asleep, so I was able to do a quick house tidy before stepping in the shower. I was just moisturising my body when I heard my doorbell ring, so I just had time to quickly slip on my Mickey Mouse onesie before getting the door.

“That was quick,” I said, as I let him in. He looked a little taller than the last time I saw him and was dressed down in a grey tracksuit.

“Hi Mickey Mouse! I love your onesie, does it have a tail? Don't tell me it has a tail,” he teased me, as he tried to investigate.

“I can't believe you just checked out my backside,” I berated him, batting him away in a playful fashion.

“And it's a fine one too – with a tail,” he replied and we both giggled. I was grateful the ice was broken earlier than anticipated.

I was just asking if he wanted some tea or coffee, when we heard Jason's rescue cry – he must have heard voices because I didn't expect him to wake up until about 10am.

“Meet my gorgeous son Jason. Jae Jae, meet my friend Funsho,” I said.

Even though it was a silly introduction, Funsho got up to greet my boy and I wondered if anyone could be as polite as he seemed to be all the time.

"I have a confession. I only have cornflakes to offer you for breakfast, unless I go out to the supermarket to get eggs and bread. I am getting used to having my freedom back, so I usually don't cook unless I have to," I explained.

"Cornflakes are perfect. But, after our paperwork exercise, you will have to feed me with some proper naija food. I miss egusi soup; it's about the only thing I can't cook."

"What about your girlfriend, what's her name again?" I asked, pretending I didn't remember.

"Tasha."

"Yes, can't she cook?" I asked.

"She is Jamaican, she can't cook Nigerian dishes but her Caribbean cooking is tantalising – she's a great cook but can't seem to grasp our style of cooking," he said, as if it was important to add that she's a great Jamaican cook.

After our meagre breakfast, I spread out the much-dreaded divorce papers on my centre table.

"Here they are! You see why I haven't been enthusiastic about completing them? The last time I spoke to Felix, he threatened to sue me for Parental Deceit and Fraud if I dared ask him for child maintenance. As if I'm interested in the little 'coins' he earns," I said, as I wondered when in our short marriage I gave him the impression of wanting his money. Yes he supported us after Jason was born, but wasn't that what any father should do. Before that I had always supported myself and, now that I had a good job again, I welcomed my financial independence back with open arms.

As I narrated the story of my life, and what led to my deceitful marriage to Felix, Funsho just listened and nodded in agreement, or shook his head to show disapproval, but it was always followed by an understanding smile. This was all I needed, I already knew how irresponsible and audacious I had been, I didn't need anyone pointing it out to me.

After baring it all in front of him, I suddenly felt naked and shy, expecting him to say something to break the silence.

"He actually sounds like a good guy. I don't think he is the one pulling the strings here, I suspect his manipulating baby mama is," Funsho said. "From what you've told me, she wears the trousers in their relationship, this is probably her own way of making sure her territory is secure and completely free of you and Jason. I can understand where she is coming from, but if they try to pull a fast one, you and I will fight to win it. In fact, let's give him a call now!"

"But there is no need for that…" I half-heartedly interjected, handing him my phone anyway, and making sure it was on speaker.

"Hi Felix, this is Mr Olabisi, Grace's lawyer," he said when Felix answered, giving me a knowing wink.

"Yes, how can I help you and why are you calling me out of office hours?" Felix asked.

"I won't take too much of your time, this is to shed some light on how the law works, in case you don't know," Funsho said, as he ruffled some of the papers on the table for sound effects.

"Grace informed me that you've been threatening to sue her for Paternity Fraud, even though she told you of the child's paternity before birth, ensured you weren't present during any of the prenatal activities, and gave her child the biological father's surname. I don't know who your lawyer is, but his advice is not optimum," Funsho said, as he paused to hear Felix's response.

"Do you know how much I invested into that boy in terms of time, money and emotion? How do I get that back?" Felix asked stroppily, realising he was out of his depth.

"I feel you, but unfortunately, the family court will do nothing to get you justice. If I were you, I would cut my losses and move on," Funsho said. The line went silent. "Are you still there?" asked Funsho.

"Yes, I'm listening, lawyer!" Felix replied, as we heard a female voice whispering in the background.

"Great! If I were you, bro, what I'd be more worried about is my house because, by law, even though Grace's name is not on the property, she has matrimonial home rights. Having consulted with her, however, she made it clear she isn't interested in the property or child maintenance, so I suggest we all behave like grown adults to minimise the stress that comes with this process. You keep your house, she keeps her sanity. I think that's a fair deal, do you?" Funsho asked.

"Yes, fair deal," sighed Felix, "Tell her to send the divorce papers over as soon as possible." Funsho gave me the thumbs up and hung up the phone.

"He knows he has no case, so there's nothing to be worried about," Funsho assured me.

"You are such a life saver, thank you very much. I didn't even know I was entitled to a stake in his house, with my name not being on the property."

"Yes, you do get a stake. No offence here, but the justice system is flawed. A man brings up another man's child for years and the woman walks away free?" Funsho said, raising his eyebrow at me.

"I don't think it's fair either," I agreed, "But men have done this for years. They have children outside their marriages and sometimes bring the child home for the wife to cater for."

"But then, the woman wouldn't be kept in the dark, she would have known what she was getting herself into," Funsho continued, into the stride of his argument.

"Let's not argue about this Funsho, it's not that simple. Most women, in Africa, for example, usually have no choice in the matter. The men just bring the mistress and her kid to their home and expect the wife to accept them. Where is the justice there? Having said that, I'm not saying tricking a man into fathering a child that isn't his is the right thing to do."

"But do you agree that the justice system is flawed, and women shouldn't be able to get away with paternity fraud," Funsho asked.

"I agree, women should be punished for it, and so should men who bring their bastard children home," I stated.

"Agreed," Funsho said, which ended our debate.

"Now that you know all about my past, tell me more about your relationship with Tasha, are you as happy as you try to make me believe?" I asked.

"I never said we were happy. Like all couples, we have our fair share of imperfections, but what I struggled with mostly was her excessive violence. Like I said, she is an amazing woman, I know she loves me deeply and I love her too, but I don't think it's enough for us to work," Funsho explained, as he shook his head vehemently. "Would you believe that I was beaten blue and black after meeting with you the last time?

"Beaten, for what?" I asked.

"Apparently, she had put a tracker in my car all this while, so when it notified her that I was at Prezzo she trailed me to find out who I was with – and of course she saw us," he said, as he showed me the marks on his shoulders and the ones on his belly.

"That's domestic violence you know?" I said, as I reached out to feel his belly; a part of it still looked sore, but he pulled his t-shirt down before I got the chance.

"You need to get out of that relationship; it's not healthy. Have you told her about Sola?" I asked.

"I can't tell her yet. Do you know how many times I have threatened her with a breakup? She keeps coming back, begging and blaming her nasty temper on her past," he said, rolling his eyes.

"Don't threaten, leave her for real. That's a toxic relationship," I said, now annoyed by his gentility.

"Leave her so I can come after you?" he asked playfully, but I didn't find it funny at all.

I shook my head, "Listen, I don't want you, you are not my type at all. I like my men strong and firm."

"And look where that got you," he retorted, and we both fell silent, both sulking for our own reasons.

Apart from the sound of Mr Tumble programme playing on the TV, you could hear a pin drop, and it lasted for quite a while before Funsho said something to break the silence. "Let's go for a walk, I know of a good African store where we can buy groceries to cook egusi."

We didn't speak much on the way there, but as Funsho pushed Jason's buggy on our way back from the grocery store he opened up to me again, "I actually broke up with her last month, that's why I've been miserable for the past few weeks. Grace, is it possible to love someone, yet hate them so much?"

"Of course, I love Adetoro, Jason's dad, and I hate him for who I think he is," I agreed, as I stopped to rearrange the bags in the buggy's basket. Funsho nodded and we fell silent again, both lost in our own thoughts about our failed relationships.

When we got home, as I watched him wash and cut the vegetables and, seeing him making himself at home in my kitchen, I wondered what it would be like if we were together. Although I wasn't ready for another relationship and Funsho would have been a most unlikely suitor, considering his son was the one responsible for my kidnap, I couldn't help but wonder.

"Have you kick-started Sola's relocation to the UK?" I asked.

"I'm on it," he replied, in a tone which implied he didn't want me to probe further, so I let it go. Where we had previously found each other's company so easy, now there was an awkwardness between us.

Throughout his visit, I made sure there was enough physical space between us too. We watched movies together, partly so we didn't have to talk anymore. I sat on the far edge of the sofa and picked Jason up, holding him on my lap like a barrier, even though the poor boy wanted to be on his own. Funsho, on the other hand, held on to my favourite cushion like it was a life jacket. When it seemed like time for Funsho to leave, I slotted another DVD into the player and, when he didn't get up from the sofa, I knew he wasn't going anywhere for another two hours. As we relaxed together, the awkwardness started to fade and we fell back into easy companionship.

It was around 7pm when I eventually let him go. At first, the plan was to walk him down my street and head straight back home. Jason wouldn't go to sleep, so I thought a walk in his buggy might help him drop off. As it was, Jason and I ended up right on his doorstep and, when he insisted that we came in for a drink, all I could do was accept his invitation. For whatever reason, we both clearly enjoyed spending time together and Jason liked him too. From being ready to run away from any man who came near me, I finally felt I had found someone I wanted to spend more time with.

This became our routine for the next two years – I saw Funsho almost every weekend and spoke to him every day. During this period, my divorce with Felix was finalised and he was married to his high school sweetheart; my little boy had started preschool; Sola had joined his father in the UK and started high school; and Adetoro kept to his promise of leaving us in peace. In my book, everything was just hunky dory.

I was able to focus on my career more than ever, and my lifetime dream of making a difference in my community was finally taking shape. With Funsho's help, I started an NGO for female teenagers and young adults, to address a matter very close to my heart and Funsho's – Paternity Fraud Awareness. We believed it was one of those family issues swept under the carpet for years, despite being rampant in everyday society, and our plan was to treat the root cause.

According to statistics shown by The Telegraph and Daily Post Nigeria, "one in fifty British fathers unknowingly raise another man's child" and "three out of ten Nigerian men are not the biological fathers of their children."

I felt the statistics were unacceptable, considering that the perpetrators were usually women who, for various reasons such as comfort, security, shame or poverty, would trick a man into raising a child who isn't theirs. Occasionally, some women would even do it out of love when they suspected their husband was infertile; it was their own way of saving him the embarrassment.

As a victim and culprit myself, I thought it was imperative that I worked with the women, especially teenagers and young women, to educate, give empowerment tips, and raise money to help support them when the need arose. The plan was to eventually take it national, but we were starting with the UK and, hopefully, would advance to other parts of the world.

The official launch date was fast approaching in my eyes, even though it was still months away. I threw myself into the preparations with great passion and military precision in the planning, feeling the need to get things organised in advance to avoid last minute disappointments. For example, my friend, DJ Tee, was no longer able to volunteer his time as he now had paid gigs, so I needed to find myself another DJ.

It was during my mission to find a new DJ that I realised I hadn't seen or heard from Funsho in two weekends, and he wasn't returning my calls either. Right there and then, I decided to stroll to his house. His car was on his driveway so I knew he was in.

"Hello Aunty Grace, where is Jason?" Sola asked, as he let me in, clearly on his own way out.

"He's at his grandma's today, where is your dad and where are you going?"

"I am off to church, it's our youth concert dress rehearsal today. Dad is in."

"Is he ok? I haven't heard from him in a while?"

"Yeah, he is ok. See you later Aunty," Sola said, ushering me into the house and closing the door behind him as he left.

After looking everywhere in the house to no avail, I eventually found Funsho moving things around in his garage.

"There you are, what are you doing in here? Why haven't you returned any of my calls?" I asked, realising I was bombarding him with too many questions.

"As you can see, I've been busy," he replied, his eyes still on the shelf and looking irritated at having been disturbed. I pushed myself in front of him so that we were face to face, then I could better gauge what was going on.

"Don't do that!" he snapped, pushing me away.

"Funsho, what's wrong, what have I done? I have never seen you like this," I said as I tried to get his attention, but he still didn't look my way. "Whatever it is I've done, you will have to tell me so I can apologise. If it's because I've been distant in the past two weeks it's because of the NGO launch, everything is going pear-shaped with the arrangements we concluded weeks ago. DJ Tee has just cancelled on me and..." I explained, before he interrupted me.

"Just stop! You know I am very much involved with the NGO as much as you are, so it's got nothing to do with that," he said, as he locked the garage and led the way into the house; and up to his bedroom.

"Then what is it Fun-Fun dear?" I asked him.

"You tell me, what are we doing here?" he snapped back, now looking me straight in the eyes.

"What do you mean?" I asked, even though I had an idea where he was going with this.

"If you are going to keep pretending, then I really have nothing to say to you," he said, before tearing his eyes away from me and in the direction of his bedroom TV.

I knew what Funsho was moaning about, in fact, I knew the exact incident and discussion that had put him in the sour mood I found him in. But I didn't know how to respond, so I kept quiet and pondered on the best way to answer his question, "You tell me, what are we doing here?"

Chapter Twenty-one

Holding Back

FUNSHO and I had been seeing each other for about six good months. Anyone who saw us together would think we were a couple, but we weren't – we were just friends who enjoyed each other's company and had similar tastes in food and hobbies. The two of us could binge on American movies, play scrabble, or go on a walk 'til thy kingdom come – we were homely like that.

One weekend, Funsho suggested we went on a weekend break to Cornwall. I thought it was a great idea, because my previous holiday with Mum, Dad, Femi and Jason, was too activity-packed. I wanted something relaxing, with less activity and more time to chill out.

"I think this resort is our best option," Funsho said, as he placed his laptop on my lap. As I scrolled down to read the holiday description, he added, "It's very child-friendly and close to the beach, I think we should go for it."

"It looks ok," I said, unsure, "But I don't want a break with children shouting and running around, we should go for something childproof," I said.

"But we've got to think about the kids," he advised.

"I didn't think we were going with them. I don't know about Sola, but I was thinking of dropping Jason off at my mum's, Sola can come too if you want."

"If that's the case, let me show you a hotel I was looking at earlier; it has a spa, it's close to the seaside and has beautiful places for walking," he grinned, as he snatched his laptop back from me.

We both agreed his new recommendation was the best holiday package available, so he promised to book it for us when he got back home. I offered to split the cost with him, but he insisted it was his treat – he was generous like that.

I didn't have the luxury of taking the whole of Friday off at work, because I had used up almost all of my holidays for childcare emergencies – I took the afternoon off instead. As planned, Funsho came to pick me up from work and off we went. Despite leaving before rush hour, we didn't get to our destination until around 7pm at night. When we got to the hotel, we went to the reception to collect our keys.

"Here you go!" the receptionist said, as she handed me the key and signalled a butler to show us our room.

"You only handed us one key," I commented, as I turned my gaze to Funsho for answers.

"Give us a minute, please," Funsho said to the receptionist, as he pulled me to one side.

"Grace, I only booked us one room."

"But why? If it's because of funds, I offered to support you!"

Funsho's face fell and I realised my mistake. "It's not about the money," he stuttered, "I thought, you know…I mean, I'm so sorry. I assumed wrongly…let's book an additional room then…"

"I'm sorry, the rooms are sold out, we can arrange twin beds for you if that helps," the receptionist suggested and so we agreed.

At dinner, things were still awkward between Funsho and I, because I thought I had overreacted and ruined the weekend break for us. But I thought it was really sneaky of him to have assumed that we would share a bed.

"We need to talk," Funsho said, as we waited for our food.

"There's nothing to talk about, just leave it," I said.

"No, I won't have this lingering between us for the whole break. We are mature adults and should be able to communicate these things," he said.

"Funsho, can we just have dinner?"

"Ok, but after dinner, we'll go for a walk and trash this out – and that's final!" he said.

The rest of our dinner was less awkward, because we had an upcoming R&B artist performing to entertain us with all of our favourite '90s songs. After dinner, we stayed longer to hum and sing along, until another artist took over.

"Let go for that walk and talk now," Funsho said, so we took our leave.

It was slightly chilly outside and all I had for insulation was a scarf around my neck.

"Here," Funsho said, as he wrapped me up with his jeans jacket. He hadn't finished doing up the buttons when he started talking.

"Grace, I apologise for my thoughtlessness, I should have asked you instead of assuming. But, in fairness to me, we've spent an ample amount of time together in the past six months. We've cried and laughed together, and shared most of our deepest and most intimate secrets. Apart from your parents, I don't think anyone knows you as well as I do, so forgive me if I assumed wrong about our relationship. When you said you were going to leave Jason at your mum's, and offered to drop Sola there too, I took that as a green light, and I shouldn't have. So, I'll ask you again, have I misread the signals?"

"No, you haven't," I said gently, as I cupped my arm in his and urged us to carry on walking. "I feel the same way, but I want to take things slow this time. I already told you, I'm prone to rushing into relationships, especially with Adetoro and Felix, and we both know the outcome of that. After all I went through, I've promised myself to look before I leap into my future relationship – note that I singularised 'relationship', so I must be totally sure before I commit."

"I understand, we've both come out of bad relationships, I get it. But there isn't anything to learn about me, what you see is what you get. However, if you must, take your time but please don't leave it too long, I'm not getting any younger," he said.

"On the contrary, I think you are still hiding your true character from me. I know you have a bad temper, but you've never lost it with me, and I have done some nasty things to deserve it."

"Grace, you're a child, nothing you do really annoys me. I'm old enough to be your father."

"No, you are not! Do eleven-year-olds have children in your village?" I asked playfully, which seemed to lighten the mood and put things back to normal between us. "Ok, old cargo, I won't waste your time, I will let you know when I'm sure."

To be honest, as fond as I was of Funsho and as much as I loved his company and how great he was with Jason, we didn't have the intense chemistry I shared with Adetoro, or the dramatic past I shared with Felix. Funsho was a lovely man, but he was also a little boring. Whilst a little boring was probably what I needed after all my adventures, I wasn't sure I could forever trade that magical spark of chemistry for comfortable companionship.

After the Cornwall trip, Funsho and I drew an invisible line that guided us through our platonic relationship, and we didn't cross that line apart from on one occasion. We had just put Jason to bed and Sola was already asleep in his room. We couldn't agree on what to watch on TV, so we rolled a dice. Funsho won the bet, but I didn't want to watch Doctor Who. I hated the programme with a passion, so I seized the remote control. He wasn't prepared to miss the beginning of the show, so he started chasing me around his living room to regain control over the remote control. When he eventually caught me, I fell on the nearest sofa so that I could hide the remote between the cushions.

Funsho rolled on top of me as he struggled to retrieve the control and we play-fought and giggled like children. All of a sudden, our laughter stopped as we realised our faces were inches apart. We gazed at each other with such focus and intensity, that I could see my own reflection in his pupils. 'Damn, his eyes are so beautiful and sincere,' I thought, 'I wonder what I look like through those enchanting eyes.' We remained still, in the same position, for a little longer before Funsho broke the silence.

"Damn, I'm in love with you G," he said.

I don't know why his profession of love came as such a shock to me and I hoped it didn't show on my face. Of all the six men I had dated in my lifetime, well, apart from Adetoro, none of them ever told me they loved me. They described their feelings in so many ways but never with the 'L' word. With Adetoro, I wasn't shocked when he said the word, because I felt the same way for him; it was just a natural love that neither of us could help, so there was no need to analyse or question it.

With Funsho, even though I loved him, I wasn't in love with him and I needed more time to be hundred percent sure I could develop those feelings for him over time – or learn to live without them. However, what confused the hell out of me was the fact that I had no reason of logic or passion to want to be with him, other than my inability to be without him. 'Is this the real definition of love?' I wondered, as tears filled my eyes and the little Grace, reflected in his beautiful eyes, became a blur.

"Oh no, what have I done, I'm sorry Grace…I didn't mean to say it out loud, it just came out. Please forget I said anything," he gushed, before I could speak, and he pulled himself up and went to get the inflatable bed he always slept on when I stayed over at his place.

"Funsho!" I called, but he ignored my cry, he just placed his bed in the middle of his living room and prepared to call it a night.

"Let's say goodnight, I have checked on the kids, they are both fine. Please turn the light off on your way out," he said, plumping up his pillow and settling down.

I felt a sharp pain in my chest, as though my heart was being ripped out of my body. I felt confused and vulnerable and desperately wanted to seek his comfort, but I couldn't bring myself to talk things through with him. As I laid in Funsho's bed that night, a part of me wanted to go back to the living room to tell him I felt exactly the same way, but I knew this was just a knee-jerk reaction to the flood of emotions I was still trying to make sense of, and I was too scared to commit to something I wasn't sure of. So I let myself doze off and didn't wake up until the following morning.

Even if we wanted to dwell on the previous night's event, we couldn't because our kids were up and ready for breakfast. So that was the end of that subject, until we were finally alone together, supposedly about to watch a movie together in his bedroom. However, Funsho turned off the TV and stared at me intensely, clearly now expecting a response to his question about our relationship.

"Are you asking about us?" I queried.

"Yes, I mean exactly that, what about us? Isn't two years enough for you to make up your mind?" he asked, as he got up to drag a chair to the edge of his bed.

"Get off my bed!" he teased, "Sit right in front of me and tell me how you feel, you already know how I feel about you, now it's your turn."

"Funsho, I'm scared," I said, as tears filled my eyes again.

"What for?" he asked, looking a little confused but keen to get to the bottom of my vulnerability. "When I tell you I love you, you cry as though I have hurt you. Why Grace?"

"I love you too," I started, choking slightly on the words, but also unable to stop myself from saying it. I trailed off, not knowing what to say next, but he wasn't going to step in as he always did when I was stuck with something. He just held his gaze steady on mine, waiting for me to continue. "My love for you is…I don't know how to explain it…different. It's kind of too good to be true and the feeling scares me; I'm going to need your help here."

"Love is a scary thing at times, but that's not a good reason to renounce or keep quiet about it. When you are in love, you should want to shout it from the rooftops," Funsho said.

"Funsho Olabisi, I love you and cannot live without you!" I shouted at the top of my voice. "Is that loud enough for you? The thought of losing you activates palpitations in my heart," I added, and we both started laughing.

"Come here," he said as he drew me against his body. "I have dreamt of this from the very moment I met you…." he added as he trailed off.

His lips on mine felt like the perfect fit; they were firm and possessive as they took over mine to satisfy my desires in a way I never knew existed. As we kissed, tears rolled down my cheeks uncontrollably – no man had ever kissed me the way Funsho did. It was more than a kiss, more than an animalistic desire. It was an act of giving and receiving love, only this time, it was with our tongues doing the job for us. When I thought my body couldn't take anymore heightened sensual sensations, Funsho's hands travelled to my left breast and his tongue on my right. I let out a soft moan, but not as powerful as the sound I made when his fingers found their way to my crotch area – whatever it was he was doing down there would have been punishable under the law if he dared to stop.

"Grace," he moaned as he came up for air. "I love you, I love your body and I'm crazily in love with you."

"But you haven't even seen my body," I said, as I clenched his upper arm.

As if I had just reminded him of the task at hand, he hurriedly went to lock the door behind us. By the time he was back, my clothes were off.

"Holy Moly, damn, you're one sexy mermaid!" he said, giving me his familiar charming grin before yanking off all of his own clothes.

"Take me, I'm all yours, for as long as you'll have me," I said, in a whisper so soft that I could barely hear myself.

"Did you just propose to me?" Funsho asked, as he raised his brows.

"No, I didn't!" I replied in a giggle, as he reached to his bedside drawer.

"I bought this before our trip to Cornwall, but you went awry on me before I had the chance to ask. You made me wait for almost two years, jeez!" he said, as he went down on one knee.

When he reached for the drawer, I had assumed he was getting condoms, but this? My heart was beating so hard I was convinced it was loud enough to wake up the entire neighbourhood.

"My amazing Grace, will you marry me?"

Again, the feeling of fear and shock overwhelmed me. I would have loved to have given some time to think about his proposal before I answered, but his eyes, so beautiful and pure, were glaring at me and waiting for an answer; so I had no choice than to respond with something pleasing to his ears.

"Yes, I will marry you, my Olufunsho Fun-Fun dear, Baba Sola. Now, slip the damn ring on and let's get back to business, I haven't had 'some' for over two years," I said seductively, as I watched his eyelids lower to my lips.

"And whose fault is that? My big daddy and I are going to make you pay for all the agony you put us through over the months," he said, as his lips met mine again.

"You must have some condoms hiding in your drawer, as well as engagement rings, right?" I asked, pulling away again for a moment. As he reached across to get one, I thanked God for bringing me Funsho. Perhaps now I would finally find true love and live happily ever after?

CHAPTER TWENTY-TWO

The Encounter

IT was Friday and I couldn't wait to be with my boys for another fun family weekend; ever since Funsho proposed, Jason and I spent more of our time at his house. As I jumped on the train after work, I spotted a woman who I thought looked like Funsho's ex, Tasha, but I wasn't too sure. I was still trying to steal glances at her to confirm my assumption, when she looked my way.

"Hi, Grace is it?" she asked, confirming my suspicions.

"Yes, and you are Tasha, right? How are you doing?" I asked with interest, as I had always wondered why she disappeared into thin air just like that. One minute she was there, the next he had ended it and she was no more. If Funsho didn't show me pictures, it was easy to assume she never even existed in the first place.

"I'm good, how is Funsho doing, are you still together?"

"Yes, we are, he is doing great. We are engaged!" I said, ensuring I was not too showy, because our meeting was pleasant thus far and I didn't want any awkwardness between us.

"Congratulations to you both, say hello to him from me," she said, looking genuinely delighted for us.

"I will, how are you doing too?" I asked.

"I'm great, I'm married now and have a two-year-old boy," she chirped.

My heart sank. "Did you just say two years?" I asked, hoping my eyebrows weren't too high as I quickly did the calculations in my head. I hadn't arrived at my result yet when she interrupted my train of thoughts.

"Don't look so worried, he isn't Funsho's, I'm married to a Scottish man," she laughed, as she shoved her phone in my face as the train swung us back and forth. To my greatest relief, her screensaver showed a beautiful family picture and we chatted for the rest of our journey, mostly about our sons.

As soon as I got off the train, I called Funsho.

"Babe, guess who I just bumped into on the train," I asked. As usual, he guessed wrong. "I just saw Tasha on the train, she is married and has a two-year-old."

"What? A two-year-old?" he gasped, and I could almost hear his heart beating over the phone.

"Relax sweetie, he is not yours. He is mixed race, she married a Scottish man."

"Phew, what a relief, he said, "Come home and let me teach you a lesson for scaring me like that."

I grinned, "You bet Fun-Fun! I'll be back soon!" I loved how open and supportive our relationship was, free from secrets and lies. Also, as our sex life got hotter and hotter, I found myself falling in love with him too. 'Things don't get much better than this, Grace!' I told myself, as I went to put the phone back in my bag. However, before I could do so, it started to ring. Assuming it was Funsho again, I picked straight up.

However, the voice on the other end was not Funsho's. I quickly looked at the screen, and saw Adetoro's number. My heart skipped a beat, as if by habit. We hadn't spoken in two years, so I wondered why he was calling.

"Hello Adetoro," I said.

"Hi, how are you and my prince doing?" he asked.

"We are fine, what do you want?"

"Abosede, you are always feisty, I guess that's one of the things I like about you. Anyway, I'm calling to inform you that we found my brother's killer. Are you free to talk?"

"No, I'm not," I said, putting my foot down from the start and showing him clear boundaries. I was not going to allow myself to get sucked into the dramas of the Cursed Palace of Ikoko again, I wasn't that woman anymore, I was a new woman, a devoted mother and wife-to-be of a successful lawyer. "I really don't care about your family issues anymore Adetoro, I have my own family to worry about now – I'm actually engaged to be married," I added, to emphasise my point.

"Congratulations, I'm engaged too – to the latest Miss Ondo beauty queen!" he laughed, as arrogant as always, "I just thought you would be interested to know who the killer was, you'll be surprised!"

"Congratulations on your engagement," I played along, of course I was curious as to who this real killer was supposed to be. "So, who connived with Simi to kill your brother?"

"You've always been so sure it was her," he began, "And you were right, it was Simi. But you will never believe who helped her." He paused for effect, "My brother was killed by Simi, with the help of Mama Soji and Soji." He went silent again, probably waiting for it to sink in for me.

I felt sick. Of all the people I had met at the palace, including my own blood father and the king himself, my ex-lover and father of my only son, Mama Soji was the one I trusted the most. I shook my head in denial, my brain racing to try and work out why Adetoro was telling me this. Was it some kind of twisted joke? "Mama Soji? I don't believe it, what is in it for her?" I stuttered, after a long pause.

"Meet me at Hilton Hotel in Golders Green, I will explain it all to you face to face. I made a stopover in London, I leave for Maryland tomorrow morning."

"Why can't you tell me over the phone?"

"Abosede, we are not enemies, are we? I am getting married in three months' time, you are also starting a new family – we are fine. But what about our son? Just like you said, whatever does or does not happen between us, we should think of our son. I brought him some African goodies to remind him of me, please drop by for a few minutes," he implored.

Adetoro was right, I had to consider Jason's interests, so I asked him to text me his hotel address. Then I called Funsho to help me get Jason from nursery, on the excuse that I had to get some groceries from the African shop. As soon as the lies left my mouth, I wondered if I should call back to tell my fiancé the truth because it was pointless hiding anything from him – but I didn't. Also, I realised I was rather fast to accept Adetoro's request to see him. Whilst I told myself it was all for Jason, the truth was I was also curious to meet with him. In lying to my fiancé and sneaking off to meet with my ex-lover, it was almost as though I was setting myself a test to pass – or a trap to fall into.

When I got to the hotel reception, I spotted Adetoro in the hotel lobby watching football on one of the screens. He had a cool new haircut, was wearing a sporty tracksuit, and adidas trainers; and anyone who saw the yellow gold chain he wore to accessorise his outfit would know it was real. As I approached the lobby, I wondered if I should go home to change the boring school teacher outfit I was wearing, but I couldn't risk bumping into Funsho on his way back from picking up Jason. So, I walked up to Adetoro and, for the first time ever, I felt inferior to him.

"Hi," I said and I could hear the nerves in my voice. I felt like a schoolgirl standing in front of the cool older boy she has a secret crush on.

As soon as he heard my voice, Adetoro leaped up to give me a hug without hesitation. The familiar smell of his aftershave hit my nostrils; as usual, it jolted me back to my time with him at Ikoko. In a room full of men, whether I was sleeping, awake, or blind, I would be able to single out Adetoro by the smell of his aftershave, and it would always have the same effect on me.

"Wow, you look good," he said, as he checked me out.

"Thanks, for the flattery," I replied self-consciously, as I looked away.

"I have never seen you in a formal outfit, I love it. You look sexy in it," he said, as he winked at me and licked his lips, like a wolf sizing up a lamb for its dinner.

"Be careful, this is someone else's fiancée, you know," I warned him, but in actual fact, I was enjoying it. I was enjoying the crazy butterfly feeling he gave me in my chest and my belly, and the fire his body heat gave to my blood. I had missed it, I had missed him.

"One can't admire God's glorious work because you belong to another man? C'mon!" he gave me a playful tap on the arm. "My room is on the third floor," he said, guiding me to the lift, "We can talk in private there."

Once inside the confined space of the lift, I felt even more awkward with Adetoro and the worse thing was, he knew it. As he gazed at me, he looked extraordinarily confident with his familiar mischievous smile playing on his handsome face.

"Please, stop looking at me like that," I requested, but he just remained quiet and continued staring at me, until the escalator door opened.

"Come on, it's this way," he said, as he led the way to his room.

As I followed behind him, guilt enveloped my entire being. I kept telling myself I was there for Jason, but it didn't seem to wash away the culpability. When we got into the room, Adetoro brought out two suitcases full of Nigerian outfits, necklaces, trainers, African books, and so much more for Jason and I.

"Adetoro, this is too much! Is this a farewell gift for Jason?" I asked, "Is this both hello and a last goodbye, as you head off into your new marriage?"

"No, he is my Prince, and these are all the things I have been buying for him for the past two years. I made a huge mistake and I realise it now; I shouldn't have allowed you put a wedge between my son and I." I watched his face darken and his smile turned into a frown.

"But you were the one who decided not to see us, how did I put a wedge between you two?" I argued.

"You accused me wrongly, I know we never spent enough time together, but you should have known I was incapable of hurting a fly. Anyway, that's bygone, tell your fiancé I am going to be involved in my son's life going forward. Make sure he is happy with it, my fiancée understands – she knows she has no choice on the matter," he said.

"Ok Adetoro," I agreed, not liking the change to his mood. I decided to distract him. "Tell me the full story, what was Mama Soji's motive for killing your big brother?"

Adetoro sat down on the bed and motioned for me to sit next to him. When we were settled, he began his story.

"Simi has been diagnosed with terminal cervical cancer; the doctors say she has six months to live. Our chief priest asked her to confess all her sins before she departs from the world if she wants a good life after death, so she did.

"According to her, after Mama Soji and Oyekan found out about my affair with Simi, he went to Simi's room that evening to talk to her, only to find Soji on top of her. The king was so upset that he grabbed Soji, started hitting him and kept saying, "I can't kill my brother, but I can kill you". Mama Soji must have heard the commotion and, to save her son, she went back into the kitchen to grab the pestle for pounding yam and hit the king from behind. Oyekan fell to the floor and, within minutes, my brother was dead.

"The three of them, Soji, his mum and Simi, carried my brother to his room and made his death look like a suicide," he paused, "That's why I'm going to the States, karma has dished out some of Simi's punishment, and it's now time to get justice for my brother by reporting Mama Soji and her son to the authorities."

As Adetoro narrated the events, I wondered what Mama Soji would say in her defence. "Well, I wouldn't call that murder, he was trying to kill my son, I did what I had to do; I've mapped my life out perfectly, something threatens to ruin it so I did something to put my life back on track?" she might say, but why she would fabricate lies and dump her callous and evil deeds on other people was something I struggled to understand. When Adetoro finished, I didn't know whether to be happy or sad that he was cleared of the crime. I wanted him to be guilty to justify my decision in following a different life path, at the same time, I was glad it wasn't him because it meant my son's father wasn't a murderer after all.

"I don't know how I'm going to carry all of this home," I said, gesturing to the pile of gifts. I didn't know how to react to his story, what he expected me to do or say.

"It's that all you've got to say? I just told you that you've made a life decision based on your wrong conclusion about me and you are asking me how you'll carry these?" Adetoro snapped, incredulous, as he paced up and down the room. "What about an apology to start with?"

"Why should I be sorry? It's your family and your mess, it's got nothing to do with me. Quit playing the victim here, you're not all that innocent either, didn't you sleep with your brother's wife?" I snapped back.

"That has always been your problem, not even the fact that I was an alleged murderer. Simi has always been the wedge between us, even after you promised you would drop the subject if I told you how we got together. But it didn't make any difference, did it? You were still as jealous as always!" he snarled, as he walked up to me with so much rage, and I kept moving backwards until I was stopped by the wall behind me. He stood in front of me, so close that I could feel his warm breath on my face. It made the hair stand up on the back of my neck, for more reasons than one.

"Adetoro!" I whispered, as I felt my knee going weak.

"Why won't you apologise?" he asked, as he tilted my chin so that we were looking into each other's eyes.

The moment our eyes met, I knew I was in trouble and was fast becoming putty in his hands, so I looked away quickly in a bid to try and regain my composure. He must have read my mind, because he took my head in his hands before I could pull away further, and ran his hand through my hair, before kissing my forehead, then my neck.

"Adetoro!" I moaned.

"Tell me to stop and I will," he groaned, but I didn't have the power to say those words.

My body yearned for his touch and not because I was sexually starved at home, rather, it was because my body had a way of taking over my mind whenever I was with Adetoro – all rules were defied when it came to me and him. Without saying another word, Adetoro carried me to his bed, where we let our bodies take over as usual, until we were left panting for air.

A part of me wanted to blame Adetoro for what had just happened, but I didn't have the strength to fight him because it was obvious I wanted it as much as he did. Instead I said, "Listen, I am in love with Funsho and sexually satisfied, so I don't understand why this just happened – but you need to understand that we can't read anything to it."

"There is a difference between sex and lovemaking," argued Adetoro, "I learnt that with you. Every woman I have been with, has been pure and simple sex, until I met you. I have great sex with the woman I'm with, but it can never come close to what we had...what we still have. With you, it's like we are in sync."

"But we can't do anything about it, we've missed this boat – maybe in another life," I mumbled, as I gathered my clothes from the floor and made to get dressed.

"Please don't leave yet," Adetoro pleaded, but I had already stayed longer than anticipated and the flush of passion was quickly being replaced by a feeling of guilt and responsibility to get home to my family.

"Thank you for all our gifts," I said, as I brushed my messy hair, "Please have them couriered to me, I will text you my address. I can't carry them home now."

"You make everything so complicated Abosede, what are cabs for? I will call one for you," he said, before adding, "Don't feel guilty about what happened here today, shit happens!"

"'Shit happens'?" I repeated, "Is that what you call what just happened? Not that long ago it was some kind of destiny and now it is 'shit'?" I knew what he meant, but my guilt and his nonchalance were making me uncomfortable and angry and I just wanted to get out of there. "I'm not a pro like you, you've been doing it for years!" I snapped back over my shoulder, as I made for the door.

"If I didn't sleep with Simi, you and I would have been married now," called Adetoro after me and I knew he was right, but I just picked up my bag and left the hotel room without saying goodbye.

As I was about to enter the lift, Adetoro came running after me with the two suitcases, whilst speaking to a cab driver on the phone. "He is asking for your address?" he said, before handing me his phone so I could take over the call. I told the cab driver my address and tossed the phone back to Adetoro without a second glance. Even though I did not turn around, I could feel his eyes burning into my back as I left.

When I got home, I picked up few foodstuffs from my pantry, put them in a blue plastic bag like the ones they gave us at African grocery shops, then I headed to Funsho's house. When I got there, Funsho and the children had already cooked and were waiting for me to join them at the table. They all looked so proud of themselves as they urged me to taste their chicken stew and rice. During dinner, I made sure I behaved as normal as possible, even though the guilt was killing me inside, gnawing at my soul and taunting me by replaying my sins on a loop, over and over in my mind's eye. I could still smell Adetoro's aftershave and manly scent in my nostrils, and I was sure Funsho would smell it too and spot me for the rat that I was.

"So, did she ask after me?" Funsho asked.

"Who?" I asked, suddenly more defensive than I had meant to be.

"You said you saw Tasha on the train?"

"Oh, yes. She did, and I told her you are doing great. I even showed her my ring before she showed me a picture of her gorgeous family," I said, as I watched Funsho's face for any sign of nostalgia. I almost hoped he would show signs of affection and longing for his ex, as though that would make me feel better about what I had just done.

"We will have our own baby to show off soon too," he said, a smile forming on his face.

"But it's not a competition honey!"

"I know, but don't you think we should stop using those condoms? Let's just throw caution to the wind and see what happens – let's have a baby!" Funsho said, before adding, "Tonight is a good night to start".

"We've talked about this," I sighed, "Please drop it Funsho. I don't want another baby right now. I want to do it right this time – wedding before baby. And please leave me be tonight, I am so tired. I have been working so hard on the launch, I just want an early night please."

What I didn't say, was that I wasn't sure I wanted his baby at all; or him, for that matter.

CHAPTER TWENTY-THREE

The Launch

The day we had all been waiting for finally arrived, it was the launch of my Paternity Fraud Awareness Campaign. Funsho was working with the hall technicians to get the sound system ready; Bolu and Funke decorated the stage, table and chairs; Mum and Dad oversaw the catering; Femi and Sola helped the DJ to set up; Tiwa looked after her twins and Jason; and all I could do was pace around, sweating, even though I was doing absolutely nothing.

"Why don't you sit down somewhere and practice your speech," Funsho advised, but I was unable to calm my nerves, even after I could see things starting to take form.

My anxiety only started to fade when teenage girls, women of various ages, and a handful of men started walking through the door. Within a very short space of time, the hall was filling up quite quickly. Like a flock of birds, they kept flooding in, and it wasn't long before I started panicking again. In my wildest imagination, I never envisaged such high turnout, so I asked Femi to get more chairs from the storage to accommodate the people standing around.

Funsho, as calm and confident as ever, was on the stage giving his welcome speech and I knew that, any moment, it would be my turn. As soon as the MC called my name, I felt my body freeze, and the hall started spinning, with the people in it. I closed my eyes as my heartbeat pounded in my ears and I willed the dizzy spell to disappear. 'Hold it together Grace,' I told myself, 'Don't fall over, you can do this, just hold it together!' Thankfully, within seconds it subsided.

Speaking in public had never been a problem for me before, but this was not just any speech; it was one which would affect many lives. So I was determined to keep it real and honest, otherwise, there was no point in doing it at all. I started by discussing the effects of Child Neglect, using Sola as an example, then I told the audience my life story as both a victim and offender of paternity deception. When I was sure I had won the crowd over, I spoke about the importance of doing the right thing, even when it hurts oneself. "For the sake of your child; poverty, convenience, comfort or shame shouldn't be an excuse!" I said, as people gave a round of applause.

"Shame is definitely not an excuse," I muttered to myself, as I cleaned up the hall with my loved ones after the event. Loved ones who had done everything to support my passion without an inkling of how selfish I had been. The same people, especially Funsho, whose heart I was going to shatter into pieces. Experience had taught me that when nature calls, you have no choice but to answer. When sleepy, you doze off; when hungry, your tummy rumbles; when you have unprotected sex, you get pregnant – it's that simple.

My body was undergoing changes very fast, and I knew for the sake of my born and unborn children, I had to talk to someone fast – "but who?" was the million-dollar question. I knew I was going to do the right thing by my fiancé and my baby daddy; I already made up my mind about having the conversations with them individually, but I couldn't decide who to speak to first.

After two weeks of careful deliberation, I decided to broach the subject with Funsho. Arsenal had just beaten Tottenham at home and Sola and Jason were spending the weekend at my mum's. If I was ever going to summon up the courage to talk to him, it was the most appropriate moment.

"Funsho, please turn the TV off, we need to talk," I said, in a voice so loud it surprised both of us.

"Is everything ok?" he asked, looking my way only briefly, before returning his gaze to the after-match commentary.

"I've messed up really badly, you need to turn that TV off and listen to me," I said, my voice sounding stronger and more determined than I felt.

"We promised not to bring work home, whatever you have done or not done will be dealt with when you get back on Monday," he advised, still watching the TV and not really paying attention.

"Funsho," I said in a serious voice, "You must listen to me now. This might be the end of the road for us, as I've unintentionally done the unforgivable. I want you to know, I never planned to do anything to hurt you, it just happened. I have cried, prayed, and even considered termination, but it goes against my beliefs. I'm afraid it is what it is," I bent down on my knees before him, my head hanging, my eyes to the ground.

"What are you talking about?" Funsho asked, finally starting to listen only when he realised I was serious. "Please get up!"

I shook my head. My shame was such that I didn't think I could have moved right then, even if I had wanted to. "If I could turn back the hands of time, this is the only thing I would love to change," I continued, "Unfortunately, I don't have that luxury. I'm prepared for whatever decision you make as long as you don't hate me – I won't be able to handle it. Funsho, you are the best thing I cannot have, that hurts already."

"G, you are scaring me now, what have you done?" he almost shouted, fear flooding his beautiful, pure eyes, as they searched my face for clues.

He looked genuinely terrified for what I was about to say.

"I accidentally slept with Jason's dad and I'm eight weeks pregnant," I garbled, before suddenly finding my feet, leaping to them and before running into the bedroom. I slammed the door behind me and leaned against it, panting as though I had just run a marathon.

"No!" shouted Funsho, "You don't get to lock yourself away after telling me the joke of the century, open the door now…Open the damn door Grace! Don't let me break my bedroom door, open up!"

I sat on his bed, shaking and fearful for my life because I could so clearly hear the rage in his voice. The anger with which he spoke to his sister was a dress rehearsal in comparison to what I heard in his voice, so I remained where I was. When I didn't hear a sound from the other side of the door, I wondered if he had gone to get a tool from the garage to force the door open.

'I better get out of this house before it's too late,' I thought, thanking God that at least Jason wasn't there at the time, so I opened the door slowly, only to find Funsho sitting on the floor.

"We've already established the fact that we don't know why it happened, please tell me how," he demanded, so I had no choice than to tell him about my little 'away match'. He just sat there while I spoke, staring at me with disgust.

"Apart from being head over heels in love with you, what hurts the most is the time I wasted with you. I warned you not to waste my time… " he hissed, before rearing up like a snake and grabbing me by my throat. I struggled back, gasping for air and trying to prise his fingers from my neck, but he was too strong for me. After what seemed like a lifetime, he released his hold and pushed me against the wall. "You did this intentionally, you whore. You never let me make love to you without protection, yet you opened your legs for him the moment he snapped his fingers. Where was he when you cried your eyes out during your divorce with your ex? Where was he when Jason took ill in the middle of the night and I had to drive you both to A&E?"

"I'm so sorry!" I whispered, with what was left of my voice. I felt stupid and small and wretched.

"You no longer have the right to speak to me!" snarled Funsho, "Ask your mother to bring my son home, get all your belongings from my house and post mine to me when you can. Do not share the same footpath as me, do not look at me, do not say my name or my child's name ever again. Grace, if you see my corpse, do not go near it unless you want me to raise from the dead and stab you in the heart until you bleed to death. Now get the hell out of my house, serpent, I curse the day I met you!"

Even though his hatred of me was the worst punishment and I knew I deserved it, I never dreamed of the day Funsho would ever actually lay his hands on me, let alone almost robbing me of my last breath. As instructed, I went back into the room to get my few belongings, and walked out of the door in silence.

If I said I knew how I got home that day, I would be lying. All I remembered was answering my mum's call in the kitchen. I was still perched on the kitchen stool, staring into space, when she arrived at my door with Jason in her arms.

"Mummy, take me home please, I'm not safe here," I cried, as I gave her and Jason a huge hug. "Funsho has gone nuts!"

"What did you do to him?" Mum asked, then stopped as she saw the red marks on my neck. "Grace, did he hurt you?" she asked.

"I will tell you when we get home," I said, as I followed her out to her car with Jason in my arms. "I just want to get home. Please can we go now and come back for my things later?"

I hoped I would have felt better after a good night's sleep in my old bedroom at my parents' house. However, I woke up the following morning feeling as unsettled as ever. In fact, the moment I opened my eyes I just wanted to close them again and go back to sleep until everything was sorted and my life was back to normal, but I knew I had to complete the second half of the task at hand. If things were about to go wrong in my life, I rather they happened all in one go so I could deal with them at the same time. Kind of like ripping off a sticking plaster in one go, rather than removing it slowly and painfully. I swung my legs out of bed and reached for my phone.

"Hey Abosede, what a surprise, how are you and my prince doing?" Adetoro asked as soon as he heard my voice on the line.

"We are good, you?"

"I'm doing great, my sweetheart and I were just talking about you actually, she thought we should give you an update about Mama Soji and her son and I told her you have the latest update, did you receive my email?" he asked.

"Yes, I did. I hope they throw the keys away," I said, "But that's not what I called you about. Since you are with your honey pie, please call me when you are free, I have something important to discuss with you."

"Hang on…" said Adetoro, before I heard him turn to his wife-to-be, "Sweetie, can you excuse me for a few minutes, this is about my son; I will be with you in a jiffy… thanks." I heard the sound of footsteps and a door slamming, and he was back on the line.

"Shoot, the coast is clear, my baby thinks I talk about you and Jason too much," he chuckled.

"Adetoro, this is no time for laughter. What I have to tell you is, my engagement has been called off. You want to know why?" I asked, sounding calmer than I felt. I had no idea how he would react and I just wanted it to be over and done with as quickly as possible.

"Why?"

"Because I'm pregnant with your child, again" I said, the words sounding hollow in my head, "Our little booty call has resulted in another human being."

Adetoro went silent. If it wasn't for the fact I could hear his breathing, I would have thought he had hung up the phone. After what felt like an age, he said, "Wow, I'm such a sharpshooter, wow! I bet it's going to be a little princess this time."

"Your barbie doll is complaining about one child, wait till she hears there is another on the way," I snapped, irritated by his insensitivity. Still, at least he wasn't angry and threatening to kill me, like Funsho was.

"Guess what angel, on the contrary, I can't wait to tell her," he chortled, "She is already annoying me, this is the perfect excuse to get rid of her!"

"Adetoro, what is wrong with you? How much alcohol have you had?" I asked, still a little upset with the way he was handling the matter. He didn't seem as though he was taking it seriously, but when he spoke again, I realised his frivolous initial reaction was most likely due to surprise, shock even.

"Things always has a way of working itself out for good, my queen," he said, in a much more reassuring tone of voice, "I'll be on the next available flight to the UK. It's high time I put a deserving diamond ring on that finger of yours, not the rubbish you were wearing when I last visited. No matter how far you run, or how much you deny it, I knew you would end up being my wife because the gods are always right!" Now, he sounded triumphant, but I didn't like that either. I realised, whatever he did or said, it still wouldn't be the right thing and I wondered whether it was emotional exhaustion, pregnancy hormones, or both which were making me feel so irritable.

"Since I set eyes on you, you've only brought me misery upon misery." I moaned, like a spoilt child, "I don't want you. I only called you to inform you so that you won't go all crazy on me like the last time. I'm capable of looking after my children on my own. I don't need any man by my side to do that, so take your beauty queen to the salon or whatever you two choose to do for the day." I hung up the phone.

He called back at least twenty times in immediate succession and, when I still refused to answer it, he decided to leave me a voicemail.

"How did you know I take her to hair salons, you've been stalking us, right? Just admit it, you are as jealous of her as she is of you. When are you going to stop fighting it? We are made for each other, love! Despite all the obstacles in our way, fate always has a way of bringing us back together. I will keep calling you until you pick up my phone, and if you don't, the next news you'll read on the Tribunal will be the announcement of my engagement to you," stated his message, with a steely air in his tone. Knowing Adetoro, he wasn't bluffing, so I decided the path of least trouble ahead would be to call him back.

"I knew that would get you to call me back, ha! What are you scared of, Abosede?" he asked, before adding, "Anyway, I've just changed my mind, I'm no longer coming to the UK, it's your turn to visit Ikoko. Tell your family to get ready for a royal wedding, we must tie the knot before you start showing and you are moving to Nigeria with my son. No argument, case closed."

"Adetoro, I can't, I have a life here," I sulked, as I wondered what kind of life was left for me in the UK now, and genuinely considered his proposal.

"Quit stalling Grace and tell me the truth," he continued, "You can't marry me, or you can't move to your rightful home?"

"I can't just up and leave like that," I said, suddenly reminded of my booming career with British Gas and my plans for the NGO. "Although if you come to the UK and ask properly, I might consider it," I added.

"Where is my laptop, I'm going to book an emergency ticket right away, you just made my day!" cheered Adetoro, and I could hear him moving around in the background.

"What are you going to tell your fiancée?" I asked.

"That it's over, any suggestions? Or do you want me to tell her I'm in love with you?" he asked.

"No, please don't!" I cried, "I don't want to make another enemy in Ikoko already!"

I could almost hear the grin spread across his face, "Then are you saying you might come back here with me someday? I have the ticket right in front of me, but before I hit 'purchase', tell me why I should make this journey. If it's because of the baby, or because you've just been jilted, they aren't good enough reasons for me to fly."

"Because you want to ask me to be your queen," I replied, knowing too well what he wanted me to admit, but refusing to say it quite yet.

"Sorry, I already have someone who is happy to be my queen, that's not a good enough reason to dump her for you," he taunted me.

"Ok, Adetoro," I began, realising now was not the time to cut off my nose to spite my face, so I swallowed my pride, "Adetoro, you should make the journey because I love you. I always have, and I always will. No matter how much I fight it, the feelings will never die." However, as the words left my mouth, I suddenly realised I had just shattered another person's dream – this time it was a fellow woman's. Felix may have deserved the pain after the way he treated me and Funsho deserved it too after placing his hands on me in anger, but this woman was innocent.

Professing our love for each other was supposed to be a thing of joy, but I couldn't help but feel guilty for all the people we've had to hurt on our journey to happily ever after. My only consolation for Miss Beauty Queen was I knew he didn't truly love her and, as they say, a broken relationship is better than a broken marriage.

As I lay in my old single bed at my parents' house, I allowed my mind to drift off and think of all the things I would do for my community when I became Queen of Ikoko. It was certain I'd continue my Paternity Fraud

Awareness campaign and, as I thought of what else I was passionate about, what else I could fill my days with when my children were at school, or off playing together somewhere. After all, they would grow up one day, they wouldn't need me forever. As Queen of Ikoko, I would have help, so would surely have some time on my hands. I suddenly remembered the book about Oshun which Adetoro had insisted I read, but I had not. Maybe now I would read it, and all of his other books too… and maybe I would write a book of my own… a book about love. As the thought crept into mind, I pulled myself up from the bed, got a pen, and an old notebook, and started to write.

'A love life is like a long journey with several stopovers. Some passengers drop off, new ones hop on, but there is this passenger who sits with you throughout the bumpy ride. You might hurt each other on occasions and hate being stuck with them, but you know that no matter what, love conquers all. So, you hang on to them through the ride called love and make it the smoothest journey you've ever embarked on…'

About the Author

Dosun Adeleye is the pseudonym of a BSc (Hons) Biomedical Scientist, who has since made a career move into project management. What keeps her awake at night, however, is writing stories which speak out about societal values and issues, with a touch of romance, passion and thrill. She is a lover of romance, as she grew up reading numerous novels ranging from romantic thrillers to Mills and Boon, and she is also a fan of hyper realistic women in fiction, where the real world collides with sheer fantasy. Dosun and her husband are parents to two young children and reside in the Buckinghamshire county of England.